Scenes And Characters

Or, Eighteen Months At Beechcroft

by

Charlotte M. Yonge

Double 9 BOOKS

Scenes And Characters
Or, Eighteen Months At Beechcroft
by Charlotte M. Yonge

ISBN: 978-93-70424-78-4

Published by

DOUBLE 9 BOOKS

2/13-B, Ansari Road
Daryaganj, New Delhi – 110002
info@double9books.com
www.double9books.com
Tel. 011-40042856

ABOUT THE AUTHOR

Charlotte M. Yonge was an English novelist and historian, born on August 11, 1823, in Otterbourne, Hampshire, England. She is best known for her prolific writing career, which spanned over 60 years and produced more than 160 works, including novels, children's books, and historical studies. Yonge's writing was strongly influenced by her deep religious beliefs and her interest in history and education. Many of her novels, such as "The Heir of Redclyffe" and "Heartsease," explore moral and religious themes and are known for their wholesome and uplifting tone. She also wrote numerous works for children, including the popular "Book of Golden Deeds," which features stories of heroism and selflessness. In addition to her writing, Yonge was a prominent figure in the Church of England and was involved in various philanthropic and educational endeavors. She founded a school for girls in her hometown and was a supporter of the National Society for Promoting Religious Education. Yonge died on May 24, 1901, in Otterbourne, Hampshire, England. Her legacy as a writer and educator continues to be celebrated, and her works remain popular with readers today.

CONTENTS

PREFACE

Of those who are invited to pay a visit to Beechcroft, there are some who, honestly acknowledging that amusement is their object, will be content to feel with Lilias, conjecture with Jane, and get into scrapes with Phyllis, without troubling themselves to extract any moral from their proceedings; and to these the Mohun family would only apologise for having led a very humdrum life during the eighteen months spent in their company.

There may, however, be more unreasonable visitors, who, professing only to come as parents and guardians, expect entertainment for themselves, as well as instruction for those who had rather it was out of sight,—look for antiques in carved cherry-stones,—and require plot, incident, and catastrophe in a chronicle of small beer.

To these the Mohuns beg respectfully to observe, that they hope their examples may not be altogether devoid of indirect instruction; and lest it should be supposed that they lived without object, aim, or principle, they would observe that the maxim which has influenced the delineation of the different *Scenes and Characters* is, that feeling, unguided and unrestrained, soon becomes mere selfishness; while the simple endeavour to fulfil each immediate claim of duty may lead to the highest acts of self-devotion.

New Court, Beechcroft,
18th *January*.

PREFACE (1886)

Perhaps this book is an instance to be adduced in support of the advice I have often given to young authors—not to print before they themselves are old enough to do justice to their freshest ideas.

Not that I can lay claim to its being a production of tender and interesting youth. It was my second actual publication, and I believe I was of age before it appeared—but I see now the failures that more experience might have enabled me to avoid; and I would not again have given it to the world if the same characters recurring in another story had not excited a certain desire to see their first start.

In fact they have been more or less my life-long companions. An almost solitary child, with periodical visits to the Elysium of a large family, it was natural to dream of other children and their ways and sports till they became almost realities. They took shape when my French master set me to write letters for him. The letters gradually became conversation and narrative, and the adventures of the family sweetened the toils of French composition. In the exigencies of village school building in those days gone by, before in every place

> "It there behoved him to set up the standard of her Grace,"

the tale was actually printed for private sale, as a link between translations of short stories.

This process only stifled the family in my imagination for a time. They awoke once more with new names, but substantially the same, and were my companions in many a solitary walk, the results of which were scribbled down in leisure moments to be poured into my mother's ever patient and sympathetic ears.

And then came the impulse to literature for young people given by the example of that memorable book the *Fairy Bower*, and followed up by *Amy Herbert*. It was felt that elder children needed something of a deeper tone than the Edgeworthian style, yet less directly religious than the Sherwood class of books; and on that wave of opinion, my little craft floated out into the great sea of the public.

Friends, whose kindness astonished me, and fills me with gratitude when I look back on it, gave me seasonable criticism and pruning, and finally launched me. My heroes and heroines had arranged themselves so as to work out a definite principle, and this was enough for us all.

Children's books had not been supposed to require a plot. Miss Edgeworth's, which I still continue to think gems in their own line, are made chronicles, or, more truly, illustrations of various truths worked out upon the same personages.

Moreover, the skill of a Jane Austen or a Mrs. Gaskell is required to produce a perfect plot without doing violence to the ordinary events of an every-day life. It is all a matter of arrangement. Mrs. Gaskell can make a perfect little plot out of a sick lad and a canary bird; and another can do nothing with half a dozen murders and an explosion; and of arranging my materials so as to build up a story, I was quite incapable. It is still my great deficiency; but in those days I did not even understand that the attempt was desirable. Criticism was a more thorough thing in those times than it has since become through the multiplicity of books to be hurried over, and it was often very useful, as when it taught that such arrangement of incident was the means of developing the leading idea.

Yet, with all its faults, the children, who had been real to me, caught, chiefly by the youthful sense of fun and enjoyment, the attention of other children; and the curious semi-belief one has in the phantoms of one's brain made me dwell on their after life and share my discoveries with my friends, not, however, writing them down till after the lapse of all these years the tenderness inspired by associations of early days led to taking up once more the old characters in *The Two Sides of the Shield*; and the kind welcome this has met with has led to the resuscitation of the crude and inexperienced tale which never pretended to be more than a mere family chronicle.

C. M. YONGE.

6th October 1886.

CHAPTER I
THE ELDER SISTER

'Return, and in the daily round Of duty and of love, Thou best wilt find that patient faith. That lifts the soul above.'

Eleanor Mohun was the eldest child of a gentleman of old family, and good property, who had married the sister of his friend and neighbour, the Marquis of Rotherwood. The first years of her life were marked by few events. She was a quiet, steady, useful girl, finding her chief pleasure in nursing and teaching her brothers and sisters, and her chief annoyance in her mamma's attempts to make her a fine lady; but before she had reached her nineteenth year she had learnt to know real anxiety and sorrow. Her mother, after suffering much from grief at the loss of her two brothers, fell into so alarming a state of health, that her husband was obliged immediately to hurry her away to Italy, leaving the younger children under the care of a governess, and the elder boys at school, while Eleanor alone accompanied them.

Their absence lasted nearly three years, and during the last winter, an engagement commenced between Eleanor and Mr. Francis Hawkesworth, rather to the surprise of Lady Emily, who wondered that he had been able to discover the real worth veiled beneath a formal and retiring manner, and to admire features which, though regular, had a want of light and animation, which diminished their beauty even more than the thinness and compression of the lips, and the very pale gray of the eyes.

The family were about to return to England, where the marriage was to take place, when Lady Emily was attacked with a sudden illness, which her weakened frame was unable to resist, and in a very few days she died, leaving the little Adeline, about eight months old, to accompany her father and sister on their melancholy journey homewards. This loss made a great change in the views of Eleanor, who, as she considered the cares and annoyances which would fall on her father, when left to bear the whole burthen of the management of the children and household, felt it was her duty to give up her own prospects of happiness, and to remain at home. How could she leave the tender little ones to the care of servants—trust her sisters to a governess, and make her brothers' home yet more dreary? She knew her father to be strong in sense and firm in judgment, but indolent, indulgent, and inattentive to details, and she could not bear to leave him to be harassed by the petty cares of a numerous family, especially when broken in spirits and weighed down with sorrow. She thought her duty was plain, and, accordingly, she wrote to Mr. Hawkesworth, to beg him to allow her to withdraw her promise.

Her brother Henry was the only person who knew what she had done, and he alone perceived something of tremulousness about her in the midst of the even cheerfulness with which she had from the first supported her father's spirits. Mr. Mohun, however, did not long remain in ignorance, for Frank Hawkesworth himself arrived at Beechcroft to plead his cause with Eleanor. He knew her value too well to give her up, and Mr. Mohun would not hear of her making such a sacrifice for his sake. But Eleanor was also firm, and after weeks of unhappiness and uncertainty, it was at length arranged that she should remain at home till Emily was old enough to take her place, and that Frank should then return from India and claim his bride.

Well did she discharge the duties which she had undertaken; she kept her father's mind at ease, followed out his views, managed the boys with discretion and gentleness, and made her sisters well-informed and accomplished girls; but, for want of fully understanding the characters of her two next sisters, Emily and Lilias, she made some mistakes with regard to them. The clouds of sorrow, to her so dark and heavy, had been to them but morning mists, and the four years which had changed her from a happy girl into a thoughtful, anxious woman, had brought them to an age which, if it is full of the follies of childhood, also partakes of the earnestness of youth; an age when deep foundations of enduring confidence may be laid by one who can enter into and direct the deeper flow of mind and feeling which lurks hid beneath the freaks and fancies of the early years of girlhood. But Eleanor had little sympathy for freaks and fancies. She knew the realities of life too well to build airy castles with younger and gayer spirits; her sisters' romance seemed to her dangerous folly, and their lively nonsense levity and frivolity. They were too childish to share in her confidence, and she was too busy and too much preoccupied to have ear or mind for visionary trifles, though to trifles of real life she paid no small degree of attention.

It might have been otherwise had Henry Mohun lived; but in the midst of the affection of all who knew him, honour from those who could appreciate his noble character, and triumphs gained by his uncommon talents, he was cut off by a short illness, when not quite nineteen, a most grievous loss to his family, and above all, to Eleanor. Unlike her, as he was joyous, high-spirited, full of fun, and overflowing with imagination and poetry, there was a very close bond of union between them, in the strong sense of duty, the firmness of purpose, and energy of mind which both possessed, and which made Eleanor feel perfect reliance on him, and look up to him with earnest admiration. With him alone she was unreserved; he was the only person who could ever make her show a spark of liveliness, and on his death, it was only with the most painful efforts that she could maintain her composed demeanour and fulfil her daily duties. Years passed on, and still she felt the blank which Harry had left, almost as much as the first day that she heard of his death, but she never spoke of him, and to her sisters it seemed as if he was forgotten. The reserve which had begun to thaw under his influence, again returning, placed her a still greater distance from the younger girls, and unconsciously she became still more of a governess and less of a sister. Little did she know of the 'blissful dreams in secret shared' between Emily, Lilias, and their brother Claude, and little did she perceive the danger that Lilias would be run away with by a lively imagination, repressed and starved, but entirely untrained.

Whatever influenced Lilias, had, through her, nearly the same effect upon Emily, a gentle girl, easily led, especially by Lilias, whom she regarded with the fondest affection and admiration. The perils of fancy and romance were not, however, to be dreaded for Jane, the fourth sister, a strong resemblance of Eleanor in her clear common sense, love of neatness, and active usefulness; but there were other dangers for her, in her tendency to faults, which, under wise training, had not yet developed themselves.

Such were the three girls who were now left to assist each other in the management of the household, and who looked forward to their new offices with the various sensations of pleasure, anxiety, self-importance, and self-mistrust, suited to their differing characters, and to the ages of eighteen, sixteen, and fourteen.

CHAPTER II
THE NEW COURT

'Just at the age 'twixt boy and youth,
When thought is speech, and speech is truth.'

The long-delayed wedding took place on the 13th of January, 1845, and the bride and bridegroom immediately departed for a year's visit among Mr. Hawkesworth's relations in Northumberland, whence they were to return to Beechcroft, merely for a farewell, before sailing for India.

It was half-past nine in the evening, and the wedding over—Mr. and Mrs. Hawkesworth gone, and the guests departed, the drawing-room had returned to its usual state. It was a very large room, so spacious that it would have been waste and desolate, had it not been well filled with handsome, but heavy old-fashioned furniture, covered with crimson damask, and one side of the room fitted up with a bookcase, so high that there was a spiral flight of library steps to give access to the upper shelves. Opposite were four large windows, now hidden by their ample curtains; and near them was at one end of the room a piano, at the other a drawing-desk. The walls were wainscoted with polished black oak, the panels reflecting the red fire-light like mirrors. Over the chimney-piece hung a portrait, by Vandyke, of a pale, dark cavalier, of noble mien, and with arched eyebrows, called by Lilias, in defiance of dates, by the name of Sir Maurice de Mohun, the hero of the family, and allowed by every one to be a striking likeness of Claude, the youth who at that moment lay, extending a somewhat superfluous length of limb upon the sofa, which was placed commodiously at right angles to the fire.

The other side of the fire was Mr. Mohun's special domain, and there he sat at his writing-table, abstracted by deafness and letter writing, from the various sounds of mirth and nonsense, which proceeded from the party round the long narrow sofa table, which they had drawn across the front of the fire, leaving the large round centre table in darkness and oblivion.

This party had within the last half hour been somewhat thinned; the three younger girls had gone to bed, the Rector of Beechcroft, Mr. Robert Devereux, had been called home to attend some parish business, and there remained Emily and Lilias—tall graceful girls, with soft hazel eyes, clear dark complexions, and a quantity of long brown curls. The latter was busily completing a guard for the watch, which Mr. Hawkesworth had presented to Reginald, a fine handsome boy of eleven, who, with his elbows on the table, sat contemplating her progress, and sometimes teasing his brother Maurice, who was earnestly engaged in constructing a model with some cards, which he had pilfered from the heap before Emily. She was putting her sister's wedding cards into their shining envelopes, and directing them in readiness for the post the next morning, while they were sealed by a youth of the same age as Claude, a small slim figure, with light complexion and hair, and dark gray eyes full of brightness and vivacity.

He was standing, so as to be more on a level with the high candle, and as Emily's writing was not quite so rapid as his sealing, he amused himself in the intervals with burning his own fingers, by twisting the wax into odd shapes.

'Why do you not seal up his eyes?' inquired Reginald, with an arch glance towards his brother on the sofa.

'Do it yourself, you rogue,' was the answer, at the same time approaching with the hot sealing-wax in his hand—a demonstration which occasioned Claude to open his eyes very wide, without giving himself any further trouble about the matter.

'Eh?' said he, 'now they try to look innocent, as if no one could hear them plotting mischief.'

'Them! it was not!—Redgie there—young ladies—I appeal—was not I as innocent?'—was the very rapid, incoherent, and indistinct answer.

'After so lucid and connected a justification, no more can be said,' replied Claude, in a kind of 'leave me, leave me to repose' tone, which occasioned Lilias to say, 'I am afraid you are very tired.'

'Tired! what has he done to tire him?'

'I am sure a wedding is a terrible wear of spirits!' said Emily—'such excitement.'

'Well—when I give a spectacle to the family next year, I mean to tire you to some purpose.'

'Eh?' said Mr. Mohun, looking up, 'is Rotherwood's wedding to be the next?'

'You ought to understand, uncle,' said Lord Rotherwood, making two stops towards him, and speaking a little more clearly, 'I thought you longed to get rid of your nephew and his concerns.'

'You idle boy!' returned Mr. Mohun, 'you do not mean to have the impertinence to come of age next year.'

'As much as having been born on the 30th of July, 1825, can make me.'

'But what good will your coming of age do us?' said Lilias, 'you will be in London or Brighton, or some such stupid place.'

'Do not be senseless, Lily,' returned her cousin. 'Devereux Castle is to be in splendour—Hetherington in amazement—the county's hair shall stand on end—illuminations, bonfires, feasts, balls, colours flying, bands playing, tenants dining, fireworks—'

'Hurrah! jolly! jolly!' shouted Reginald, dancing on the ottoman, 'and mind there are lots of squibs.'

'And that Master Reginald Mohun has a new cap and bells for the occasion,' said Lord Rotherwood.

'Let me make some fireworks,' said Maurice.

'You will begin like a noble baron of the hospitable olden time,' said Lily.

'It will be like the old days, when every birthday of yours was a happy day for the people at Hetherington,' said Emily.

'Ah! those were happy old days,' said Lord Rotherwood, in a graver tone.

'These are happy days, are not they?' said Lily, smiling.

Her cousin answered with a sigh, 'Yes, but you do not remember the old ones, Lily;' then, after a pause, he added, 'It was a grievous mistake to shut up the castle all these years. We have lost sight of everybody. I do not even know what has become of the Aylmers.'

'They went to live in London,' said Emily, 'Aunt Robert used to write to them there.'

'I know, I know, but where are they now?'

'In London, I should think,' said Emily. 'Some one said Miss Aylmer was gone out as a governess.'

'Indeed! I wish I could hear more! Poor Mr. Aylmer! He was the first man who tried to teach me Latin. I wonder what has become of that mad fellow Edward, and Devereux, my father's godson! Was not Mrs. Aylmer badly off? I cannot bear that people should be forgotten!'

'It is not so very long that we have lost sight of them,' said Emily.

'Eight years,' said Lord Rotherwood. 'He died six weeks after my father. Well! I have made my mother promise to come home.'

'Really?' said Lilias, 'she has been coming so often.'

'Aye—but she is coming this time. She is to spend the winter at the castle, and make acquaintance with all the neighbourhood.'

'His lordship is romancing,' said Claude to Lily in a confidential tone.

'I'll punish you for suspecting me of talking hyperborean language—hyperbolical, I mean,' cried Lord Rotherwood; 'I'll make you dance the Polka with all the beauty and fashion.'

'Then I shall stay at Oxford till it is over,' said Claude.

'You do not know what a treasure you will be,' said the Marquis, 'ladies like nothing so well as dancing with a fellow twice the height he should be.'

'Beware of putting me forward,' said Claude, rising, and, as he leant against the chimney-piece, looking down from his height of six feet three, with a patronising air upon his cousin, 'I shall be taken for the hero, and you for my little brother.'

'I wish I was,' said Lord Rotherwood, 'it would be much better fun. I should escape the speechifying, the worst part of it.'

'Yes,' said Claude, 'for one whose speeches will be scraps of three words each, strung together with the burthen of the apprentices' song, Radara tadara, tandore.'

'Radaratade,' said the Marquis, laughing. 'By the bye, if Eleanor and Frank Hawkesworth manage well, they may be here in time.'

'Because they are so devoted to gaiety?' said Claude. 'You will say next that William is coming from Canada, on purpose.'

'That tall captain!' said Lord Rotherwood. 'He used to be a very awful person.'

'Ah! he used to keep the spoilt Marquis in order,' said Claude.

'To say nothing of the spoilt Claude,' returned Lord Rotherwood.

'Claude never was spoilt,' said Lily.

'It was not Eleanor's way,' said Emily.

'At least she cannot be accused of spoiling me,' said Lord Rotherwood. 'I shall never dare to write at that round table again—her figure will occupy the chair like Banquo's ghost, and wave me off with a knitting needle.'

'Ah! that stain of ink was a worse blot on your character than on the new table cover,' said Claude.

'She was rigidly impartial,' said Lord Rotherwood.

'No,' said Claude, 'she made exceptions in favour of Ada and me. She left the spoiling of the rest to Emily.'

'And well Emily will perform it! A pretty state you will be in by the 30th of July, 1846,' said Lord Rotherwood.

'Why should not Emily make as good a duenna as Eleanor?' said Lily.

'Why should she not? She will not—that is all,' said the Marquis. 'Such slow people you all are! You would all go to sleep if I did not sometimes rouse you up a little—grow stagnant.'

'Not an elegant comparison,' said Lilias; 'besides, you must remember that your hasty brawling streams do not reflect like tranquil lakes.'

'One of Lily's poetical hits, I declare!' said Lord Rotherwood, 'but she need not have taken offence—I did not refer to her—only Claude and Emily, and perhaps—no, I will not say who else.'

'Then, Rotherwood, I will tell you what I am—the Lily that derives all its support from the calm lake.'

'Well done, Lily, worthy of yourself,' cried Lord Rotherwood, laughing, 'but you know I am always off when you talk poetry.'

'I suspect it is time for us all to be off,' said Claude, 'did I not hear it strike the quarter?'

'And to-morrow I shall be off in earnest,' said Lord Rotherwood. 'Half way to London before Claude has given one turn to "his sides, and his shoulders, and his heavy head."'

'Shall we see you at Easter?' said Emily.

'No, I do not think you will. I am engaged to stay with somebody somewhere, I forget the name of place and man; besides, Grosvenor Square is more tolerable then than at any other time of the year, and I shall spend a fortnight with my mother and Florence. It is after Easter that you come to Oxford, is it not, Claude?'

'Yes, my year of idleness will be over. And there is the Baron looking at his watch.'

The 'Baron' was the title by which the young people were wont to distinguish Mr. Mohun, who, as Lily believed, had a right to the title of Baron of Beechcroft. It was certain that he was the representative of a family which had been settled at Beechcroft ever since the Norman Conquest, and Lily was very proud of the name of Sir William de Moune in the battle roll, and of Sir John among the first Knights of the Garter. Her favourite was Sir Maurice, who had held out Beechcroft Court for six weeks against the Roundheads, and had seen the greater part of the walls battered down. Witnesses of the strength of the old castle yet remained in the massive walls and broad green ramparts, which enclosed what was now orchard and farm-yard, and was called the Old Court, while the dwelling-house, built by Sir Maurice after the Restoration, was named the New Court. Sir Maurice had lost many an acre in the cause of King Charles, and his new mansion was better suited to the honest squires who succeeded him, than to the mighty barons his ancestors. It was substantial and well built, with a square gravelled court in front, and great, solid, folding gates opening into a lane, bordered with very tall well-clipped holly hedges, forming a polished, green, prickly wall. There was a little door in one of these gates, which was scarcely ever shut, from whence a well-worn path led to the porch, where generally reposed a huge Newfoundland dog, guardian of the hoops and walkingsticks that occupied the corners. The front door was of heavy substantial oak, studded with nails, and never closed in the daytime, and the hall, wainscoted and floored with slippery oak, had a noble open fireplace, with a wood fire burning on the hearth.

On the other side of the house was a terrace sloping down to a lawn and bowling-green, hedged in by a formal row of evergreens. A noble plane-tree was in the middle of the lawn, and beyond it a pond renowned for water-lilies. To the left was the kitchen garden, terminating in an orchard, planted on the ramparts and moat of the Old Court; then came the farm buildings, and beyond them a field, sloping upwards to an extensive wood called Beechcroft Park. In the wood was the cottage of Walter Greenwood, gamekeeper and woodman by hereditary succession, but able and willing to turn his hand to anything, and, in fact, as Adeline once elegantly termed him, the 'family tee totum.'

To the right of the house there was a field, called Long Acre, bounded on the other side by the turnpike road to Raynham, which led up the hill to the village green, surrounded by well-kept cottages and gardens. The principal part of the village was, however, at the foot of the hill, where the Court lane crossed the road, led to the old church, the school, and parsonage, in its little garden, shut in by thick yew hedges. Beyond was the blacksmith's shop, more cottages, and Mrs. Appleton's wondrous village warehouse; and the lane, after passing by the handsome old farmhouse of Mr. Harrington, Mr. Mohun's principal tenant, led to a bridge across a clear trout stream, the boundary of the parish of Beechcroft.

CHAPTER III
THE NEW PRINCIPLE

'And wilt thou show no more, quoth he,
  Than doth thy duty bind?
I well perceive thy love is small.'

On the Sunday evening which followed Eleanor's wedding, Lilias was sitting next to Emily, and talking in very earnest tones, which after a time occasioned Claude to look up and say, 'What is all this about? Something remarkably absurd I suspect.'

'Only a new principle,' said Emily.

'New!' cried Lily, 'only what must be the feeling of every person of any warmth of character?'

'Now for it then,' said Claude.

'No, no, Claude, I really mean it (and Lily sincerely thought she did). I will not tell you if you are going to laugh.'

'That depends upon what your principle may chance to be,' said Claude. 'What is it, Emily? She will be much obliged to you for telling.'

'She only says she cannot bear people to do their duty, and not to act from a feeling of love,' said Emily.

'That is not fair,' returned Lily, 'all I say is, that it is better that people should act upon love for its own sake, than upon duty for its own sake.'

'What comes in rhyme with Lily?' said Claude.

'Don't be tiresome, Claude, I really want you to understand me.'

'Wait till you understand yourself,' said the provoking brother, 'and let me finish what I am reading.'

For about a quarter of an hour he was left in peace, while Lily was busily employed with a pencil and paper, under the shadow of a book, and at length laid before him the following verses:—

'What is the source of gentleness,
The spring of human blessedness,
Bringing the wounded spirit healing,
The comforts high of heaven revealing,
The lightener of each daily care,

The wing of hope, the life of prayer,
The zest of joy, the balm of sorrow,
Bliss of to-day, hope of to-morrow,
The glory of the sun's bright beam,
The softness of the pale moon stream,
The flow'ret's grace, the river's voice,
The tune to which the birds rejoice;
Without it, vain each learned page,
Cold and unfelt each council sage,
Heavy and dull each human feature,
Lifeless and wretched every creature;
In which alone the glory lies,
Which value gives to sacrifice?
'Tis that which formed the whole creation,
Which rests on every generation.
Of Paradise the only token
Just left us, 'mid our treasures broken,
Which never can from us be riven,
Sure earnest of the joys of Heaven.
And which, when earth shall pass away,
Shall be our rest on the last day,
When tongues shall fail and knowledge cease,
And throbbing hearts be all at peace:
When faith is sight, and hope is sure,
That which alone shall still endure
Of earthly joys in heaven above,
'Tis that best gift, eternal Love!'

'What have you there?' said Mr. Mohun, who had come towards them while Claude was reading the lines. Taking the paper from Claude's hand, he read it to himself, and then saying, 'Tolerable, Lily; there are some things to alter, but you may easily make it passable,' he went on to his own place, leaving Lilias triumphant.

'Well, Claude, you see I have the great Baron on my side.'

'I am of the Baron's opinion,' said Claude, 'the only wonder is that you doubted it.'

'You seemed to say that love was good for nothing.'

'I said nothing but that Lily has a rhyme.'

'And saying that I was silly, was equivalent to saying that love was nothing,' said Lily.

'O Lily, I hope not,' said Claude, with a comical air.

'Well, I know I often am foolish, but not in this,' said Lily; 'I do say that mere duty is not lovable.'

'Say it if you will then,' said Claude, yawning, 'only let me finish this sermon.'

Lily set herself to reconsider some of her lines: but presently Emily left the room, Claude looked up, and Lily exclaimed, 'Now, Claude, let us make a trial of it.'

'Well,' said Claude, yawning again, and looking resigned.

'Think how Eleanor went on telling us of duty, duty, duty—never making allowances—never relaxing her stiff rules about trifles—never unbending from her duenna-like dignity—never showing one spark of enthusiasm—making great sacrifices, but only because she thought them her duty—because it was right—good for herself—only a higher kind of selfishness—not because her feeling prompted her.'

'Certainly, feeling does not usually prompt people to give up their lovers for the sake of their brothers and sisters.'

'She did it because it was her duty,' said Lily, 'quite as if she did not care.'

'I wonder whether Frank thought so,' said Claude.

'At any rate you will confess that Emily is a much more engaging person,' said Lily.

'Certainly, I had rather talk nonsense to her,' said Claude.

'You feel it, though you will not allow it,' said Lily. 'Now think of Emily's sympathy, and gentleness, and sweet smile, and tell me if she is not a complete personification of love. And then Eleanor, unpoetical—never thrown off her balance by grief or joy, with no ups and downs—no enthusiasm—no appreciation of the beautiful—her highest praise "very right," and tell me if there can be a better image of duty.'

Claude might have had some chance of bringing Lily to her senses, if he had allowed that there was some truth in what she had said; but he thought the accusation so unjust in general, that he would not agree to any part of it, and only answered, 'You have very strange views of duty and of Eleanor.'

'Well!' replied Lily, 'I only ask you to watch; Emily and I are determined to act on the principle of love, and you will see if her government is not more successful than that of duty.'

Such was the principle upon which Lily intended her sister to govern the household, and to which Emily listened without knowing what she meant much better than she did herself. Emily's own views, as far as she possessed any, were to get on as smoothly as she could, and make everybody pleased and happy, without much trouble to herself, and also to make the establishment look a little more as if a Lady Emily had lately been its mistress, than had been the case in Eleanor's time. Mr. Mohun's property was good, but he wished to avoid unnecessary display and expense, and he expected his daughters to follow out these views, keeping a wise check upon Emily, by looking over her accounts every Saturday, and turning a deaf ear when she talked of the age of the drawing-room carpet, and the ugliness of the old chariot. Emily had a good deal on her hands, requiring sense and activity, but Lilias and Jane were now quite old enough to assist her. Lily however, thought fit to despise all household affairs, and bestowed the chief of her attention on her own department—the village school and poor people; and she was also much engrossed by her music and drawing, her German and Italian, and her verse writing.

Claude had more power over her than any one else. He was a gentle, amiable boy, of high talent, but disposed to indolence by ill health. In most matters he was, however, victorious over this propensity, which was chiefly visible in his love of easy chairs, and his dislike of active sports, which made him the especial companion of his sisters. A dangerous illness had occasioned his removal from Eton, and he had since been at home, reading with his cousin Mr. Devereux, and sharing his sisters' amusements.

Jane was in her own estimation an important member of the administration, and in fact, was Emily's chief assistant and deputy. She was very small and trimly made, everything fitted her precisely, and she had tiny dexterous fingers, and active little feet, on which she darted about noiselessly and swiftly as an arrow; an oval brown face, bright colour, straight features, and smooth dark hair, bright sparkling black eyes, a little mouth, wearing an arch subdued smile, very white teeth, and altogether the air of a woman in miniature. Brisk, bold, and blithe—ever busy and ever restless, she was generally known by the names of Brownie and Changeling, which were not inappropriate to her active and prying disposition.

Excepting Claude and Emily, the young party were early risers, and Lily especially had generally despatched a good deal of business before the eight o'clock breakfast.

At nine they went to church, Mr. Devereux having restored the custom of daily service, and after this, Mr. Mohun attended to his multitudinous affairs; Claude went to the parsonage,—Emily to the storeroom, Lily to the village, the younger girls to the schoolroom, where they were presently joined by Emily. Lily remained in her own room till one o'clock, when she joined the others in the schoolroom, and they read aloud some book of history till two, the hour of dinner for the younger, and of luncheon for the elder. They then went out, and on their return from evening service, which began at half-past four, the little ones had their lessons to learn, and the others were variously employed till dinner, the time of which was rather uncertain but always late. The evening passed pleasantly and quickly away in reading, work, music, and chatter.

As Emily had expected, her first troubles were with Phyllis; called, not the neat handed, by her sisters; Master Phyl, by her brothers; and Miss Tomboy, by the maids. She seemed born to be a trial of patience to all concerned with her; yet without many actual faults, except giddiness, restlessness, and unrestrained spirits. In the drawing-room, schoolroom, and nursery she was continually in scrapes, and so often reproved and repentant, that her loud roaring fits of crying were amongst the ordinary noises of the New Court. She was terribly awkward when under constraint, or in learning any female accomplishment, but swift and ready when at her ease, and glorying in the boyish achievements of leaping ditches and climbing trees. Her voice was rather highly pitched, and she had an inveterate habit of saying, 'I'll tell you what,' at the beginning of all her speeches. She was not tall, but strong, square, firm, and active; she had a round merry face, a broad forehead, and large bright laughing eyes, of a doubtful shade between gray and brown. Her mouth was wide, her nose turned up, her complexion healthy, but not rosy, and her stiff straight brown hair was more apt to hang over her eyes, than to remain in its proper place behind her ears.

Adeline was very different; her fair and brilliant complexion, her deep blue eyes and golden ringlets, made her a very lovely little creature; her quietness was a relief after her sister's boisterous merriment, and her dislike of dirt and brambles, continually contrasted with poor Phyllis's recklessness of such impediments. Ada readily learnt lessons, which cost Phyllis and her teacher hours of toil; Ada worked deftly when Phyllis's stiff fingers never willingly touched a needle; Ada played with a doll, drew on scraps of paper, or put up dissected maps, while Phyllis was in mischief or in the way. A book was the only chance of interesting her; but very few books took her fancy enough to occupy her long;—those few, however, she read over and over again, and when unusual tranquillity reigned in the drawing-room, she was sure to be found curled up at the top of the library steps, reading one of three books—*Robinson Crusoe*, *Little Jack*, or *German Popular Tales*. Then Emily blamed her ungraceful position, Jane laughed at her uniform taste, and Lily proposed some story about modern children, such as Phyllis never could like, and the constant speech was repeated, 'Only look at Ada!' till Phyllis considered her sister as a perfect model, and sighed over her own naughtiness.

German Popular Tales were a recent introduction of Claude's, for Eleanor had carefully excluded all fairy tales from her sisters' library; so great was her dread of works of fiction, that Emily and Lilias had never been allowed to read any of the Waverley Novels, excepting *Guy Mannering*, which their brother Henry had insisted upon reading aloud to them the last time he was at home, and that had taken so strong a hold on their imagination, that Eleanor was quite alarmed.

One day Mr. Mohun chanced to refer to some passage in *Waverley*, and on finding that his daughters did not understand him, he expressed great surprise at their want of taste.

Poor things,' said Claude, 'they cannot help it; do not you know that Eleanor thinks the Waverley Novels a sort of slow poison? They know no more of them than their outsides.'

'Well, the sooner they know the inside the better.'

'Then may we really read them, papa?' cried Lily.

'And welcome,' said her father.

This permission once given, the young ladies had no idea of moderation; Lily's heart and soul were wrapped up in whatever tale she chanced to be reading—she talked of little else, she neglected her daily occupations, and was in a kind of trance for about three weeks. At length she was recalled to her senses by her father's asking her why she had shown him no drawings lately. Lily hesitated for a moment, and then said, 'Papa, I am sorry I was so idle.'

'Take care,' said Mr. Mohun, 'let us be able to give a good account of ourselves when Eleanor comes.'

'I am afraid, papa,' said Lily, 'the truth is, that my head has been so full of *Woodstock* for the last few days, that I could do nothing.'

'And before that?'

'*The Bride of Lammermoor.*'

'And last week?'

'*Waverley.* Oh! papa, I am afraid you must be very angry with me.'

'No, no, Lily, not yet,' said Mr. Mohun, 'I do not think you quite knew what an intoxicating draught you had got hold of; I should have cautioned you. Your negligence has not yet been a serious fault, though remember, that it becomes so after warning.'

'Then,' said Lily, 'I will just finish *Peveril* at once, and get it out of my head, and then read no more of the dear books,' and she gave a deep sigh.

'Lily would take the temperance pledge, on condition that she might finish her bottle at a draught,' said Mr. Mohun.

Lily laughed, and looked down, feeling quite unable to offer to give up *Peveril* before she had finished it, but her father relieved her, by saying in his kind voice, 'No, no, Lily, take my advice, read those books, for most of them are very good reading, and very pretty reading, and very useful reading, and you can hardly be called a well-educated person if you do not know them; but read them only after the duties of the day are done—make them your pleasure, but do not make yourself their slave.'

'Lily,' said Claude the next morning, as he saw her prepare her drawing-desk, 'why are you not reading *Peveril*?'

'You know what papa said yesterday,' was the answer.

'Oh! but I thought your feelings were with poor Julian in the Tower,' said Claude.

'My feelings prompt me to sacrifice my pleasure in reading about him to please papa, after he spoke so kindly.'

‘If that is always the effect of your principle, I shall think better of it,’ said Claude.

Lily, whether from her new principle, or her old habits of obedience, never ventured to touch one of her tempters till after five o’clock, but, as she was a very rapid reader, she generally contrived to devour more than a sufficient quantity every evening, so that she did not enjoy them as much as she would, had she been less voracious in her appetite, and they made her complain grievously of the dulness of the latter part of Russell’s *Modern Europe*, which was being read in the schoolroom, and yawn nearly as much as Phyllis over the ‘Pragmatic Sanction.’ However, when that book was concluded, and they began Palgrave’s *Anglo Saxons*, Lily was seized within a sudden historical fever. She could hardly wait till one o’clock, before she settled herself at the schoolroom table with her work, and summoned every one, however occupied, to listen to the reading.

CHAPTER IV
HONEST PHYL

'Multiplication
Is a vexation.'

It was a bright and beautiful afternoon in March, the song of the blackbird and thrush, and the loud chirp of the titmouse, came merrily through the schoolroom window, mixed with the sounds of happy voices in the garden; the western sun shone brightly in, and tinged the white wainscoted wall with yellow light; the cat sat in the window-seat, winking at the sun, and sleepily whisking her tail for the amusement of her kitten, which was darting to and fro, and patting her on the head, in the hope of rousing her to some more active sport.

But in the midst of all these joyous sights and sounds, was heard a dolorous voice repeating, 'three and four are—three and four are—oh dear! they are—seven, no, but I do not think it is a four after all, is it not a one? Oh dear!' And on the floor lay Phyllis, her back to the window, kicking her feet slowly up and down, and yawning and groaning over her slate.

Presently the door opened, and Claude looked in, and very nearly departed again instantly, for Phyllis at that moment made a horrible squeaking with her slate-pencil, the sound above all others that he disliked. He, however, stopped, and asked where Emily was.

'Out in the garden,' answered Phyllis, with a tremendous yawn.

'What are you doing here, looking so piteous?' said Claude.

'My sum,' said Phyllis.

'Is this your time of day for arithmetic?' asked he.

'No,' said Phyllis, 'only I had not done it by one o'clock to-day, and Lily said I must finish after learning my lessons for to-morrow, but I do not think I shall ever have done, it is so hard. Oh!' (another stretch and a yawn, verging on a howl), 'and Jane and Ada are sowing the flower-seeds. Oh dear! Oh dear!' and Phyllis's face contracted, in readiness to cry.

'And is that the best position for doing sums?' said Claude.

'I was obliged to lie down here to get out of the way of Ada's sum,' said Phyllis, getting up.

'Get out of the way of Ada's sum?' repeated Claude.

'Yes, she left it on the table where I was sitting, where I could see it, and it is this very one, so I must not look at it; I wish I could do sums as fast as she can.'

'Could you not have turned the other side of the slate upwards?' said Claude, smiling.

'So I could!' said Phyllis, as if a new light had broken in upon her. 'But then I wanted to be out of sight of pussy, for I could not think a bit, while the kitten was at play so prettily, and I kicked my heels to keep from hearing the voices in the garden, for it does make me so unhappy!'

Some good-natured brothers would have told the little girl not to mind, and sent her out to enjoy herself, but Claude respected Phyllis's honesty too much to do so, and he said, 'Well, Phyl, let me see the sum, and we will try if we cannot conquer it between us.'

Phyllis's face cleared up in an instant, as she brought the slate to her brother.

'What is this?' said he; 'I do not understand.'

'Compound Addition,' said Phyllis, 'I did one with Emily yesterday, and this is the second.'

'Oh! these are marks between the pounds, shillings, and pence,' said Claude, 'I took them for elevens; well, I do not wonder at your troubles, I could not do this sum as it is set.'

'Could not you, indeed?' cried Phyllis, quite delighted.

'No, indeed,' said Claude. 'Suppose we set it again, more clearly; but how is this? When I was in the schoolroom we always had a sponge fastened to the slate.'

'Yes,' said Phyllis, 'I had one before Eleanor went, but my string broke, and I lost it, and Emily always forgets to give me another. I will run and wash the slate in the nursery; but how shall we know what the sum is?'

'Why, I suppose I may look at Ada's slate, though you must not,' said Claude, laughing to himself at poor little honest simplicity, as he applied himself to cut a new point to her very stumpy slate-pencil, and she scampered away, and returned in a moment with her clean slate.

'Oh, how nice and fresh it all looks!' said she as he set down the clear large figures. 'I cannot think how you can do it so evenly.'

'Now, Phyl, do not let the pencil scream if you can help it.'

Claude found that Phyllis's great difficulty was with the farthings. She could not understand the fractional figures, and only knew thus far, that 'Emily said it never meant four.'

Claude began explaining, but his first attempt was far too scientific. Phyllis gave a desponding sigh, looking so mystified, that he began to believe that she was hopelessly dull, and to repent of having offered to help her; but at last, by means of dividing a card into four pieces, he succeeded in making her comprehend him, and her eyes grew bright with the pleasure of understanding.

Even then the difficulties were not conquered, her addition was very slow, and dividing by twelve and twenty seemed endless work; at length the last figure of the pounds was set down, the slate was compared with Adeline's, and the sum pronounced to be right. Phyllis capered up to the kitten and tossed it up in the air in her joy, then coming slowly back to her brother, she said with a strange, awkward air, hanging down her head, 'Claude, I'll tell you what—'

'Well, what?' said Claude.

'I should like to kiss you.'

Then away she bounded, clattered down stairs, and flew across the lawn to tell every one she met that Claude had helped her to do her sum, and that it was quite right.

'Did you expect that it would be too hard for him, Phyl?' said Jane, laughing.

'No,' said Phyllis, 'but he said he could not do it as it was set.'

'And whose fault was that?' said Jane.

'Oh! but he showed me how to set it better,' said Phyllis, 'and he said that when he learnt the beginning of fractions, he thought them as hard as I do.'

'Fractions!' said Jane, 'you do not fancy you have come to fractions yet! Fine work you will make of them when you do!'

In the evening, as soon as the children were gone to bed, Jane took a paper out of her work-basket, saying, 'There, Emily, is my account of Phyl's scrapes through this whole week; I told you I should write them all down.'

'How kind!' muttered Claude.

Regardless of her brother, who had not looked up from his book, Jane began reading her list of poor Phyllis's misadventures. 'On Monday she tore her frock by climbing a laurel-tree, to look at a blackbird's nest.'

'I gave her leave,' said Emily. 'Rachel had ordered her not to climb; and she was crying because she could not see the nest that Wat Greenwood had found.'

'On Tuesday she cried over her French grammar, and tore a leaf out of the old spelling-book.'

'That was nearly out before,' said Emily, 'Maurice and Redgie spoilt that long ago.'

'I do not know of anything on Wednesday, but on Thursday she threw Ada down the steps out of the nursery.'

'Oh! that accounts for the dreadful screaming that I heard,' said Claude; 'I forgot to ask the meaning of it.'

'I am sure it was Phyl that was the most dismayed, and cried the loudest,' said Lily.

'That she always does,' said Jane. 'On Friday we had an uproar in the schoolroom about her hemming, and on Saturday she tumbled into a wet ditch, and tore her bonnet in the brambles; on Sunday, she twisted her ancles together at church.'

'Well, there I did chance to observe her,' said Lily, 'there seemed to be a constant struggle between her ancles and herself, they were continually coming lovingly together, but were separated the next moment.'

'And to-day this sum,' said Jane; 'seven scrapes in one week! I really am of opinion, as Rachel says when she is angry, that school is the best place for her.'

'I think so too,' said Claude.

'I do not know,' said Emily, 'she is very troublesome, but—'

'Oh, Claude!' cried Lily, 'you do not mean that you would have that poor dear merry Master Phyl sent to school, she would pine away like a wild bird in a cage; but papa will never think of such a thing.'

'If I thought of her being sent to school,' said Claude, 'it would be to shield her from—the rule of love.'

'Oh! you think we are too indulgent,' said Emily; 'perhaps we are, but you know we cannot torment a poor child all day long.'

'If you call the way you treat her indulgent, I should like to know what you call severe.'

'What do you mean, Claude?' said Emily.

'I call your indulgence something like the tender mercies of the wicked,' said Claude. 'On a fine day, when every one is taking their pleasure in the garden, to shut an unhappy child up in the schoolroom, with a hard sum that you have not taken the trouble to teach her how to do, and late in the day, when no one's head is clear for difficult arithmetic—'

'Hard sum do you call it?' said Jane.

'Indeed I explained it to her,' said Emily.

'And well she understood you,' said Claude.

'She might have learnt if she had attended,' said Emily; 'Ada understood clearly, with the same explanation.'

'And do not you be too proud of the effect of your instructions, Claude,' said Jane, 'for when honest Phyl came into the garden, she did not know farthings from fractions.'

'And pray, Mrs. Senior Wrangler,' said Claude, 'will you tell me where is the difference between a half-penny and half a penny?'

After a good laugh at Jane's expense, Emily went on, 'Now, Claude, I will tell you how it happened; Phyllis is so slow, and dawdles over her lessons so long, that it is quite a labour to hear her; Ada is quick enough, but if you were to hear Phyllis say one column of spelling, you would know what misery is. Then before she has half finished, the clock strikes one, it is time to read, and the lessons are put off till the afternoon. I certainly did not know that she was about her sum all that time, or I would have sent her out as I did on Saturday.'

'And the reading at one is as fixed as fate,' said Claude.

'Oh, no!' said Jane, 'when we were about old "Russell," we did not begin till nearly two, but since we have been reading this book, Lily will never let us rest till we begin; she walks up and down, and hurries and worries and—'

'Yes,' said Emily, in a murmuring voice, 'we should do better if Lily would not make such a point of that one thing; but she never minds what else is cut short, and she never thinks of helping me. It never seems to enter her head how much I have on my hands, and no one does anything to help me.'

'Oh, Emily! you never asked me,' said Lily.

'I knew you would not like it,' said Emily. 'No, it is not my way to complain, people may see how to help me if they choose to do it.'

'Lily, Lily, take care,' said Claude, in a low voice; 'is not the rule you admire, the rule of love of yourself?'

'Oh, Claude!' returned Lily, 'do not say so, you know it was Emily that I called an example of it, not myself, and see how forbearing she has been. Now I see that I am really wanted, I will help. It must be love, not duty, that calls me to the schoolroom, for no one ever said that was my province.'

'Poor duty! you give it a very narrow boundary.'

Lilias, who, to say the truth, had been made more careful of her own conduct, by the wish to establish her principle, really betook herself to the schoolroom for an hour every morning, with a desire to be useful. She thought she did great things in undertaking those tasks of Phyllis's which Emily most disliked. But Lilias was neither patient nor humble enough to be a good teacher, though she could explain difficult rules in a sensible way. She could not, or would not, understand the difference between dulness and inattention; her sharp hasty manner would frighten away all her pupil's powers of comprehension; she sometimes fell into the great error of scolding, when Phyllis was doing her best, and the poor child's tears flowed more frequently than ever.

Emily's gentle manner made her instructions far more agreeable, though she was often neither clear nor correct in her explanations; she was contented if the lessons were droned through in any manner, so long as she could say they were done; she disliked a disturbance, and overlooked or half corrected mistakes rather than cause a cry. Phyllis naturally preferred being taught by her, and Lily was vexed and unwilling to persevere. She went to the schoolroom expecting to be annoyed, created vexation for herself, and taught in anything but a loving spirit. Still, however, the thought of Claude, and the wish to do more than her duty, kept her constant to her promise, and her love of seeing things well done was useful, though sadly counterbalanced by her deficiency in temper and patience.

CHAPTER V
VILLAGE GOSSIP

'The deeds we do, the words we say,
  Into still air they seem to fleet;
We count them past,
  But they shall last.'

Soon after Easter, Claude went to Oxford. He was much missed by his sisters, who wanted him to carve for them at luncheon, to escort them when they rode or walked, to hear their music, talk over their books, advise respecting their drawings, and criticise Lily's verses. A new subject of interest was, however, arising for them in the neighbours who were shortly expected to arrive at Broom Hill, a house which had lately been built in a hamlet about a mile and a half from the New Court.

These new comers were the family of a barrister of the name of Weston, who had taken the house for the sake of his wife, her health having been much injured by her grief at the loss of two daughters in the scarlet fever. Two still remained, a grown-up young lady, and a girl of eleven years old, and the Miss Mohuns learnt with great delight that they should have near neighbours of their own age. They had never had any young companions as young ladies were scarce among their acquaintance, and they had not seen their cousin, Lady Florence Devereux, since they were children.

It was with great satisfaction that Emily and Lilias set out with their father to make the first visit, and they augured well from their first sight of Mrs. Weston and her daughters. Mrs. Weston was alone, her daughters being out walking, and Lily spent the greater part of the visit in silence, though her mind was made up in the first ten minutes, as she told Emily on leaving the house, 'that Miss Weston's tastes were in complete accordance with her own.'

'Rapid judgment,' said Emily. 'Love before first sight. But Mrs. Weston is a very sweet person.'

'And, Emily, did you see the music-book open at "Angels ever bright and fair?" If Miss Weston sings that as I imagine it!'

'How could you see what was in the music-book at the other end of the room? I only saw it was a beautiful piano. And what handsome furniture! it made me doubly ashamed of our faded carpet and chairs, almost as old as the house itself.'

'Emily!' said Lily, in her most earnest tones, 'I would not change one of those dear old chairs for a king's ransom!'

The visit was in a short time returned, and though it was but a formal morning call, Lilias found her bright expectations realised by the sweetness of Alethea Weston's manners, and the next time they met it was a determined thing in her mind that, as Claude would have said, they had sworn an eternal friendship.

She had the pleasure of lionising the two sisters over the Old Court, telling all she knew and all she imagined about the siege, Sir Maurice Mohun, and his faithful servant, Walter Greenwood. 'Miss Weston,' said she in conclusion, 'have you read *Old Mortality*?'

'Yes,' said Alethea, amused at the question.

'Because they say I am as bad as Lady Margaret about the king's visit.'

'I have not heard the story often enough to think so,' said Miss Weston, 'I will warn you if I do.'

In the meantime Phyllis and Adeline were equally charmed with Marianne, though shocked at her ignorance of country manners, and, indeed, Alethea was quite diverted with Lily's pity at the discovery that she had never before been in the country in the spring. 'What,' she cried, 'have you never seen the tufts of red on the hazel, nor the fragrant golden palms, and never heard the blackbird rush twittering out of the hedge, nor the first nightingale's note, nor the nightjar's low chirr, nor the chattering of the rooks? O what a store of sweet memories you have lost! Why, how can you understand the beginning of the Allegro?'

Both the Miss Westons had so much pleasure in making acquaintance with 'these delights,' as quite to compensate for their former ignorance, and soon the New Court rang with their praises. Mr. Mohun thought very highly of the whole family, and rejoiced in such society for his daughters, and they speedily became so well acquainted, that it was the ordinary custom of the Westons to take luncheon at the New Court on Sunday. On her side, however, Alethea Weston felt some reluctance to become intimate with the young ladies of the New Court. She was pleased with Emily's manners, interested by Lily's earnestness and simplicity, and thought Jane a clever and amusing little creature, but even their engaging qualities gave her pain, by reminding her of the sisters she had lost, or by making her think how they would have liked them. A country house and neighbours like these had been the objects of many visions of their childhood, and now all the sweet sights and sounds around her only made her think how she should have enjoyed them a year ago. She felt almost jealous of Marianne's liking for her new friends, lest they should steal her heart from Emma and Lucy; but knowing that these were morbid and unthankful feelings, she struggled against them, and though she missed her sisters even more than when her mother and Marianne were in greater need of her attention, she let no sign of her sorrowful feeling appear, and seeing that Marianne was benefited in health and spirits, by intercourse with young companions, she gave no hint of her disinclination to join in the walks and other amusements of the Miss Mohuns.

She also began to take interest in the poor people. By Mrs. Weston's request, Mr. Devereux had pointed out the families which were most in need of assistance, and Alethea made it her business to find out the best way of helping them. She visited the village school with Lilias, and when requested by her and by the Rector to give her aid in teaching, she did not like to refuse what might be a duty, though she felt very diffident of her powers of instruction. Marianne, like Phyllis and Adeline, became a Sunday scholar, and was catechised with the others in church. Both Mr. Mohun and his nephew thought very highly of the family, and the latter was particularly glad that Lily should have some older person to assist her in those parish matters which he left partly in her charge.

Mr. Devereux had been Rector of Beechcroft about a year and a half, and had hitherto been much liked. His parishioners had known him from a boy, and were interested about him, and though very young, there was something about him that gained their respect. Almost all his plans were going on well, and things were, on the whole, in a satisfactory state, though no one but Lilias expected even Cousin Robert to make a Dreamland of Beechcroft, and there were days when he looked worn and anxious, and the girls suspected that some one was behaving ill.

'Have you a headache, Robert?' asked Emily, a few evenings before Whit-Sunday, 'you have not spoken three words this evening.'

'Not at all, thank you,' said Mr. Devereux, smiling, 'you need not think to make me your victim, now you have no Claude to nurse.'

'Then if it is not bodily, it is mental,' said Lily.

'I am in a difficulty about the christening of Mrs. Naylor's child.'

'Naylor the blacksmith?' said Jane. 'I thought it was high time for it to be christened. It must be six weeks old.'

'Is it not to be on Whit-Sunday?' said Lily, disconsolately.

'Oh no! Mrs. Naylor will not hear of bringing the child on a Sunday, and I could hardly make her think it possible to bring it on Whit-Tuesday.'

'Why did you not insist?' said Lily.

'Perhaps I might, if there was no other holy day at hand, or if there was not another difficulty, a point on which I cannot give way.'

'Oh! the godfathers and godmothers,' said Lily, 'does she want that charming brother of hers, Edward Gage?'

'Yes, and what is worse, Edward Gage's dissenting wife, and Dick Rodd, who shows less sense of religion than any one in the parish, and has never been confirmed.'

'Could you make them hear reason?'

'They were inclined to be rather impertinent,' said Mr. Devereux. 'Old Mrs. Gage—'

'Oh!' interrupted Jane, 'there is no hope for you if the sour Gage is in the pie.'

'The sour Gage told me people were not so particular in her younger days, and perhaps they should not have the child christened at all, since I was such a *contrary* gentleman. Tom Naylor was not at home, I am to see him to-morrow.'

'Well, I do not think Tom Naylor is as bad as the rest,' said Lily; 'he would have been tolerable, if he had married any one but Martha Gage.'

'Yes, he is an open good-natured fellow, and I have hopes of making an impression on him.'

'If not,' said Lily, 'I hope papa will take away his custom.'

'What?' said Mr. Mohun, who always heard any mention of himself. Mr. Devereux repeated his history, and discussed the matter with his uncle, only once interrupted by an inquiry from Jane about the child's name, a point on which she could gain no intelligence. His report the next day was not decidedly unfavourable, though he scarcely hoped the christening would be so soon as Tuesday. He had not seen the father, and suspected he had purposely kept out of the way.

Jane, disappointed that the baby's name remained a mystery, resolved to set out on a voyage of discovery. Accordingly, as soon as her cousin was gone, she asked Emily if she had not been saying that Ada wanted some more cotton for her sampler.

'Yes,' said Emily, 'but I am not going to walk all the way to Mrs. Appleton's this afternoon.'

'Shall I go?' said Jane. 'Ada, run and fetch your pattern.' Emily and Ada were much obliged by Jane's disinterested offer, and in a quarter of an hour Ada's thoughts and hands were busy in Mrs. Appleton's drawer of many-coloured cotton.

'What a pity this is about Mrs. Naylor's baby,' began Jane.

'It is a sad story indeed, Miss Jane, I am sure it must be grievous to Mr. Devereux,' said Mrs. Appleton. 'Betsy Wall said he had been there three times about it.'

'Ah! we all know that Walls have ears,' said Jane; 'how that Betsy does run about gossiping!'

'Yes, Miss Jane, there she bides all day long at the stile gaping; not a stitch does she do for her mother; I cannot tell what is to be the end of it.'

'And do you know what the child's name is to be, Mrs. Appleton?'

'No, Miss Jane,' answered Mrs. Appleton. 'Betsy did say they talked of naming him after his uncle, Edward Gage, only Mr. Devereux would not let him stand.'

'No,' said Jane. 'Since he married that dissenting wife he never comes near the church; he is too much like the sour Gage, as we call his mother, to be good for much. But, after all, he is not so bad as Dick Rodd, who has never been confirmed, and has never shown any sense of religion in his life.'

'Yes, Miss, Dick Rodd is a sad fellow: did you hear what a row there was at the Mohun Arms last week, Miss Jane?'

'Aye,' said Jane, 'and papa says he shall certainly turn Dick Rodd out of the house as soon as the lease is out, and it is only till next Michaelmas twelve-months.'

'Yes, Miss, as I said to Betsy Wall, it would be more for their interest to behave well.'

'Indeed it would,' said Jane. 'Robert and papa were talking of having their horses shod at Stoney Bridge, if Tom Naylor will be so obstinate, only papa does not like to give Tom up if he can help it, because his father was so good, and Tom would not be half so bad if he had not married one of the Gages.'

'Here is Cousin Robert coming down the lane,' said Ada, who had chosen her cotton, and was gazing from the door. Jane gave a violent start, took a hurried leave of Mrs. Appleton, and set out towards home; she could not avoid meeting her cousin.

'Oh, Jenny! have you been enjoying a gossip with your great ally?' said he.

'We have only been buying pink cotton,' said Ada, whose conscience was clear.

'Ah!' said Mr. Devereux, 'Beechcroft affairs would soon stand still, without those useful people, Mrs. Appleton, Miss Wall, and Miss Jane Mohun,' and he passed on. Jane felt her face colouring, his freedom from suspicion made her feel very guilty, but the matter soon passed out of her mind.

Blithe Whit-Sunday came, the five Miss Mohuns appeared in white frocks, new bonnets were plenty, the white tippets of the children, and the bright shawls of the mothers, made the village look gay; Wat Greenwood stuck a pink between his lips, and the green boughs of hazel and birch decked the dark oak carvings in the church.

And Whit-Monday came. At half-past ten the rude music of the band of the Friendly Society came pealing from the top of the hill, then appeared two tall flags, crowned with guelder roses and peonies, then the great blue drum, the clarionet blown by red-waist-coated and red-faced Mr. Appleton, the three flutes and the triangle, all at their loudest, causing some of the spectators to start, and others to dance. Then behold the whole procession of labourers, in white round frocks, blue ribbons in their hats, and tall blue staves in their hands. In the rear, the confused mob, women and children, cheerful faces and mirthful sounds everywhere. These were hushed as the flags were lowered to pass under the low-roofed gateway of the churchyard, and all was still, except the trampling of feet on the stone floor. Then the service began, the responses were made in full and hearty tones, almost running into a chant, the old 133rd Psalm was sung as loudly and as badly as usual, a very short but very earnest sermon was preached, and forth came the troop again.

Mr. Devereux always dined with the club in a tent, at the top of the hill, but his uncle made him promise to come to a second dinner at the New Court in the evening.

'Robert looks anxious,' said Lily, as she parted with him after the evening service; 'I am afraid something is going wrong.'

'Trust me for finding out what it is,' said Jane.

'No, no, Jenny, do not ask him,' said Lily; 'if he tells us to relieve his mind, I am very glad he should make friends of us, but do not ask. Let us talk of other things to put it out of his head, whatever it may be.'

Jane soon heard more of the cause of the depression of her cousin's spirits than even she had any desire to do. After dinner, the girls were walking in the garden, enjoying the warmth of the evening, when Mr. Devereux came up to her and drew her aside from the rest, telling her that he wished to speak to her.

'Oh!' said Jane, 'when am I to meet you at school again? You never told me which chapter I was to prepare; I cannot think what would become of your examinations if it was not for me, you could not get an answer to one question in three.'

'That was not what I wished to speak to you about,' said Mr. Devereux. 'What had you been saying to Mrs. Appleton when I met you at her door on Saturday?'

The colour rushed into Jane's cheeks, but she replied without hesitation, 'Oh! different things, *La pluie et le beau temps*, just as usual.'

'Cannot you remember anything more distinctly?'

'I always make a point of forgetting what I talk about,' said Jane, trying to laugh.

'Now, Jane, let me tell you what has happened in the village—as I came down the hill from the club-dinner—'

'Oh,' said Jane, hoping to make a diversion, 'Wat Greenwood came back about a quarter of an hour ago, and he—'

Mr. Devereux proceeded without attending to her, 'As I came down the hill from the club-dinner, old Mrs. Gage came out of Naylor's house, and her daughter with her, in great anger, calling me to account for having spoken of her in a most unbecoming way, calling her the sour Gage, and trying to set the Squire against them.'

'Oh, that abominable chattering woman!' Jane exclaimed; 'and Betsy Wall too, I saw her all alive about something. What a nuisance such people are!'

'In short,' said Mr. Devereux, 'I heard an exaggerated account of all that passed here on the subject the other day. Now, Jane, am I doing you any injustice in thinking that it must have been through you that this history went abroad into the village?'

'Well,' said Jane, 'I am sure you never told us that it was any secret. When a story is openly told to half a dozen people they cannot be expected to keep it to themselves.'

'I spoke uncharitably and incautiously,' said he, 'I am willing to confess, but it is nevertheless my duty to set before you the great matter that this little fire has kindled.'

'Why, it cannot have done any great harm, can it?' asked Jane, the agitation of her voice and laugh betraying that she was not quite so careless as she wished to appear. 'Only the sour Gage will ferment a little.'

'Oh, Jane! I did not expect that you would treat this matter so lightly.'

'But tell me, what harm has it done?' asked she.

'Do you consider it nothing that the poor child should remain unbaptized, that discord should be brought into the parish, that anger should be on the conscience of your neighbour, that he should be driven from the church?'

'Is it as bad as that?' said Jane.

'We do not yet see the full extent of the mischief our idle words may have done,' said Mr. Devereux.

'But it is their own fault, if they will do wrong,' said Jane; 'they ought not to be in a rage, we said nothing but the truth.'

'I wish I was clear of the sin,' said her cousin.

'And after all,' said Jane, 'I cannot see that I was much to blame; I only talked to Mrs. Appleton, as I have done scores of times, and no one minded it. You only laughed at me on Saturday, and papa and Eleanor never scolded me.'

'You cannot say that no one has ever tried to check you,' said the Rector.

'And how was I to know that that mischief-maker would repeat it?' said Jane.

'I do not mean to say,' said Mr. Devereux, 'that you actually committed a greater sin than you may often have done, by talking in a way which you knew would displease your father. I know we are too apt to treat lightly the beginnings of evil, until some sudden sting makes us feel what a serpent we have been fostering. Think this a warning, pray that the evil we dread may be averted; but should it ensue, consider it as a punishment sent in mercy. It will be better for you not to come to school to-morrow; instead of the references you were to have looked out, I had rather you read over in a humble spirit the Epistle of St. James.'

Jane's tears by this time were flowing fast, and finding that she no longer attempted to defend herself, her cousin said no more. He joined the others, and Jane, escaping to her own room, gave way to a passionate fit of crying. Whether her tears were of true sorrow or of anger she could not have told herself; she was still sobbing on her bed when the darkness came on, and her two little sisters came in on their way to bed to wish her good-night.

'Oh, Jane, Jane! what is the matter? have you been naughty?' asked the little girls in great amazement.

'Never mind,' said Jane, shortly; 'good-night,' and she sat up and wiped away her tears. The children still lingered. 'Go away, do,' said she. 'Is Robert gone?'

'No,' said Phyllis, 'he is reading the newspaper.'

Phyllis and Adeline left the room, and Jane walked up and down, considering whether she should venture to go down to tea; perhaps her cousin had waited till the little girls had gone before he spoke to Mr. Mohun, or perhaps her red eyes might cause questions on her troubles; she was still in doubt when Lily opened the door, a lamp in her hand.

'My dear Jenny, are you here? Ada told me you were crying, what is the matter?'

'Then you have not heard?' said Jane.

'Only Robert began just now, "Poor Jenny, she has been the cause of getting us into a very awkward scrape," but then Ada came to tell me about you, and I came away.'

'Yes,' said Jane, angrily, 'he will throw all the blame upon me, when I am sure it was quite as much the fault of that horrible Mrs. Appleton, and papa will be as angry as possible.'

'But what has happened?' asked Lily.

'Oh! that chatterer, that worst of gossipers, has gone and told the Naylors and Mrs. Gage all we said about them the other day.'

'So you told Mrs. Appleton?' said Lily; 'so that was the reason you were so obliging about the marking thread. Oh, Jane, you had better say no more about Mrs. Appleton! And has it done much mischief?'

'Oh! Mrs. Gage "pitched" into Robert, as Wat Greenwood would say, and the christening is off again.'

'Jane, this is frightful,' said Lily; 'I do not wonder that you are unhappy.'

'Well, I daresay it will all come right again,' said Jane; 'there will only be a little delay, papa and Robert will bring them to their senses in time.'

'Suppose the baby was to die,' said Lily.

'Oh, it will not die,' said Jane, 'a great fat healthy thing like that likely to die indeed!'

'I cannot make you out, Jane,' said Lily. 'If I had done such a thing, I do not think I could have a happy minute till it was set right.'

'Well, I told you I was very sorry,' said Jane, 'only I wish they would not all be so hard upon me. Robert owns that he should not have said such things if he did not wish them to be repeated.'

'Does he?' cried Lily. 'How exactly like Robert that is, to own himself in fault when he is obliged to blame others. Jane, how could you hear him say such things and not be overcome with shame? And then to turn it against him! Oh, Jane, I do not think I can talk to you any more.'

'I do not mean to say it was not very good of him,' said Jane.

'Good of him—what a word!' cried Lily. 'Well, good-night, I cannot bear to talk to you now. Shall I say anything for you downstairs?'

'Oh, tell papa and Robert I am very sorry,' said Jane. 'I shall not come down again, you may leave the lamp.'

On her way downstairs in the dark Lilias was led, by the example of her cousin, to reflect that she was not without some share in the mischief that had been done; the words which report imputed to Mr. Devereux were mostly her own or Jane's. There was no want of candour in Lily, and as soon as she entered the drawing-room she went straight up to her father and cousin, and began, 'Poor Jenny is very unhappy; she desired me to tell you how sorry she is. But I really believe that I did the mischief, Robert. It was I who said those foolish things that were repeated as if you had said them. It is a grievous affair, but who could have thought that we were doing so much harm?'

'Perhaps it may not do any,' said Emily. 'The Naylors have a great deal of good about them.'

'They must have more than I suppose, if they can endure what Robert is reported to have said of them,' said Mr. Mohun.

'What did you say, Robert,' said Lily, 'did you not tell them all was said by your foolish young cousins?'

'I agreed with you too much to venture on contradicting the report; you know I could not even deny having called Mrs. Gage by that name.'

'Oh, if I could do anything to mend it!' cried Lily.

But wishes had no effect. Lilias and Jane had to mourn over the full extent of harm done by hasty words. After the more respectable men had left the Mohun Arms on the evening of Whit-Monday, the rest gave way to unrestrained drunkenness, not so much out of reckless self-indulgence, as to defy the clergyman and the squire. They came to the front of the parsonage, yelled and groaned for some time, and ended by breaking down the gate.

This conduct was repeated on Tuesday, and on many Saturdays following; some young trees in the churchyard were cut, and abuse of the parson written on the walls the idle young men taking this opportunity to revenge their own quarrels, caused by Mr. Devereux's former efforts for their reformation.

On Sunday several children were absent from school; all those belonging to Farmer Gage's labourers were taken away, and one man was turned off by the farmers for refusing to remove his child.

Now that the war was carried on so openly, Mr. Mohun considered it his duty to withdraw his custom from one who chose to set his pastor at defiance. He went to the forge, and had a long conversation with the blacksmith, but though he was listened to with respect, it was not easy to make much impression on an ignorant, hot-tempered man, who had been greatly offended, and prided himself on showing that he would support the quarrel of his wife and her relations against both squire and parson; and though Mr. Mohun did persuade him to own that it was wrong to be at war with the clergyman, the effect of his arguments was soon done away with by the Gages, and no ground was gained.

Mr. Gage's farm was unhappily at no great distance from a dissenting chapel and school, in the adjoining parish of Stoney Bridge, and thither the farmer and blacksmith betook themselves, with many of the cottagers of Broom Hill.

One alone of the family of Tom Naylor refused to join him in his dissent, and that was his sister, Mrs. Eden, a widow, with one little girl about seven years old, who, though in great measure dependent upon him for subsistence, knew her duty too well to desert the church, or to take her child from school, and continued her even course, toiling hard for bread, and uncomplaining, though often munch distressed. All the rest of the parish who were not immediately under Mr. Mohun's influence were in a sad state of confusion.

Jane was grieved at heart, but would not confess it, and Lilias was so restless and unhappy, that Emily was quite weary of her lamentations. Her best comforter was Miss Weston, who patiently listened to her, sighed with her over the evident sorrow of the Rector, and the mischief in the parish, and proved herself a true friend, by never attempting to extenuate her fault.

CHAPTER VI
THE NEW FRIEND

'Maidens should be mild and meek,
Swift to hear, and slow to speak.'

Miss Weston had been much interested by what she heard respecting Mrs. Eden, and gladly discovered that she was just the person who could assist in some needlework which was required at Broom Hill. She asked Lilias to tell her where to find her cottage, and Lily replied by an offer to show her the way; Miss Weston hesitated, thinking that perhaps in the present state of things Lily had rather not see her; but her doubts were quickly removed by this speech, 'I want to see her particularly. I have been there three times without finding her. I think I can set this terrible matter right by speaking to her.'

Accordingly, Lilias and Phyllis set out with Alethea and Marianne one afternoon to Mrs. Eden's cottage, which stood at the edge of a long field at the top of the hill. Very fast did Lily talk all the way, but she grew more silent as she came to the cottage, and knocked at the door; it was opened by Mrs. Eden herself, a pale, but rather pretty young woman, with a remarkable gentle and pleasing face, and a manner which was almost ladylike, although her hands were freshly taken out of the wash-tub. She curtsied low, and coloured at the sight of Lilias, set chairs for the visitors, and then returned to her work.

'Oh! Mrs. Eden,' Lily began, intending to make her explanation, but feeling confused, thought it better to wait till her friend's business was settled, and altered her speech into 'Miss Weston is come to speak to you about some work.'

Mrs. Eden looked quite relieved, and Alethea proceeded to appoint the day for her coming to Broom Hill, and arrange some small matters, during which Lily not only settled what to say, but worked herself into a fit of impatience at the length of Alethea's instructions. When they were concluded, however, and there was a pause, her words failed her, and she wished that she was miles from the cottage, or that she had never mentioned her intentions. At last she stammered out, 'Oh! Mrs. Eden—I wanted to speak to you about—about Mr. Devereux and your brother.'

Mrs. Eden bent over her wash-tub, Miss Weston examined the shells on the chimney-piece, Marianne and Phyllis listened with all their ears, and poor Lily was exceedingly uncomfortable.

'I wished to tell you—I do not think—I do not mean—It was not his saying. Indeed, he did not say those things about the Gages.'

'I told my brother I did not think Mr. Devereux would go for to say such a thing,' said Mrs. Eden, as much confused as Lily.

'Oh! that was right, Mrs. Eden. The mischief was all my making and Jane's. We said those foolish things, and they were repeated as if it was he. Oh! do tell your brother so, Mrs. Eden. It was very good of you to think it was not Cousin Robert. Pray tell Tom Naylor. I cannot bear that things should go on in this dreadful way.'

'Indeed, Miss, I am very sorry,' said Mrs. Eden.

'But, Mrs Eden, I am sure that would set it right again,' said Lily, 'are not you? I would do anything to have that poor baby christened.'

Lily's confidence melted away as she saw that Mrs. Eden's tears were falling fast, and she ended with, 'Only tell them, and we shall see what will happen.'

'Very well, Miss Lilias,' said Mrs. Eden. 'I am very sorry.'

'Let us hope that time and patience will set things right,' said Miss Weston, to relieve the embarrassment of both parties. 'Your brother must soon see that Mr. Devereux only wishes to do his duty.'

Alethea skilfully covered Lily's retreat, and the party took leave of Mrs. Eden, and turned into their homeward path.

Lily at first seemed disposed to be silent, and Miss Weston therefore amused herself with listening to the chatter of the little girls as they walked on before them.

'There are only thirty-six days to the holidays,' said Phyllis; 'Ada and I keep a paper in the nursery with the account of the number of days. We shall be so glad when Claude, and Maurice, and Redgie come home.'

'Are they not very boisterous?' said Marianne.

'Not Maurice,' said Phyllis.

'No, indeed,' said Lily, 'Maurice is like nobody else. He takes up some scientific pursuit each time he comes home, and cares for nothing else for some time, and then quite forgets it. He is an odd-looking boy too, thick and sturdy, with light flaxen hair, and dark, overhanging eyebrows, and he makes the most extraordinary grimaces.'

'And Reginald?' said Alethea.

'Oh! Redgie is a noble-looking fellow. But just eleven, and taller than Jane. His complexion so fair, yet fresh and boyish, and his eyes that beautiful blue that Ada's are—real blue. Then his hair, in dark brown waves, with a rich auburn shine. The old knights must have been just like Redgie. And Claude—Oh! Miss Weston, have you ever seen Claude?'

'No, but I have seen your eldest brother.'

'William? Why, he has been in Canada these three years. Where could you have seen him?'

'At Brighton, about four years ago.'

'Ah! the year before he went. I remember that his regiment was there. Well, it is curious that you should know him; and did you ever hear of Harry, the brother that we lost?'

'I remember Captain Mohun's being called away to Oxford by his illness,' said Alethea.

'Ah, yes! William was the only one of us who was with him, even papa was not there. His illness was so short.'

'Yes,' said Alethea, 'I think it was on a Tuesday that Captain Mohun left Brighton, and we saw his death in the paper on Saturday.'

'William only arrived the evening that he died. Papa was gone to Ireland to see about Cousin Rotherwood's property. Robert, not knowing that, wrote to him at Beechcroft; Eleanor forwarded the letter without opening it, and so we knew nothing till Robert came to tell us that all was over.'

'Without any preparation?'

'With none. Harry had left home about ten days before, quite well, and looking so handsome. You know what a fine-looking person William is. Well, Harry was very like him, only not so tall and strong, with the same clear hazel eyes, and more pink in his cheeks—fairer altogether. Then Harry wrote, saying that he had caught one of his bad colds. We did not think much of it, for he was always having coughs. We heard no more for a week, and then one morning Eleanor was sent for out of the schoolroom, and there was Robert come to tell us. Oh! it was such a thunderbolt. This was what did the mischief. You know papa and mamma being from home so long, the elder boys had no settled place for the holidays; sometimes they stayed with one friend, sometimes with another, and so no one saw enough of them to find out how delicate poor Harry really was. I think papa had been anxious the only winter they were at home together, and Harry had been talked to and advised to take care; but in the summer and autumn he was well, and did not think about it. He went to Oxford by the coach—it was a bitterly cold frosty day—there was a poor woman outside, shivering and looking very ill, and Harry changed places with her. He was horribly chilled, but thinking he had only a common cold, he took no care. Robert, coming to Oxford about a week after, found him very ill, and wrote to papa and William, but William scarcely came in time. Harry just knew him, and that was all. He could not speak, and died that night. Then William stayed at Oxford to receive papa, and Robert came to tell us.'

'It must have been a terrible shock.'

'Such a loss—he was so very good and clever. Every one looked up to him—William almost as much as the younger ones. He never was in any scrape, had all sorts of prizes at Eton, besides getting his scholarship before he was seventeen.'

Whenever Lily could get Miss Weston alone, it was her way to talk in this manner. She loved the sound of her own voice so well, that she was never better satisfied than when engrossing the whole conversation. Having nothing to talk of but her books, her poor people, and her family, she gave her friend the full benefit of all she could say on each subject, while Alethea had kindness enough to listen with real interest to her long rambling discourses, well pleased to see her happy.

The next time they met, Lilias told her all she knew or imagined respecting Eleanor, and of her own debate with Claude, and ended, 'Now, Miss Weston, tell me your opinion, which would you choose for a sister, Eleanor or Emily?'

'I have some experience of Miss Mohun's delightful manners, and none of Mrs. Hawkesworth's, so I am no fair judge,' said Alethea.

'I really have done justice to Eleanor's sterling goodness,' said Lily. 'Now what should you think?'

'I can hardly imagine greater proofs of affection than Mrs. Hawkesworth has given you,' said Miss Weston, smiling.

'It was because it was her duty,' said Lilias. 'You have only heard the facts, but you cannot judge of her ways and looks. Now only think, when Frank came home, after seven years of perils by field and flood—there she rose up to receive him as if he had been Mr. Nobody making a morning call. And all the time before they were married, I do believe she thought more of showing Emily how much tea we were to use in a week than anything else.'

'Perhaps some people might have admired her self-command,' said Alethea.

'Self-command, the refuge of the insensible? And now, I told you about dear Harry the other day. He was Eleanor's especial brother, yet his death never seemed to make any difference to her. She scarcely cried: she heard our lessons as usual, talked in her quiet voice—showed no tokens of feeling.'

'Was her health as good as before?' asked Miss Weston.

'She was not ill,' said Lily; 'if she had, I should have been satisfied. She certainly could not take long walks that winter, but she never likes walking. People said she looked ill, but I do not know.'

'Shall I tell you what I gather from your history?'

'Pray do.'

'Then do not think me very perverse, if I say that perhaps the grief she then repressed may have weighed down her spirits ever since, so that you can hardly remember any alteration.'

'That I cannot,' said Lily. 'She is always the same, but then she ought to have been more cheerful before his death.'

'Did not you lose him soon after your mother?' said Alethea.

'Two whole years,' said Lily. 'Oh! and aunt, Robert too, and Frank went to India the beginning of that year; yes, there was enough to depress her, but I never thought of grief going on in that quiet dull way for so many years.'

'You would prefer one violent burst, and then forgetfulness?'

'Not exactly,' said Lily; 'but I should like a little evidence of it. If it is really strong, it cannot be hid.'

Little did Lily think of the grief that sat heavy upon the spirit of Alethea, who answered—'Some people can do anything that they consider their duty.'

'Duty: what, are you a duty lover?' exclaimed Lilias. 'I never suspected it, because you are not disagreeable.'

'Thank you,' said Alethea, laughing, 'your compliment rather surprises me, for I thought you told me that your brother Claude was on the duty side of the question.'

'He thinks he is,' said Lily, 'but love is his real motive of action, as I can prove to you. Poor Claude had a very bad illness when he was about three years old; and ever since he has been liable to terrible headaches, and he is not at all strong. Of course he cannot always study hard, and when first he went to school, every one scolded him for being idle. I really believe he might have done more, but then he was so clever that he could keep up without any trouble, and, as Robert says, that was a great temptation; but still papa was not satisfied, because he said Claude could do better. So said Harry. Oh! you cannot think what a person Harry was, as high-spirited as William, and as gentle as Claude; and in his kind way he used to try hard to make Claude exert himself, but it never would do—he was never in mischief, but he never took pains. Then Harry died, and when Claude came home, and saw how changed things were, how gray papa's hair had turned, and how silent and melancholy William had grown, he set himself with all his might to make up to papa as far as he could. He thought only of doing what Harry would have wished, and papa himself says that he has done wonders. I cannot see that Henry himself could have been more than Claude is now; he has not spared himself in the least, his tutor says, and he would have had the Newcastle Scholarship last year, if he had not worked so hard that he brought on one of his bad illnesses, and was obliged to come home. Now I am sure that he has acted from love, for it was as much his duty to take pains while Harry was alive as afterwards.'

'Certainly,' said Miss Weston, 'but what does he say himself?'

'Oh! he never will talk of himself,' said Lily.

'Have you not overlooked one thing which may be the truth,' said Alethea, as if she was asking for information, 'that duty and love may be identical? Is not St. Paul's description of charity very like the duty to our neighbour?'

'The practice is the same, but not the theory,' said Lily.

'Now, what is called duty, seems to me to be love doing unpleasant work,' said Miss Weston; 'love disguised under another name, when obliged to act in a way which seems, only seems, out of accordance with its real title.'

'That is all very well for those who have love,' said Lily. 'Some have not who do their duty conscientiously—another word which I hate, by the bye.'

'They have love in a rough coat, perhaps,' said Alethea, 'and I should expect it soon to put on a smoother one.'

CHAPTER VII
SIR MAURICE

'Shall thought was his, in after time,
Thus to be hitched into a rhyme;
The simple sire could only boast
That he was loyal to his cost,
The banished race of kings revered,
And lost his land.'

The holidays arrived, and with them the three brothers, for during the first few weeks of the Oxford vacation Claude accompanied Lord Rotherwood on visits to some college friends, and only came home the same day as the younger ones.

Maurice did not long leave his sisters in doubt as to what was to be his reigning taste, for as soon as dinner was over, he made Jane find the volume of the Encyclopædia containing Entomology, and with his elbows on the table, proceeded to study it so intently, that the young ladies gave up all hopes of rousing him from it. Claude threw himself down on the sofa to enjoy the luxury of a desultory talk with his sisters; and Reginald, his head on the floor, and his heels on a chair, talked loud and fast enough for all three, with very little regard to what the damsels might be saying.

'Oh! Claude,' said Lily, 'you cannot think how much we like Miss Weston, she lets us call her Alethea, and—'

Here came an interruption from Mr. Mohun, who perceiving the position of Reginald's dusty shoes, gave a loud 'Ah—h!' as if he was scolding a dog, and ordered him to change them directly.

'Here, Phyl!' said Reginald, kicking off his shoes, 'just step up and bring my shippers, Rachel will give them to you.'

Away went Phyllis, well pleased to be her brother's fag.

'Ah! Redgie does not know the misfortune that hangs over him,' said Emily.

'What?' said Reginald, 'will not the Baron let Viper come to the house?'

'Worse,' said Emily, 'Rachel is going away.'

'Rachel?' cried Claude, starting up from the sofa.

'Rachel?' said Maurice, without raising his eyes.

'Rachel! Rachel! botheration!' roared Reginald, with a wondrous caper.

'Yes, Rachel,' said Emily; 'Rachel, who makes so much of you, for no reason that I could ever discover, but because you are the most troublesome.'

'You will never find any one to mend your jackets, and dress your wounds like Rachel,' said Lily, 'and make a baby of you instead of a great schoolboy. What will become of you, Redgie?'

'What will become of any of us?' said Claude; 'I thought Rachel was the mainspring of the house.'

'Have you quarrelled with her, Emily?' said Reginald.

'Nonsense,' said Emily, 'it is only that her brother has lost his wife, and wants her to take care of his children.'

'Well,' said Reginald, 'her master has lost his wife, and wants her to take care of his children.'

'I cannot think what I shall do,' said Ada; 'I cry about it every night when I go to bed. What is to be done?'

'Send her brother a new wife,' said Maurice.

'Send him Emily,' said Reginald; 'we could spare her much better.'

'Only I don't wish him joy,' said Maurice.

'Well, I hope you wish me joy of my substitute,' said Emily; 'I do not think you would ever guess, but Lily, after being in what Rachel calls quite a way, has persuaded every one to let us have Esther Bateman.'

'What, the Baron?' said Claude, in surprise.

'Yes,' said Lily, 'is it not delightful? He said at first, Emily was too inexperienced to teach a young servant; but then we settled that Hannah should be upper servant, and Esther will only have to wait upon Phyl and Ada. Then he said Faith Longley was of a better set of people, but I am sure it would give one the nightmare to see her lumbering about the house, and then he talked it over with Robert and with Rachel.'

'And was not Rachel against it, or was she too kind to her young ladies?'

'Oh! she was cross when she talked it over with us,' said Lily; 'but we coaxed her over, and she told the Baron it would do very well.'

'And Robert?'

'He was quite with us, for he likes Esther as much as I do,' said lily.

'Now, Lily,' said Jane, 'how can you say he was quite with you, when he said he thought it would be better if she was farther from home, and under some older person?'

'Yes, but he allowed that she would be much safer here than at home,' said Lily.

'But I thought she used to be the head of all the ill behaviour in school,' said Claude.

'Oh! that was in Eleanor's time,' said Lily; 'there was nothing to draw her out, she never was encouraged; but since she has been in my class, and has found that her wishes to do right are appreciated and met by affection, she has been quite a new creature.'

'Since she has been in MY class,' Claude repeated.

'Well,' said Lily, with a slight blush, 'it is just what Robert says. He told her, when he gave her her prize Bible on Palm Sunday, that she had been going on very well, but she must take great care when removed from those whose influence now guided her, and who could he have meant but me? And now she is to go on with me always. She will be quite one of the old sort of faithful servants, who feel that they owe everything to their masters, and will it not be pleasant to have so sweet and expressive a face about the house?'

'Do I know her face?' said Claude. 'Oh yes! I do. She has black eyes, I think, and would be pretty if she did not look pert.'

'You provoking Claude!' cried Lily, 'you are as bad as Alethea, who never will say that Esther is the best person for us.'

'I was going to inquire for the all-for-love principle,' said Claude, 'but I see it is in full force. And how are the verses, Lily? Have you made a poem upon Michael Moone, or Mohun, the actor, our uncle, whom I discovered for you in Pepys's Memoirs?'

'Nonsense,' said Lily; 'but I have been writing something about Sir Maurice, which you shall hear whenever you are not in this horrid temper.'

The next afternoon, as soon as luncheon was over, Lily drew Claude out to his favourite place under the plane-tree, where she proceeded to inflict her poem upon his patient ears, while he lay flat upon the grass looking up to the sky; Emily and Jane had promised to join them there in process of time, and the four younger ones were, as usual, diverting themselves among the farm buildings at the Old Court.

Lily began: 'I meant to have two parts about Sir Maurice going out to fight when he was very young, and then about his brothers being killed, and King Charles knighting him, and his betrothed, Phyllis Crossthwayte, embroidering his black engrailed cross on his banner, and then the taking the castle, and his being wounded, and escaping, and Phyllis not thinking it right to leave her father; but I have not finished that, so now you must hear about his return home.'

> 'A romaunt in six cantos, entitled Woe woe,
> By Miss Fanny F. known more commonly so,'

muttered Claude to himself; but as Lily did not understand or know whence his quotation came, it did not hurt her feelings, and she went merrily on:—

"'Tis the twenty-ninth of merry May;
Full cheerily shine the sunbeams to-day,
  Their joyous light revealing
Full many a troop in garments gay,
With cheerful steps who take their way
  By the green hill and shady lane,
While merry bells are pealing;
  And soon in Beechcroft's holy fane
The villagers are kneeling.
Dreary and mournful seems the shrine
Where sound their prayers and hymns divine;
  For every mystic ornament
  By the rude spoiler's hand is rent;
  Scarce is its ancient beauty traced
  In wood-work broken and defaced,
  Reft of each quaint device and rare,
  Of foliage rich and mouldings fair;
  Yet happy is each spirit there;
    The simple peasantry rejoice
  To see the altar decked with care,
    To hear their ancient Pastor's voice
  Reciting o'er each well-known prayer,
  To view again his robe of white,
  And hear the services aright;
  Once more to chant their glorious Creed,
  And thankful own their nation freed
  From those who cast her glories down,
  And rent away her Cross and Crown.
  A stranger knelt among the crowd,
  And joined his voice in praises loud,
  And when the holy rites had ceased,
  Held converse with the aged Priest,
  Then turned to join the village feast,
  Where, raised on the hill's summit green,
  The Maypole's flowery wreaths were seen;
  Beneath the venerable yew
  The stranger stood the sports to view,
  Unmarked by all, for each was bent
  On his own scheme of merriment,

On talking, laughing, dancing, playing—
There never was so blithe a Maying.
So thought each laughing maiden gay,
Whose head-gear bore the oaken spray;
So thought that hand of shouting boys,
Unchecked in their best joy—in noise;
But gray-haired men, whose deep-marked scars
Bore token of the civil wars,
And hooded dames in cloaks of red,
At the blithe youngsters shook the head,
Gathering in eager clusters told
How joyous were the days of old,
When Beechcroft's lords, those Barons bold,
Came forth to join their vassals' sport,
And here to hold their rustic court,
Throned in the ancient chair you see
Beneath our noble old yew tree.
Alas! all empty stands the throne,
Reserved for Mohun's race alone,
And the old folks can only tell
Of the good lords who ruled so well.
"Ah! I bethink me of the time,
The last before those years of crime,
When with his open hearty cheer,
The good old squire was sitting here."
"'Twas then," another voice replied,
"That brave young Master Maurice tried
To pitch the ball with Andrew Grey—
We ne'er shall see so blithe a day—
All the young squires have long been dead."
"No, Master Webb," quoth Andrew Grey,
"Young Master Maurice safely fled,
At least so all the Greenwoods say,
And Walter Greenwood with him went
To share his master's banishment;
And now King Charles is ruling here,
Our own good landlord may be near."
"Small hope of that," the old man said,
And sadly shook his hoary head,
"Sir Maurice died beyond the sea,

Last of his noble line was he."
"Look, Master Webb!" he turned, and there
The stranger sat in Mohun's chair;
At ease he sat, and smiled to scan
The face of each astonished man;
Then on the ground he laid aside
His plumed hat and mantle wide.
One moment, Andrew deemed he knew
Those glancing eyes of hazel hue,
But the sunk cheek, the figure spare,
The lines of white that streak the hair—
How can this he the stripling gay,
Erst, victor in the sports of May?
Full twenty years of cheerful toil,
And labour on his native soil,
On Andrew's head had left no trace—
  The summer's sun, the winter's storm,
They had but ruddier made his face,
  More hard his hand, more strong his form.
Forth from the wandering, whispering crowd,
A farmer came, and spoke aloud,
With rustic bow and welcome fair,
But with a hesitating air—
He told how custom well preserved
The throne for Mohun's race reserved;
The stranger laughed, "What, Harrington,
Hast thou forgot thy landlord's son?"
Loud was the cry, and blithe the shout,
On Beechcroft hill that now rang out,
And still remembered is the day,
That merry twenty-ninth of May,
When to his father's home returned
That knight, whose glory well was earned.
In poverty and banishment,
His prime of manhood had been spent,
A wanderer, scorned by Charles's court,
One faithful servant his support.
And now, he seeks his home forlorn,
Broken in health, with sorrow worn.
And two short years just passed away,

Between that joyous meeting-day,
And the sad eve when Beechcroft's bell
Tolled forth Sir Maurice's funeral knell;
And Phyllis, whose love was so constant and tried,
Was a widow the year she was Maurice's bride;
Yet the path of the noble and true-hearted knight,
Was brilliant with honour, and glory, and light,
And still his descendants shall sing of the fame
Of Sir Maurice de Mohun, the pride of his name.'

'It is a pity they should sing of it in such lines as those last four,' said Claude. 'Let me see, I like your bringing in the real names, though I doubt whether any but Greenwood could have been found here.'

'Oh! here come Emily and Jane,' said Lily, 'let me put it away.'

'You are very much afraid of Jane,' said Claude.

'Yes, Jane has no feeling for poetry,' said Lily, with simplicity, which made her brother smile.

Jane and Emily now came up, the former with her work, the latter with a camp-stool and a book. 'I wonder,' said she, 'where those boys are! By the bye, what character did they bring home from school?'

'The same as usual,' said Claude. 'Maurice's mind only half given to his work, and Redgie's whole mind to his play.'

'Maurice's talent does not lie in the direction of Latin and Greek,' said Emily.

'No,' said Jane, 'it is nonsense to make him learn it, and so he says.'

'Perhaps he would say the same of mathematics and mechanics, if as great a point were made of them,' said Lily.

'I think not,' said Claude; 'he has more notion of them than of Latin verses.'

'Then you are on my side,' said Jane, triumphantly.

'Did I say so?' said Claude.

'Why not?' said Jane. 'What is the use of his knowing those stupid languages? I am sure it is wasting time not to improve such a genius as he has for mechanics and natural history. Now, Claude, I wish you would answer.'

'I was waiting till you had done,' said Claude.

'Why do you not think it nonsense?' persisted Jane.

'Because I respect my father's opinion,' said Claude, letting himself fall on the grass, as if he had done with the subject.

'Pooh!' said Jane, 'that sounds like a good little boy of five years old!'

'Very likely,' said Claude.

'But you have some opinion of your own,' said Lily.

'Certainly.'

'Then I wish you would give it,' said Jane.

'Come, Emily,' said Claude, 'have you brought anything to read?'

'But your opinion, Claude,' said Jane. 'I am sure you think with me, only you are too grand, and too correct to say so.'

Claude made no answer, but Jane saw she was wrong by his countenance; before she could say anything more, however, they were interrupted by a great outcry from the Old Court regions.

'Oh,' said Emily, 'I thought it was a long time since we had heard anything of those uproarious mortals.'

'I hope there is nothing the matter,' said Lily.

'Oh no,' said Jane, 'I hear Redgie's laugh.'

'Aye, but among that party,' said Emily, 'Redgie's laugh is not always a proof of peace: they are too much in the habit of acting the boys and the frogs.'

'We were better off,' said Lily, 'with the gentle Claude, as Miss Middleton used to call him.'

'Miss Molly, as William used to call him with more propriety,' said Claude, 'not half so well worth playing with as such a fellow as Redgie.'

'Not even for young ladies?' said Emily.

'No, Phyllis and Ada are much the better for being teased,' said Claude. 'I am convinced that I never did my duty by you in that respect.'

'There were others to do it for you,' said Jane.

'Harry never teased,' said Emily, 'and William scorned us.'

'His teasing was all performed upon Claude,' said Lily, 'and a great shame it was.'

'Not at all,' said Claude, 'only an injudicious attempt to put a little life into a tortoise.'

'A bad comparison,' said Lily; 'but what is all this? Here come the children in dismay! What is the matter, my dear child?'

This was addressed to Phyllis, who was the first to come up at full speed, sobbing, and out of breath, 'Oh, the dragon-fly! Oh, do not let him kill it!'

'The dragon-fly, the poor dear blue dragon-fly!' screamed Adeline, hiding her face in Emily's lap, 'Oh, do not let him kill it! he is holding it; he is hurting it! Oh, tell him not!'

'I caught it,' said Phyllis, 'but not to have it killed. Oh, take it away!'

'A fine rout, indeed, you chicken,' said Reginald; 'I know a fellow who ate up five horse-stingers one morning before breakfast.'

'Stingers!' said Phyllis, 'they do not sting anything, pretty creatures.'

'I told you I would catch the old pony and put it on him to try,' said Reginald.

In the meantime, Maurice came up at his leisure, holding his prize by the wings. 'Look what a beautiful Libellulla Puella,' said he to Jane.

'A demoiselle dragon-fly,' said Lily; 'what a beauty! what are you going to do with it?'

'Put it into my museum,' said Maurice. 'Here, Jane, put it under this flower-pot, and take care of it, while I fetch something to kill it with.'

'Oh, Maurice, do not!' said Emily.

'One good squeeze,' said Reginald. 'I will do it.'

'How came you be so cruel?' said Lily.

'No, a squeeze will not do,' said Maurice; 'it would spoil its beauty; I must put it ever the fumes of carbonic acid.'

'Maurice, you really must not,' said Emily.

'Now do not, dear Maurice,' said Ada, 'there's a dear boy; I will give you such a kiss.'

'Nonsense; get out of the way,' said Maurice, turning away.

'Now, Maurice, this is most horrid cruelty,' said Lily; 'what right have you to shorten the brief, happy life which—'

'Well,' interrupted Maurice, 'if you make such a fuss about killing it, I will stick a pin through it into a cork, and let it shift for itself.'

Poor Phyllis ran away to the other end of the garden, sat down and sobbed, Ada screamed and argued, Emily complained, Lily exhorted Claude to interfere, while Reginald stood laughing.

'Such useless cruelty,' said Emily.

'Useless!' said Maurice. 'Pray how is any one to make a collection of natural objects without killing things?'

'I do not see the use of a collection,' said Lily; 'you can examine the creatures and let them go.'

'Such a young lady's tender-hearted notion,' said Reginald.

'Who ever heard of a man of science managing in such a ridiculous way?'

'Man of science!' exclaimed Lily, 'when he will have forgotten by next Christmas that insects ever existed.'

It was not convenient to hear this speech, so Maurice turned an empty flower-pot over his prisoner, and left it in Jane's care while he went to fetch the means of destruction, probably choosing the lawn for the place of execution, in order to show his contempt for his sisters.

'Fair damsel in boddice blue,' said Lily, peeping in at the hole at the top of the flower-pot, 'I wish I could avert your melancholy fate. I am very sorry for you, but I cannot help it.'

'You might help it now, at any rate,' muttered Claude.

'No,' said Lily, 'I know Monsieur Maurice too well to arouse his wrath so justly. If you choose to release the pretty creature, I shall be charmed.'

'You forget that I am in charge,' said Jane.

'There is a carriage coming to the front gate,' cried Ada. 'Emily, may I go into the drawing-room? Oh, Jenny, will you undo my brown holland apron?'

'That is right, little mincing Miss,' said Reginald, with a low bow; 'how fine we are to-day.'

'How visitors break into the afternoon,' said Emily, with a languid turn of her head.

'Jenny, brownie,' called Maurice from his bedroom window, 'I want the sulphuric acid.'

Jane sprang up and ran into the house, though her sisters called after her, that she would come full upon the company in the hall.

'They shall not catch me here,' cried Reginald, rushing off into the shrubbery.

'Are you coming in, Claude?' said Emily.

'Send Ada to call me, if there is any one worth seeing,' said Claude

'They will see you from the window,' said Emily.

'No,' said Claude, 'no one ever found me out last summer, under these friendly branches.'

The old butler, Joseph, now showed himself on the terrace; and the young ladies, knowing that he had no intention of crossing the lawn, hastened to learn from him who their visitors were, and entered the house. Just then Phyllis came running back from the kitchen garden, and without looking round, or perceiving Claude, she took up the flower-pot and released the captive, which, unconscious of its peril, rested on a blade of grass, vibrating its gauzy wings and rejoicing in the restored sunbeams.

'Fly away, fly away, you pretty creature,' said Phyllis; 'make haste, or Maurice will come and catch you again. I wish I had not given you such a fright. I thought you would have been killed, and a pin stuck all through that pretty blue and black body of yours. Oh! that would be dreadful. Make haste and go away! I would not have caught you, you beautiful thing, if I had known what he wanted to do. I thought he only wanted to look at your beautiful body, like a little bit of the sky come down to look at the flowers, and your delicate wings, and great shining eyes. Oh! I am very glad God made you so beautiful. Oh! there is Maurice coming. I must blow upon you to make you go. Oh, that is right—up quite high in the air—quite safe,' and she clapped her hands as the dragon-fly rose in the air, and disappeared behind the laurels, just as Maurice and Reginald emerged from the shrubbery, the former with a bottle in his hand.

'Well, where is the Libellulla?' said he.

'The dragon-fly?' said Phyllis. 'I let it out.'

'Sold, Maurice!' cried Reginald, laughing at his brother's disaster.

'Upon my word, Phyl, you are very kind!' said Maurice, angrily. 'If I had known you were such an ill-natured crab—'

'Oh! Maurice dear, don't say so,' exclaimed Phyllis. 'I thought I might let it out because I caught it myself; and I told you I did not catch it for you to kill; Maurice, indeed, I am sorry I vexed you.'

'What else did you do it for?' said Maurice. 'It is horrid not to be able to leave one's things a minute—'

'But I did not know the dragon-fly belonged to you, Maurice,' said Phyllis.

'That is a puzzler, Mohun senior,' said Reginald.

'Now, Redgie, do get Maurice to leave off being angry with me,' implored his sister.

'I will leave off being angry,' said Maurice, seeing his advantage, 'if you will promise never to let out my things again.'

'I do not think I can promise,' said Phyllis.

'O yes, you can,' said Reginald, 'you know they are not his.'

'Promise you will not let out any insects I may get,' said Maurice, 'or I shall say you are as cross as two sticks.'

'I'll tell you what, Maurice,' said Phyllis, 'I do wish you would not make me promise, for I do not think I *can* keep it, for I cannot bear to see the beautiful live things killed.'

'Nonsense,' said Maurice, fiercely, 'I am very angry indeed, you naughty child; promise—'

'I cannot,' said Phyllis, beginning to cry.

'Then,' said Maurice, 'I will not speak to you all day.'

'No, no,' shouted Reginald, 'we will only treat her like the horse-stinger; you wanted a puella, Maurice—here is one for you, here, give her a dose of the turpentine.'

'Yes,' said Maurice, advancing with his bottle; 'and do you take the poker down to Naylor's to be sharpened, it will just do to stick through her back. Oh! no, not Naylor's—the girls have made a hash there, as they do everything else; but we will settle her before they come out again.'

Phyllis screamed and begged for mercy—her last ally had deserted her.

'Promise!' cried the boys.

'Oh, don't!' was all her answer.

Reginald caught her and held her fast, Maurice advanced upon her, she struggled, and gave a scream of real terror. The matter was no joke to any one but Reginald, for Maurice was very angry and really meant to frighten her.

'Hands off, boys, I will not have her bullied,' said Claude, half rising.

Maurice gave a violent start, Reginald looked round laughing, and exclaimed, 'Who would have thought of Claude sneaking there?' and Phyllis ran to the protecting arm, which he stretched out. To her great surprise, he drew her to him, and kissed her forehead, saying, 'Well done, Phyl!'

'Oh, I knew he was not going to hurt me,' said Phyllis, still panting from the struggle.

'To be sure not,' said Maurice, 'I only meant to have a little fun.'

Claude, with his arm still round his sister's waist, gave Maurice a look, expressing, 'Is that the truth?' and Reginald tumbled head over heels, exclaiming, 'I would not have been Phyl just them.'

Ada now came running up to them, saying, 'Maurice and Redgie, you are to come in; Mr. and Mrs. Burnet heard your voices, and begged to see you, because they never saw you last holidays.'

'More's the pity they should see us now,' said Maurice.

'I shall not go,' said Reginald.

'Papa is there, and he sent for you,' said Ada.

'Plague,' was the answer.

'See what you get by making such a row,' said Claude. 'If you had been as orderly members of society as I am—'

'Oh, but Claude,' said Ada, 'papa told me to see if I could find you. Dear Claude, I wish,' she proceeded, taking his hand, and looking engaging, 'I wish you would put your arm round me as you do round Phyl.'

'You are not worth it, Ada,' said Reginald, and Claude did not contradict him.

CHAPTER VIII
THE BROTHERS

'But smiled to hear the creatures he had known
So long were now in class and order shown—
Genus and species. "Is it meet," said he,
"This creature's name should one so sounding be—
'Tis but a fly, though first-born of the spring,
Bombylius Majus, dost thou call the thing?"

It was not till Sunday, that Lily's eager wish was fulfilled, of introducing her friend and her brothers; but, as she might have foreseen, their first meeting did not make the perfections of either party very clear to the other. Claude never spoke to strangers more than he could help, Maurice and Reginald were in the room only a short time; so that the result of Miss Weston's observations, when communicated in reply to Lily's eager inquiries, was only that Claude was very like his father and eldest brother, Reginald very handsome, and Maurice looked like a very funny fellow.

On Monday, Reginald and Maurice were required to learn what they had always refused to acknowledge, that the holidays were not intended to be spent in idleness. A portion of each morning was to be devoted to study, Claude having undertaken the task of tutor—and hard work he found it; and much did Lily pity him, when, as not unfrequently happened, the summons to the children's dinner would bring him from the study, looking thoroughly fagged—Maurice in so sulky a mood that he would hardly deign to open his lips—Reginald talking fast enough, indeed, but only to murmur at his duties in terms, which, though they made every one laugh, were painful to hear. Then Claude would take his brothers back to the study, and not appear for an hour or more, and when he did come forth, it was with a bad headache. Sometimes, as if to show that it was only through their own fault that their tasks were wearisome, one or both boys would finish quite early, when Reginald would betake himself to the schoolroom and employ his idle time in making it nearly impossible for Ada and Phyllis to learn, by talking, laughing, teasing the canary, overturning everything in pursuing wasps, making Emily fretful by his disobedience, and then laughing at her, and, in short, proving his right to the title he had given himself at the end of the only letter he had written since he first went to school, and which he had subscribed, 'Your affectionate bother, R. Mohun.' So that, for their own sake, all would have preferred the inattentive mornings.

Lily often tried to persuade Claude to allow her to tell her father how troublesome the boys were, but never with any effect. He once took up a book he had been using with them, and pointing to the name in the first page, in writing, which Lily knew full well, 'Henry Mohun,' she perceived that he meant to convince her that it was useless to try to dissuade him, as he thought the patience and forbearance his brother had shown to him must be repaid by his not shrinking from the task he had imposed upon himself with his young brothers, though he was often obliged to sit up part of the night to pursue his own studies.

If Claude had rather injudiciously talked too much to Lilias of 'her principle,' and thus kept it alive in her mind, yet his example might have made its fallacy evident. She believed that what she called love had been the turning point in his character, that it had been his earnest desire to follow in Henry's steps, and so try to comfort his father for his loss, that had roused him from his indolence; but she was beginning to see that nothing but a sense of duty could have kept up the power of that first impulse for six years. Lily began to enter a little into his principle, and many things that occurred during these holidays made her mistrust her former judgment. She saw that without the unvarying principle of right and wrong, fraternal love itself would fail in outward acts and words. Forbearance, though undeniably a branch of love, could not exist without constant remembrance of duty; and which of them did not sometimes fail in kindness, meekness, and patience? Did Emily show that softness, which was her most agreeable characteristic, in her whining reproofs—in her complaints that 'no one listened to a word she said'—in her refusal to do justice even to those who had vainly been seeking for peace? Did Lily herself show any of her much valued love, by the sharp manner in which she scolded the boys for roughness towards herself? or for language often used by them on purpose to make her displeasure a matter of amusement? She saw that her want of command of temper was a failure both in love and duty, and when irritated, the thought of duty came sooner to her aid than the feeling of love.

And Maurice and Reginald were really very provoking. Maurice loved no amusement better than teasing his sisters, and this was almost the only thing in which Reginald agreed with him. Reginald was affectionate, but too reckless and violent not to be very troublesome, and he too often flew into a passion if Maurice attempted to laugh at him; the little girls were often frightened and made unhappy; Phyllis would scream and roar, and Ada would come sobbing to Emily, to be comforted after some rudeness of Reginald's. It was not very often that quarrels went so far, but many a time in thought, word, and deed was the rule of love transgressed, and more than once did Emily feel ready to give up all her dignity, to have Eleanor's hand over the boys once more. Claude, finding that he could do much to prevent mischief, took care not to leave the two boys long together with the elder girls. They were far more inoffensive when separate, as Maurice never practised his tormenting tricks when no one was present to laugh with him, and Reginald was very kind to Phyllis and Ada, although somewhat rude.

It was a day or two after they returned that Phyllis was leaning on the window-sill in the drawing-room, watching a passing shower, and admiring the soft bright tints of a rainbow upon the dark gray mass of cloud. 'I do set my bow in the cloud,' repeated she to herself over and over again, until Adeline entering the room, she eagerly exclaimed, 'Oh Ada, come and look at this beautiful rainbow, green, and pink, and purple. A double one, with so many stripes, Ada. See, there is a little bit more green.'

'There is no green in a rainbow,' said Ada.

'But look, Ada, that is green.'

'It is not real green. Blue, red, and yellow are the pragmatic colours,' said Ada, with a most triumphant air. 'Now are not they, Maurice?' said she, turning to her brother, who was, as usual, deep in entomology.

'Pragmatic, you foolish child,' said he. 'Prismatic you mean. I am glad you remember what I tell you, however; I think I might teach you some science in time. You are right in saying that blue, red, and yellow are the prismatic colours. Now do you know what causes a rainbow?'

'It is to show there is never to be another flood,' said Phyllis, gravely.

'Oh, I did not mean that,' said Maurice, addressing himself to Ada, whose love of hard words made him deem her a promising pupil, and whom he could lecture without interruption. 'The rainbow is caused by—'

'But, Maurice!' exclaimed Phyllis, remaining with mouth wide open.

'The rainbow is occasioned by the refraction of the rays of the sun in the drops of water of which a cloud is composed.'

'But, Maurice!' again said Phyllis.

'Well, what do you keep on "but, Mauricing," about?'

'But, Maurice, I thought it said, "I do set my bow in the cloud." Is not that right? I will look.'

'I know that, but I know the iris, or rainbow, is a natural phenomenon occasioned by the refraction.'

'But, Maurice, I can't bear you to say that;' and poor Phyllis sat down and began to cry.

Ada interfered. 'Why, Maurice, you believe the Bible, don't you?'

This last speech was heard by Lilias, who just now entered the room, and greatly surprised her. 'What can you be talking of?' said she.

'Only some nonsense of the children's,' said Maurice, shortly.

'But only hear what he says,' cried Ada. 'He says the rainbow was not put there to show there is never to be another flood!'

'Now, Lily,' said Maurice, 'I do not think there is much use in talking to you, but I wish you to understand that all I said was, that the rainbow, or iris, is a natural phenomenon occasioned by the refraction of the solar—'

'You will certainly bewilder yourself into something dreadful with that horrid science,' said Lily. 'What is the matter with Phyl?'

'Only crying because of what I said,' answered Maurice. 'So childish, and you are just as bad.'

'But do you mean to say,' exclaimed Lily, 'that you set this human theory above the authority of the Bible?'

'It is common sense,' said Maurice; 'I could make a rainbow any day.'

Whereupon Phyllis cried the more, and Lily looked infinitely shocked. 'This is philosophy and vain deceit,' said she; 'the very thing that tends to infidelity.'

'I can't help it—it is universally allowed,' said the boy doggedly.

It was fortunate that the next person who entered the room was Claude, and all at once he was appealed to by the four disputants, Lily the loudest and most vehement. 'Claude, listen to him, and tell him to throw away these hateful new lights, which lead to everything that is shocking!'

'Listen to him, with three ladies talking at once?' said Claude. 'No, not Phyl—her tears only are eloquent; but it is a mighty war about the token of peace and *love*, Lily.'

'The love would be in driving these horrible philosophical speculations out of Maurice's mind,' said Lily.

'No one can ever drive out the truth,' said Maurice, with provoking coolness. 'Don't let her scratch out my eyes, Claude.'

'I am not so sure of that maxim,' said Claude. 'Truth is chiefly injured—I mean, her force weakened, by her own supporters.'

'Then you agree with me,' said Maurice, 'as, in fact, every rational person must.'

'Then you are with me,' said Lily, in the same breath; 'and you will convince Maurice of the danger of this nonsense.'

'Umph,' sighed Claude, throwing himself into his father's arm-chair, ''tis a Herculean labour! It seems I agree with you both.'

'Why, every Christian must be with me, who has not lost his way in a mist of his own raising,' said Lilias.

'Do you mean to say,' said Maurice, 'that these colours are not produced by refraction? Look at them on those prisms;' and he pointed to an old-fashioned lustre on the chimney-piece. 'I hope this is not a part of the Christian faith.'

'Take care, Maurice,' and Claude's eyes were bent upon him in a manner that made him shrink. And he added, 'Of course I do believe that chapter about Noah. I only meant that the immediate cause of the rainbow is the refraction of light. I did not mean to be irreverent, only the girls took me up in such a way.'

'And I know well enough that you can make those colours by light on drops of water,' said Lily.

'So you agreed all the time,' said Claude.

'But,' added Lily, 'I never liked to know it; for it always seemed to be explaining away the Bible, and I cannot bear not to regard that lovely bow as a constant miracle.'

'You will remember,' said Claude, 'that some commentators say it should be, "I *have* set my bow in the cloud," which would make what already existed become a token for the future.

'I don't like that explanation,' said Lily.

'Others say,' added Claude, 'that there might have been no rain at all till the windows of heaven were opened at the flood, and, in that case, the first recurrence of rain must have greatly alarmed Noah's family, if they had not been supported and cheered by the sight of the rainbow.'

'That is reasonable,' said Maurice.

'I hate reason applied to revelation,' said Lily.

'It is a happier state of mind which does not seek to apply it,' said Claude, looking at Phyllis, who had dried her tears, and stood in the window gazing at him, in the happy certainty that he was setting all right. Maurice respected Claude for his science as much as his character, and did not make game of this observation as he would if it had been made by one of his sisters, but he looked at him with an odd expression of perplexity. 'You do not think ignorant credulity better than reasonable belief?' said he at length.

'It is not I only who think most highly of child-like unquestioning faith, Maurice,' said Claude—'faith, that is based upon love and reverence,' added he to Lily. 'But come, the shower is over, and philosophers, or no philosophers, I invite you to walk in the wood.'

'Aye,' said Maurice, 'I daresay I can find some of the Arachne species there. By the bye, Claude, do you think papa would let me have a piece of plate-glass, eighteen by twenty, to cover my case of insects?'

'Ask, and you will discover,' said Claude.

Accordingly, Maurice began the next morning at breakfast, 'Papa, may I have a piece of plate-glass, eighteen by—?'

But no one heard, for Emily was at the moment saying, 'The Westons are to dine here to-day.'

Claude and Maurice both looked blank.

'I persuaded papa to ask the Westons,' said Lily, 'because I am determined that Claude shall like Alethea.'

'You must expect that I shall not, you have given me so many orders on the subject,' said Claude.

'Take care it has not the same effect as to tell Maurice to like a book,' said Emily; 'nothing makes his aversion so certain.'

'Except when he takes it up by mistake, and forgets that it has been recommended to him,' said Claude.

'Take care, Redgie, with your knife; don't put out my eyes in your ardour against that wretched wasp. Wat Greenwood may well say "there is a terrible sight of waspses this year."'

'I killed twenty-nine yesterday,' said Reginald.

'And I will tell you what I saw,' said Phyllis; 'I was picking up apples, and the wasps were flying all round, and there came a hornet.'

'Vespa Crabro!' cried Maurice; 'oh, I must have one!'

'Well, what of the hornet?' said Mr. Mohun.

'I'll tell you what,' resumed Phyllis, 'he saw a wasp flying, and so he went up in the air, and pounced on the poor wasp as the hawk did on Jane's bantam. So then he hung himself up to the branch of a tree by one of his legs, and held the wasp with the other five, and began to pack it up. First he bit off the yellow tail, then the legs, and threw them away, and then there was nothing left but the head, and so he flew away with it to his nest.'

'Which way did he go?' said Maurice.

'To the Old Court,' answered Phyllis; 'I think the nest is in the roof of the old cow-house, for they were flying in and out there yesterday, and one was eating out the wood from the old rails.'

'Well,' said Mr. Mohun, 'you must show me a hornet hawking for wasps before the nest is taken, Phyllis; I suppose you have seen the wasps catching flies?'

'Oh yes, papa! but they pack them up quite differently. They do not hang by one leg, but they sit down quite comfortably on a branch while they bite off the wings and legs.'

'There, Maurice,' said Mr. Mohun, 'I had rather hear of one such well-observed fact than of a dozen of your hard names and impaled insects.'

Phyllis looked quite radiant with delight at his approbation.

'But, papa,' said Maurice, 'may I have a piece of plate-glass, eighteen by twenty?'

'When you observe facts in natural history, perhaps I may say something to your entomology,' said Mr. Mohun.

'But, papa, all my insects will be spoilt if I may not have a piece of glass, eighteen by—'

He was interrupted by the arrival of the post-bag, which Jane, as usual, opened. 'A letter from Rotherwood,' said she; 'I hope he is coming at last.'

'He is,' said Claude, reading the letter, 'but only from Saturday till Wednesday.'

'He never gave us so little of his good company as he has this summer,' said Emily.

'You will have them all in the autumn, to comfort you,' said Claude, 'for he hereby announces the marvellous fact, that the Marchioness sends him to see if the castle is fit to receive her.'

'Are you sure he is not only believing what he wishes?' said Mr. Mohun.

'I think he will gain his point at last,' said Claude.

'How stupid of him to stay no longer!' said Reginald.

'I think he has some scheme for this vacation,' said Claude, 'and I suppose he means to crowd all the Beechcroft diversions of a whole summer into those few days.'

'Emily,' said Mr. Mohun, 'I wish him to know the Carringtons; invite them and the Westons to dinner on Tuesday.'

'Oh don't!' cried Reginald. 'It will be so jolly to have him to take wasps' nests; and may I go out rabbit-shooting with him?'

'If he goes.'

'And may I carry a gun?'

'If it is not loaded,' said his father.

'Indeed, I would do no mischief,' said Reginald.

'Let me give you one piece of advice, Reginald,' said Mr. Mohun, with a mysterious air—'never make rash promises.'

Lilias was rather disappointed in her hopes that Miss Weston and Claude would become better acquainted. At dinner the conversation was almost entirely between the elder gentlemen; Claude scarcely spoke, except when referred to by his father or Mr. Devereux. Miss Weston never liked to incur the danger of having to repeat her insignificant speeches to a deaf ear, and being interested in the discussion that was going on, she by no means seconded Lily's attempt to get up an under-current of talk. In general, Lily liked to listen to conversation in silence, but she was now in very high spirits, and could not be quiet; fortunately, she had no interest in the subject the gentlemen were discussing, so that she could not meddle with that, and finding Alethea silent and Claude out of reach, she turned to Reginald, and talked and tittered with him all dinner-time.

In the drawing-room she had it all her own way, and talked enough for all the sisters.

'Have you heard that Cousin Rotherwood is coming?'

'Yes, you said so before dinner.'

'We hope,' said Emily, 'that you and Mr. Weston will dine here on Tuesday. The Carringtons are coming, and a few others.'

'Thank you,' said Alethea; 'I daresay papa will be very glad to come.'

'Have you ever seen Rotherwood?' said Lilias.

'Never,' was the reply.

'Do not expect much,' said Lily, laughing, though she knew not why; 'he is a very little fellow; no one would suppose him to be twenty, he has such a boyish look. Then he never sits down—'

'Literally?' said Emily.

'Literally,' persisted Lily; 'such a quick person you never did see.'

'Is he at Oxford?'

'Oh yes! it was all papa's doing that he was sent to Eton. Papa is his guardian. Aunt Rotherwood never would have parted with him.'

'He is the only son,' interposed Emily.

'Uncle Rotherwood put him quite in papa's power; Aunt Rotherwood wanted to keep him at home with a tutor, and what she would have made of him I cannot think,' said Lily; and regardless of Emily's warning frowns, and Alethea's attempt to change the subject, she went on: 'When he was quite a child he used to seem a realisation of all the naughty Dicks and Toms in story-books. Miss Middleton had a perfect horror of his coming here, for he would mind no one, and played tricks and drew Claude into mischief; but he is quite altered since papa had the management of him—Oh! such talks as papa has had with Aunt Rotherwood—do you know, papa says no one knows what it is to lose a father but those who have the care of his children, and Aunt Rotherwood is so provoking.'

Here Alethea determined to put an end to this oration, and to Emily's great relief, she cut short the detail of Lady Rotherwood's offences by saying, 'Do you think Faith Longley likely to suit us, if we took her to help the housemaid?'

'Are you thinking of taking her?' cried Lily. 'Yes, for steady, stupid household work, Faith would do very well; she is just the stuff to make a servant of—"for dulness ever must be regular"—I mean for those who like mere steadiness better than anything more lovable.'

As Alethea said, laughing, 'I must confess my respect for that quality,' Mr. Devereux and Claude entered the room.

'Oh, Robert!' cried Lily, 'Mrs. Weston is going to take Faith Longley to help the housemaid.'

'You are travelling too fast, Lily,' said Alethea, 'she is only going to think about it.'

'I should be very glad,' said Mr. Devereux, 'that Faith should have a good place; the Longleys are very respectable people, and they behaved particularly well in refusing to let this girl go and live with some dissenters at Stoney Bridge.'

'I like what I have seen of the girl very much,' said Miss Weston.

'In spite of her sad want of feeling,' said Robert, smiling, as he looked at Lily.

'Oh! she is a good work-a-day sort of person,' said Lily, 'like all other poor people, hard and passive. Now, do not set up your eyebrows, Claude, I am quite serious, there is no warmth about any except—'

'So this is what Lily is come to!' cried Emily; 'the grand supporter of the poor on poetical principles.'

'The poor not affectionate!' said Alethea.

'Not, compared within people whose minds and affections have been cultivated,' said Lily. 'Now just hear what Mrs. Wall said to me only yesterday; she asked for a black stuff gown out of the clothing club, "for," said she, "I had a misfortune, Miss;" I thought it would be, "and tore my gown," but it was, "I had a misfortune, Miss, and lost my brother."'

'A very harsh conclusion on very slight grounds,' said Mr. Devereux.

'Prove the contrary,' said Lily.

'Facts would scarcely demonstrate it either way,' said Mr. Devereux. 'They would only prove what was the case with individuals who chanced to come in our way, and if we are seldom able to judge of the depth of feeling of those with whom we are familiar, how much less of those who feel our presence a restraint.'

'Intense feeling mocks restraint,' said Lily.

'Violent, not intense,' said Mr. Devereux. 'Besides, you talk of cultivating the affections. Now what do you mean? Exercising them, or talking about them?'

'Ah!' said Emily, 'the affection of a poor person is more tried; we blame a poor man for letting his old mother go to the workhouse, without considering how many of us would do the same, if we had as little to live upon.'

'Still,' said Alethea, 'the same man who would refuse to maintain her if poor, would not bear with her infirmities if rich.'

'Are the poor never infirm and peevish?' said Mr. Devereux.

'Oh! how much worse it must be to bear with ill-temper in poverty,' said Emily, 'when we think it quite wonderful to see a young lady kind and patient with a cross old relation; what must it be when she is denying herself, not only her pleasure, but her food for her sake; not merely sitting quietly with her all day, and calling a servant to wait upon her, but toiling all day to maintain her, and keeping awake half the night to nurse her?'

'Those are realities, indeed,' said Alethea; 'our greatest efforts seem but child's play in comparison.'

Lilias could hardly have helped being sobered by this conversation if she had attended to it, but she had turned away to repeat the story of Mrs. Walls to Jane, and then, fancying that the others were still remarking upon it, she said in a light, laughing tone, 'Well, so far I agree with you. I know of a person who may well be called one of ourselves, who I could quite fancy making such a speech.'

'Whom do you mean?' said Mr. Devereux. Alethea wished she did not know.

'No very distant relation,' said Jane.

'Do not talk nonsense, Jane,' said Claude, gravely.

'No nonsense at all, Claude,' cried Jane in her very very pertest tone, 'it is exactly like Eleanor; I am sure I can see her with her hands before her, saying in her prim voice, "I must turn my old black silk and trim it with crape, for I have had a misfortune, and lost my brother."'

'Lilias,' said Miss Weston, somewhat abruptly, 'did you not wish to sing with me this evening?'

And thus she kept Lilias from any further public mischief that evening.

Claude, exceedingly vexed by what had passed, with great injustice, laid the blame upon Miss Weston, and instead of rendering her the honour which she really deserved for the tact with which she had put an end to the embarrassment of all parties, he fancied she was anxious to display her talents for music, and thus only felt fretted by the sounds.

Mr. Weston and his daughter intended to walk home that evening, as it was a beautiful moonlight night.

'Oh, let us convoy you!' exclaimed Lilias; 'I do long to show Alethea a glow-worm. Will you come, Claude? May we, papa? Feel how still and warm it is. A perfect summer night, not a breath stirring.'

Mr. Mohun consented, and Lily almost hurried Alethea upstairs, to put on her bonnet and shawl. When she came down she found that the walking party had increased. Jane and Reginald would both have been in despair to have missed such a frolic; Maurice hoped to fall in with the droning beetle, or to lay violent hands on a glow-worm; Emily did not like to be left behind, and even Mr. Mohun was going, being in the midst of an interesting conversation with Mr. Weston. Lily, with an absurd tragic gesture, told Alethea that amongst so many, such a crowd, all the grace and sweet influence of the walk was ruined. The 'sweet influence' was ruined as far as Lily was concerned, but not by the number of her companions. It was the uneasy feeling caused by her over-strained spirits and foolish chattering that prevented her from really entering into the charm of the soft air, the clear moon, the solemn deep blue sky, the few stars, the white lilies on the dark pond, the long shadows of the trees, the freshness of the dewy fields. Her simplicity, and her genuine delight in the loveliness of the scene, was gone for the time, and though she spoke much of her enjoyment, it was in a high-flown affected style.

When the last good-night had been exchanged, and Lily had turned homeward, she felt the stillness which succeeded their farewells almost oppressive; she started at the dark shadow of a tree which lay across the path, and to shake off a sensation of fear which was coming over her, she put her arm within Claude's, exclaiming, 'You naughty boy, you will be stupid and silent, say what I will.'

'I heard enough to-night to strike me dumb,' said Claude.

For one moment Lily thought he was in jest, but the gravity of his manner showed her that he was both grieved and displeased, and she changed her tone as she said, 'Oh! Claude, what do you mean?'

'Do you not know?' said Claude.

'What, you mean about Eleanor?' said Lily; 'you must fall upon Miss Jenny there—it was her doing.'

'Jane's tongue is a pest,' said Claude; 'but she was not the first to speak evil falsely of one to whom you owe everything. Oh! Lily, I cannot tell you how that allusion of yours sounded.'

'What allusion?' asked Lily in alarm, for she had never seen her gentle brother so angry.

'You know,' said he.

'Indeed, I do not,' exclaimed Lily, munch frightened. 'Claude, Claude, you must mistake, I never could have said anything so very shocking.'

'I hope I do,' said Claude; 'I could hardly believe that one of the little ones who cannot remember him, could have referred to him in that way—but for you!'

'Him?' said Lilias.

'I do not like to mention his name to one who regards him so lightly,' said Claude. 'Think over what passed, if you are sufficiently come to yourself to remember it.'

After a little pause Lily said in a subdued voice, 'Claude, I hope you do not believe that I was thinking of what really happened when I said that.'

'Pray what were you thinking of?'

'The abstract view of Eleanor's character.'

'Abstract nonsense!' said Claude. 'A fine demonstration of the rule of love, to go about the world slandering your sister!'

'To go about the world! Oh! Claude, it was only Robert, one of ourselves, and Alethea, to whom I tell everything.'

'So much the worse. I always rejoiced that you had no foolish young lady friend to make missish confidences to.'

'She is no foolish young lady friend,' said Lilias, indignant in her turn; 'she is five years older than I am, and papa wishes us to be intimate with her.'

'Then the fault is in yourself,' said Claude. 'You ought not to have told such things if they were true, and being utterly false—'

'But, Claude, I cannot see that they are false.'

'Not false, that Eleanor cared not a farthing for Harry!' cried Claude, shaking off Lily's arm, and stopping short.

'Oh!—she cared, she really did care,' said Lily, as fast as she could speak. 'Oh! Claude, how could you think that? I told you I did not mean what really happened, only that—Eleanor is cold—not as warm as some people—she did care for him, of course she did—I know that—I believe she loved him with all her heart—but yet—I mean she did not—she went on as usual—said nothing—scarcely cried—looked the same—taught us—never—Oh! it did not make half the difference in her that it did in William.'

'I cannot tell how she behaved at the time,' said Claude, 'I only know I never had any idea what a loss Harry was till I came home and saw her face. I used never to trouble myself to think whether people looked ill or well, but the change in her did strike me. She was bearing up to comfort papa, and to cheer William, and to do her duty by all of us, and you could take such noble resignation for want of feeling!'

Lilias looked down and tried to speak, but she was choked by her tears; she could not bear Claude's displeasure, and she wept in silence. At last she said in a voice broken by sobs, 'I was unjust—I know Eleanor was all kindness—all self-sacrifice—I have been very ungrateful—I wish I could help it—and you know well, Claude, how far I am from regarding dear Harry with indifference—how the thought of him is a star in my mind—how happy it makes me to think of him at the end of the Church Militant Prayer; do not believe I was dreaming of him.'

'And pray,' said Claude, laughing in his own good-humoured way, 'which of us is it that she is so willing to lose?'

'Oh! Claude, no such thing,' said Lily, 'you know what I meant, or did not mean. It was nonsense—I hope nothing worse.' Lily felt that she might take his arm again. There was a little silence, and then Lily resumed in a timid voice, 'I do not know whether you will be angry, Claude, but honestly, I do not think that if—that Eleanor would be so wretched about you as I should.'

'Eleanor knew Harry better than you did; no, Lily, I never could have been what Harry was, even if I had never wasted my time, and if my headaches had not interfered with my best efforts.'

'I do not believe that, say what you will,' said Lily.

'Ask William, then,' said Claude, sighing.

'I am sure papa does not think so,' said Lily; 'no, I cannot feel that Harry is such a loss when we still have you.'

'Oh! Lily, it is plain that you never knew Harry,' said Claude. 'I do not believe you ever did—that is one ting to be said for you.'

'Not as you did,' said Lily; 'remember, he was six years older. Then think how little we saw of him whilst they were abroad; he was always at school, or spending the holidays with Aunt Robert, and latterly even farther off, and only coming sometimes for an hour or two to see us. Then he used to kiss us all round, we went into the garden with him, looked at him, and were rather afraid of him; then he walked off to Wat Greenwood, came back, wished us good-bye, and away he went.'

'Yes,' said Claude, 'but after they came home?'

'Then he was a tall youth, and we were silly girls,' said Lilias; 'he avoided Miss Middleton, and we were always with her. He was good-natured, but he could not get on with us; he did very well with the little ones, but we were of the wrong age. He and William and Eleanor were one faction, we were another, and you were between both—he was too old, too sublime, too good, too grave for us.'

'Too grave!' said Claude; 'I never heard a laugh so full of glee, except, perhaps, Phyllis's.'

'The last time he was at home,' continued Lily, 'we began to know him better; there was no Miss Middleton in the way, and after you and William were gone, he used to walk with us, and read to us. He read *Guy Mannering* to us, and told us the story of Sir Maurice de Mohun; but the loss was not the same to us as to you elder ones; and then sorrow was almost lost in admiration, and in pleasure at the terms in which every one spoke of him. Claude, I have no difficulty in not wishing it otherwise; he is still my brother, and I would not change the feeling which the thought of his death gives me—no, not for himself in life and health.'

'Ah!' sighed Claude, 'you have no cause for self-reproach—no reason to lament over "wasted hours and love misspent."'

'You will always talk of your old indolence, as if it was a great crime,' said Lily.

'It was my chief temptation,' said Claude. 'As long as we know we are out of the path of duty it does not make much difference whether we have turned to the right hand or to the left.'

'Was it Harry's death that made you look upon it in this light?' said Lily.

'I knew it well enough before,' said Claude, 'it was what he had often set before me. Indeed, till I came home, and saw this place without him, I never really knew what a loss he was. At Eton I did not miss him more than when he went to Oxford, and I did not dwell on what he was to papa, or what I ought to be; and even when I saw what home was without him, I should have contented myself with miserable excuses about my health, if it had not been for my confirmation; then I awoke, I saw my duty, and the wretched way in which I had been spending my time. Thoughts of Harry and of my father came afterwards; I had not vigour enough for them before.'

Here they reached the house, and parted—Claude, ashamed of having talked of himself for the first time in his life, and Lily divided between shame at her own folly and pleasure at Claude's having thus opened his mind.

Jane, who was most in fault, escaped censure. Her father was ignorant of her improper speech. Emily forgot it, and it was not Claude's place to reprove his sisters, though to Lily he spoke as a friend. It passed away from her mind like other idle words, which, however, could not but leave an impression on those who heard her.

An unlooked-for result of the folly of this evening was, that Claude was prevented from appreciating Miss Weston He could not learn to like her, nor shake off an idea, that she was prying into their family concerns; he thought her over-praised, and would not even give just admiration to her singing, because he had once fancied her eager to exhibit it. It was unreasonable to dislike his sister's friend for his sister's folly, but Claude's wisdom was not yet arrived at its full growth, and he deserved credit for keeping his opinion to himself.

CHAPTER IX
THE WASP

'Whom He hath blessed and called His own,
He tries them early, look and tone,
  Bent brow and throbbing heart,
Tries them with pain.'

The next week Lily had the pleasure of fitting out Faith Longley for her place at Mrs. Weston's. She rejoiced at this opportunity of patronising her, because in her secret soul she felt that she might have done her a little injustice in choosing her own favourite Esther in her stead. Esther's popularity at the New Court, however, made Lilias confident in her own judgment; the servants liked her because she was quick and obliging, Mr. Mohun said she looked very neat, Phyllis liked her because a mischance to her frock was not so brave an offence with her as with Rachel, and Ada was growing very fond of her, because she was in the habit of bestowing great admiration on her golden curls as she arranged them, and both little girls were glad not to be compelled to put away the playthings they took out.

Maurice and Reginald had agreed to defer their onslaught on the wasps till Lord Rotherwood's arrival, and the war was now limited to attacks on foraging parties. Reginald most carefully marked every nest about the garden and farm, and, on his cousin's arrival on Saturday evening, began eagerly to give him a list of their localities. Lord Rotherwood was as ardent in the cause as even Reginald could desire, and would have instantly set out with him to reconnoitre had not the evening been rainy.

Then turning to Claude, he said, 'But I have not told you what brought me here; I came to persuade you to make an expedition with me up the Rhine; I set off next week; I would not write about it, because I knew you would only say you should like it very much, but—some but, that meant it was a great deal too much trouble.'

'How fast the plan has risen up,' said Claude, 'I heard nothing of it when I was with you.'

'Oh! it only came into my head last week, but I do not see what there is to wait for, second thoughts are never best.'

'Oh! Claude, how delightful,' said Lily.

Claude stirred his tea meditatively, and did not speak.

'It is too much trouble, I perceive,' said Lord Rotherwood; 'just as I told you.'

'Not exactly,' said Claude.

Lord Rotherwood now detailed his plan to his uncle, who said with a propitious smile, 'Well, Claude, what do you think of it?

'Mind you catch a firefly for me,' said Maurice.

'Why don't you answer, Claude?' said Lilias; 'only imagine seeing Undine's Castle!'

'Eh, Claude?' said his father.

'It would be very pleasant,' said Claude, slowly, 'but—'

'What?' said Mr. Mohun.

'Only a but,' said the Marquis. 'I hope he will have disposed of it by the morning; I start next Tuesday week; I would not go later for the universe; we shall be just in time for the summer in its beauty, and to have a peep at Switzerland. We shall not have time for Mont Blanc, without rattling faster than any man in his senses would do. I do not mean to leave any place till I have thoroughly seen twice over everything worth seeing that it contains.'

'Then perhaps you will get as far as Antwerp, and spend the rest of the holidays between the Cathedral and Paul Potter's bull. No, I shall have nothing to say to you at that rate,' said Claude.

'Depend upon it, it will be you that will wish to stand still when I had rather be on the move,' said the Marquis.

'Then you had better leave me behind. I have no intention of being hurried over the world, and never having my own way,' said Claude, trying to look surly.

'I am sure I should not mind travelling twice over the world to see Cologne Cathedral, or the field of Waterloo,' said Lily.

'Let me only show him my route,' said Lord Rotherwood. 'Redgie, look in my greatcoat pocket in the hall for Murray's Handbook, will you?'

'Go and get it, Phyl,' said Reginald, who was astride on the window-sill, peeling a stick.

Away darted Lord Rotherwood to fetch it himself, but Phyllis was before him; her merry laugh was heard, as he chased her round the hall to get possession of his book, throwing down two or three cloaks to intercept her path. Mr. Mohun took the opportunity of his absence to tell Claude that he need not refuse on the score of expense.

'Thank you,' was all Claude's answer.

Lord Rotherwood returned, and after punishing the discourteous Reginald by raising him up by his ears, he proceeded to give a full description of the delights of his expedition, the girls joining heartily with him in declaring it as well arranged as possible, and bringing all their knowledge of German travels to bear upon it. Claude sometimes put in a word, but never as if he cared much about the matter, and he was not to be persuaded to give any decided answer as to whether he would accompany the Marquis.

The next morning at breakfast Lord Rotherwood returned to the charge, but Claude seemed even more inclined to refuse than the day before. Lilias could not divine what was the matter with him, and lingered long after her sisters had gone to school, to hear what answer he would make; and when Mr. Mohun looked at his watch, and asked her if she knew how late it was, she rose from the breakfast-table with a sigh, and thought while she was putting on her bonnet how much less agreeable the school had been since the schism in the parish. And besides, now that Faith and Esther, and one or two others of her best scholars, had gone away from school, there seemed to be no one of any intelligence or knowledge left in the class, except Marianne Weston, who knew too much for the others, and one or two clever inattentive little girls: Lily almost disliked teaching them.

Phyllis and Adeline were in Miss Weston's class, and much did they delight in her teaching. There was a quiet earnestness in her manner which attracted her pupils, and fixed their attention, so as scarcely to allow the careless room for irreverence, while mere cleverness seemed almost to lose its advantage in learning what can only truly be entered into by those whose conduct agrees with their knowledge.

Phyllis never dreamt that she could be happy while standing still and learning, till Miss Weston began to teach at the Sunday school. Obedience at school taught her to acquire habits of reverent attention, which gradually conquered the idleness and weariness which had once possessed her at church. First, she learnt to be interested in the Historical Lessons, then never to lose her place in the Psalms, then to think about and follow some of the Prayers; by this time she was far from feeling any fatigue at all on week-days; she had succeeded in restraining any contortions to relieve herself from the irksomeness of sitting still, and had her thoughts in tolerable order through the greater part of the Sunday service, and now it was her great wish, unknown to any one, to abstain from a single yawn through the whole service, including the sermon!

Her place (chosen for her by Eleanor when first she had begun to go to Church, as far as possible from Reginald) was at the end of the seat, between her papa and the wall. This morning, as she put her arm on the book-board, while rising from kneeling, she felt a sudden thrill of sharp pain smear her left elbow, which made her start violently, and would have caused a scream, had she not been in church. She saw a wasp fall on the ground, and was just about to put her foot on it, when she recollected where she was. She had never in her life intentionally killed anything, and this was no time to begin in that place, and when she was angry. The pain was severe—more so perhaps than any she had felt before—and very much frightened, she pulled her papa's coat to draw his attention. But her first pull was so slight that he did not feel it, and before she gave a second she remembered that she could not make him hear what was the matter, without more noise than was proper. No, she must stay where she was, and try to bear the pain, and she knew that if she did try, help would be given her. She proceeded to find out the Psalm and join her voice with the others, though her heart was beating very fast, her forehead was contracted, and she could not help keeping her right hand clasped round her arm, and sometimes shifting from one foot to the other. The sharpness of the pain soon went off; she was able to attend to the Lessons, and hoped it would soon be quite well; but as soon as she began to think about it, it began to ache and throb, and seemed each moment to be growing hotter. The sermon especially tried her patience, her cheeks were burning, she felt sick and hardly able to hold up her head, yet she would not lean it against the wall, because she had often been told not to do so. She was exceedingly alarmed to find that her arm had swelled so much that she could hardly bend it, and it had received the impression of the gathers of her sleeve; she thought no sermon had ever been so long, but she sat quite still and upright, as she could not have done, had she not trained herself unconsciously by her efforts to leave off the trick of kicking her heels together. She did not speak till she was in the churchyard, and then she made Emily look at her arm.

'My poor child, it is frightful,' said Emily, 'what is the matter?'

'A wasp stung me just before the Psalms,' said Phyllis, 'and it goes on swelling and swelling, and it does pant!'

'What is the matter?' asked Mr. Mohun.

'Papa, just look,' said Emily, 'a wasp stung this dear child quite early in the service, and she has been bearing it all this time in silence. Why did you not show me, Phyl?'

'Because it was in church,' said the little girl.

'Why, Phyllis, you are a very Spartan,' said Lord Rotherwood.

'Something better than a Spartan,' said Mr. Mohun. 'Does it give you much pain now, my dear?'

'Not so bad as in church,' said Phyllis, 'only I am very tired, and it is so hot.'

'We will help you home, then,' said Mr. Mohun. As he took her up in his arms, Phyllis laughed, thanked him, replied to various inquiries from her sisters and the Westons—laughed again at sundry jokes from her brothers, then became silent, and was almost asleep, with her head on her papa's shoulder, by the time they reached the hall-door. She thought it very strange to be laid down on the sofa in the drawing-room, and to find every one attending to her. Mrs. Weston bathed her forehead with lavender-water, and Lily cut open the sleeve of her frock; Jane fetched all manner of remedies, and Emily pitied her. She was rather frightened: she thought such a fuss would not be made about her unless she was very ill; she was faint and tired, and was glad when Mrs. Weston proposed that they should all come away, and leave her to go to sleep quietly.

Marianne was so absorbed in admiration of Phyllis that she did not speak one word all the way from church to the New Court, and stood in silence watching the operations upon her friend, till Mrs. Weston sent every one away.

Adeline rather envied Phyllis; she would willingly have endured the pain to be made of so much importance, and said to be better than a Spartan, which must doubtless be something very fine indeed!

Phyllis was waked by the bells ringing for the afternoon service; Mrs. Weston was sitting by her, reading, Claude came to inquire for her, and to tell her that as she had lost her early dinner, she was to join the rest of the party at six. To her great surprise she felt quite well and fresh, and her arm was much better; Mrs. Weston pinned up her sleeve, and she set off with her to church, wondering whether Ada would remember to tell her what she had missed that afternoon at school. Those whose approbation was valuable, honoured Phyllis for her conduct, but she did not perceive it, or seek for it; she did not look like a heroine while running about and playing with Reginald and the dogs in the evening, but her papa had told her she was a good child, Claude had given her one of his kindest smiles, and she was happy. Even when Esther was looking at the mark left by the sting, and telling her that she was sure Miss Marianne Weston would have not been half so good, her simple, humble spirit came to her aid, and she answered, 'I'll tell you what, Esther, Marianne would have behaved much better, for she is older, and never fidgets, and she would not have been angry like me, and just going to kill the wasp.'

CHAPTER X
COUSIN ROTHERWOOD

'We care not who says
And intends it dispraise,
That an Angler to a fool is next neighbour.'

In the evening Lord Rotherwood renewed his entreaties to Claude to join him on his travels. He was very much bent on taking him, for his own pleasure depended not a little on his cousin's company. Claude lay on the glassy slope of the terrace, while Lord Rotherwood paced rapidly up and down before him, persuading him with all the allurements he could think of, and looking the picture of impatience. Lily sat by, adding her weight to all his arguments. But Claude was almost contemptuous to all the beauties of Germany, and all the promised sights; he scarcely gave himself the trouble to answer his tormentors, only vouchsafing sometimes to open his lips to say that he never meant to go to a country where people spoke a language that sounded like cracking walnuts; that he hated steamers; had no fancy for tumble-down castles; that it was so common to travel; there was more distinction in staying at home; that the field of Waterloo had been spoilt, and was not worth seeing; his ideas of glaciers would be ruined by the reality; and he did not care to see Cologne Cathedral till it was finished.

On this Lily set up an outcry of horror.

'One comfort is, Lily,' said Lord Rotherwood, 'he does not mean it; he did not say it from the bottom of his heart. Now, confess you did not, Claude.'

Claude pretended to be asleep.

'I see plainly enough,' said the Marquis to Lily, 'it is as Wat Greenwood says, "Mr. Reynold and the grapes."'

'But it is not,' said Lily, 'and that is what provokes me; papa says he is quite welcome to go if he likes, and that he thinks it will do him a great deal of good, but that foolish boy will say nothing but "I will think about it," and "thank you".'

'Then I give him up as regularly dense.'

'It is the most delightful plan ever thought of,' said Lily, 'so easily done, and just bringing within his compass all he ever wished to see.'

'Oh! his sole ambition is to stretch those long legs of his on the grass, like a great vegetable marrow,' said Lord Rotherwood. 'It is vegetating like a plant that makes him so much taller than any rational creature with a little animal life.'

'I think Jane has his share of curiosity,' said Lily, 'I am sure I had no idea that anything belonging to us could be so stupid.'

'Well,' said the Marquis, 'I shall not go.'

'No?' said Lily.

'No, I shall certainly not go.'

'Nonsense,' said Claude, waking from his pretended sleep, 'why do you not ask Travers to go with you? He would like nothing better.'

'He is a botanist, and would bore me with looking for weeds. No, I will have you, or stay at home.'

Claude proposed several others as companions, but Lord Rotherwood treated them all with as much disdain as Claude had shown for Germany, and ended with 'Now, Claude, you know my determination, only tell me why you will not go?'

'Then I do tell you, Rotherwood, the truth is, that those boys, Maurice and Reginald, are perfectly unmanageable when they are left alone with the girls.'

'Have a tutor for them,' said the Marquis.

'Very much obliged to you they would be for the suggestion,' said Claude.

'Oh! but Claude,' said Lily.

'I really cannot go. They mind no one but the Baron and me, and besides that, it would be no small annoyance to the house; ten tutors could not keep them from indescribable bits of mischief. I undertook them these holidays, and I mean to keep them.'

Lilias was just flying off to her father, when Claude caught hold of her, saying, 'I desire you will not,' and she stood still, looking at her cousin in dismay.

'It is all right,' cried the Marquis, joyfully, 'it is only to set off three weeks later.'

'Oh! I thought you would not go a week later for the universe,' said Claude, smiling.

'Not for the Universe, but for U—,' said Lord Rotherwood.

'Worthy of a companion true, of the University of Gottingen,' said Claude; 'but, Rotherwood, do you really mean that it will make no difference to you?'

'None whatever; I meant to spend three weeks with my mother at the end of the tour, and I shall spend them now instead. I only talked of going immediately, because nothing is done at all that is not done quickly, and I hate delays, but it is all the same, and now it stands for Tuesday three weeks. Now we shall see what he says to Cologne, Lily.'

Claude sprung up, and began talking over arrangements and possibilities with zest, which showed what his wishes had been from the first. All was quickly settled, and as soon as his father had given his cordial approbation to the scheme, it was amusing to see how animated and active Claude became, and in how different a style he talked of the once slighted Rhine.

Lord Rotherwood told the boys that their brother was a great deal too good for them, but they never troubled themselves to ask in what respect; Lilias took very great delight in telling Emily of the sacrifice which he had been willing to make, and looked forward to talking it over with Alethea, but she refrained, as long as he was at home, as she knew it would greatly displease him, and she had heard enough about missish confidences.

The Marquis of Rotherwood was certainly the very reverse of his chosen travelling companion, in the matter of activity. He made an appointment with the two boys to get up at half-past four on Monday morning for some fishing, before the sun was too high—Maurice not caring for the sport, but intending to make prize of any of the 'insect youth' which might prefer the sunrise for their gambols; and Reginald, in high delight at the prospect of real fishing, something beyond his own performances with a stick and a string, in pursuit of minnows in the ditches. Reginald was making contrivances for tying a string round his wrist and hanging the end of it from the window, that Andrew Grey might give it a pull as he went by to his work, to wake him, when Lord Rotherwood exclaimed, 'What! cannot you wake yourself at any time you please?'

'No,' said Reginald, 'I never heard of any one that could.'

'Then I advise you to learn the art; in the meantime I will call you to-morrow.'

Loud voices and laughter in the hall, and the front door creaking on its hinges at sunrise, convinced the household that this was no vain boast; before breakfast was quite over the fishermen were seen approaching the house. Lord Rotherwood was an extraordinary figure, in an old shooting jacket of his uncle's, an enormous pair of fishing-boots of William's, and the broad-brimmed straw hat, which always hung up in the hall, and was not claimed by any particular owner.

Maurice displayed to Jane the contents of two phials, strange little creatures, with stranger names, of which he was as proud as Reginald of his three fine trout. Lord Rotherwood did not appear till he had made himself look like other people, which he did in a surprisingly short time. He began estimating the weight of the fish, and talking at his most rapid rate, till at last Claude said, 'Phyllis told us just now that you were coming back, for that she heard Cousin Rotherwood talking, and it proved to be Jane's old turkey cock gobbling.'

'No bad compliment,' said Emily, 'for Phyllis was once known to say, on hearing a turkey cock, "How melodiously that nightingale sings."'

'No, no! that was Ada,' said Lilias.

'I could answer for that,' said Claude. 'Phyllis is too familiar with both parties to mistake their notes. Besides, she never was known to use such a word as melodiously.'

'Do you remember,' said the Marquis, 'that there was some great lawyer who had three kinds of handwriting, one that the public could read, one that only his clerk could read, and one that nobody could read?'

'I suppose I am the clerk,' said Claude, 'unless I divide the honour with Florence.'

'I do not think I am unintelligible anywhere but here,' said Lord Rotherwood. 'There is nothing sufficiently exciting at home, if Grosvenor Square is to be called home.'

'Sometimes you do it without knowing it,' said Lily.

'Yes,' said Claude, 'when you do not exactly know what you are going to say.'

'Then it is no bad plan,' said Lord Rotherwood. 'People are satisfied, and you don't commit yourself.'

'I'll tell you what, Cousin Rotherwood,' exclaimed Phyllis, 'your hand is bleeding.'

'Is it? Thank you, Phyllis, I thought I had washed it off: now do find me some sealing-wax—India-rub her—sticking-plaster, I mean.'

'Oh! Rotherwood,' said Emily, 'what a bad cut, how did it happen?'

'Only, I am the victim to Maurice's first essay in fishing.'

'Just fancy what an awkward fellow Maurice is,' said Reginald, 'he had but one throw, and he managed to stick the hook into Rotherwood's hand.'

'One of those barbed hooks? Oh! Rotherwood, how horrid!' said Emily.

'And he cut it out with his knife, and caught that great trout with it directly,' said Reginald.

'And neither half drowned Maurice, nor sent him home again?' asked Lily.

'I contented myself with taking away his weapon,' said the Marquis; 'and he wished for nothing better than to poke about in the gutters for insects; it was only Redgie that teased him into the nobler sport.'

Emily was inclined to make a serious matter of the accident, but her cousin said ten words while she said one, and by the time her first sentence was uttered, she found him talking about his ride to Devereux Castle.

He and Claude set out as soon as breakfast was over, and came back about three o'clock; Claude was tired with the heat, and betook himself to the sofa, where he fell asleep, under pretence of reading, but the indefatigable Marquis was ready and willing to set out with Reginald and Wat Greenwood to shoot rabbits.

Dinner-time came, and Emily sat at the drawing-room window with Claude and Lilias, lamenting her cousin's bad habits. 'Nothing will ever make him punctual,' said she.

'I am in duty bound to let you say nothing against him,' said Claude.

'It is very good-natured in him to wait for you,' said Lily, 'but it would be horribly selfish to leave you behind.'

'Delay is his great horror,' said Claude, 'and the wonder of his character is, that he is not selfish. No one had ever better training for it.'

'He does like his own way very much,' said Lilias.

'Who does not?' said Claude.

'Nothing shows his sense so much,' said Emily, 'as his great attachment to papa—the only person who ever controlled him.'

'And to Claude—his opposite in everything,' said Lilias.

'I think he will tire you to death in Germany,' said Emily.

'Never fear,' said Claude, 'my *vis inertiæ* is enough to counterbalance any amount of restlessness.'

'Here they come,' said Lily; 'how Wat Greenwood is grinning at Rotherwood's jokes!'

'A happy day for Wat,' said Emily. 'He will be quite dejected if William is not at home next shooting season. He thinks you a degenerate Mohun, Claude.'

'He must comfort himself with Redgie,' said Claude.

'Rotherwood is only eager about shooting in common with everything else,' said Lily, 'but Redgie, I fear, will care for nothing else.'

Lord Rotherwood came in, accounting for being late, as, in passing through a harvest field, he could not help attempting to reap. The Beechcroft farming operations had been his especial amusement from very early days, and his plans were numerous for farming on a grand scale as soon as he should be of age. His talk during dinner was of turnips and wheat, till at length Mr. Mohun asked him what he thought of the appearance of the castle. He said it was very forlorn; the rooms looked so dreary and deserted that he could not bear to be in them, and had been out of doors almost all the time. Indeed, he was afraid he had disappointed the housekeeper by not complimenting her as she deserved, for the freezing dismal order in which she kept everything. 'And really,' said he, 'I must go again to-morrow and make up for it, and Emily, you must come with me and try to devise something to make the unhappy place less like the abode of the Prince of the Black Islands.'

Emily willingly promised to go, and she went on talking to him, and telling him whom he was to meet on the next day, when an unusual silence making her look up, she beheld him more than half asleep.

Reginald fidgeted and sighed, and Maurice grew graver and graver as they thought of the wasps. Maurice wanted to take a nest entire, and began explaining his plan to Claude.

'You see, Claude, burning some straw and then digging, spoils the combs, as Wat does it; now I have got some puff-balls and sulphur to put into the hole, and set fire to them with a lucifer match, so as to stifle the wasps, and then dig them out quietly to-morrow morning.'

'It is all of no use, if that Rotherwood will do nothing but sleep,' said Reginald, in a disconsolate tone.

'You should not have made him get up at four,' said Emily.

'Who! I?' exclaimed the Marquis. 'I never was wider awake. What are you waiting for, Reginald? I thought you were going to take wasps' nests.'

'You are much too tired, I am sure,' said Emily.

'Tired! not in the least, I have done nothing to-day to tire me,' said Lord Rotherwood, walking up and down the room to keep himself awake.

The whole party went out, and found Wat Greenwood waiting for them with a bundle of straw, a spade, and a little gunpowder. Maurice carried a basket containing all his preparations, on which Wat looked with supreme contempt, telling him that his puffs were too green to make a smeech. Maurice, not condescending to argue the point, ran on to a nest which Reginald had marked on one of the green banks of the ancient moat.

'Take care that the wasps are all come in; mind what you are about, Maurice,' called his father.

'Master Maurice,' shouted Wat, 'you had better take a green bough.'

'Never mind, Wat,' said Lord Rotherwood, 'he would not stay long enough to use it if he had it.'

Reginald ran after Maurice, who had just reached the nest.

'There is one coming in, the evening is so warm they are not quiet yet.'

'I'll quiet them,' said Maurice, kneeling down, and putting his first puff-ball into the hole.

Reginald stood by with a sly smile, as he pulled a branch off a neighbouring filbert-tree. The next moment Maurice gave a sudden yell, 'The wasps! the wasps!' and jumping up, and tripping at his first step, rolled down the bank, and landed safely at Lord Rotherwood's feet. The shouts of laughter were loud, but he regarded them not, and as soon as he recovered his feet, rushed past his sisters, and never stopped till he reached the house. Redgie stood alone, in the midst of a cloud of wasps, beating them off with a bough, roaring with laughter, and calling Wat to bring the straw to burn them.

'No, no, Redgie, come away, leave them for Maurice to try again,' said his father.

'The brute, he stung me,' cried Reginald, knocking down a wasp or two as he came down. 'What is this?' added he, as he stumbled over something at the bottom of the slope. 'Oh! Maurice's basket; look here—laudanum—did he mean to poison the wasps?'

'No,' said Jane, 'to cure their stings.'

'The poor unhappy quiz!' cried Reginald.

While the others were busy over a nest, Mr. Mohun asked Emily how the boy got at the medicine chest. Emily looked confused, and said she supposed Jane had given him a bottle.

'Jane is too young to be trusted there,' said Mr. Mohun, 'I thought you knew better; do not let the key be out of your possession again.'

After a few more nests had been taken in the usual manner, they returned to the house. Maurice was lying on the sofa reading the *Penny Magazine*, from which he raised his eyes no more that evening, in spite of all the jokes which flew about respecting wounded knights, courage, and the balsam of Fierabras. He called Jane to teach her how flies were made, and as soon as tea was over he went to bed. Reginald, after many yawns, prepared to follow his example, and as he was wishing his sisters good-night, Emily said, 'Now, Redgie, do not go out at such a preposterous hour to-morrow morning.'

'What is that to you?' was Reginald's courteous inquiry.

'I do not wish to see every one fast asleep to-morrow evening,' said Emily, and she looked at her cousin, whose head was far back over his chair.

'He is a Trojan,' said Reginald.

'Is a Trojan better than a Spartan?' asked Ada, meditatively.

'Helen thought so,' said Claude.

'"When Greek meets Greek, then comes the tug of war,"' muttered the Marquis.

'You are all talking Greek,' said Jane.

'Arabic,' said Claude.

As far as it could be comprehended, Lord Rotherwood's answer related to Maurice and the wasps.

'There,' said Emily, 'what is to be done if he is in that condition to-morrow?'

'I am not asleep; what makes you think I am?'

'I wish you would sit in that great chair,' said Emily, 'I am afraid you will break your neck; you look so uncomfortable, I cannot bear to see you.'

'I never was more comfortable in my life,' said Lord Rotherwood, asleep while finishing the sentence; but this time, happily with his elbows on the table, and his head in a safer position.

The next day was spent rather more rationally. Lord Rotherwood met with a book of Irish Tales, with which he became so engrossed that he did not like to leave it when Emily and Claude were ready to ride to Devereux Castle with him. When there he was equally eager and vehement about each matter that came under consideration, and so many presented themselves, that Emily began to be in agonies lest she should not be at home in time to dress and receive her guests. They did, however, reach the house before Lilias, who had been walking with Miss Weston, came in, and when she went upstairs, she found Emily full of complaints at the inconvenience of having no Rachel to assist her in dressing, and to see that everything was in order, and that Phyllis was fit to appear when she came down in the evening; but, by the assistance of Lily and Jane, she got over her troubles, and when she went into the drawing-room, she was much relieved to find her two gentlemen quite safe and dressed. She had been in great fear of Lord Rotherwood's straying away to join in some of Reginald's sports, and was grateful to the Irish book for keeping him out of mischief.

Emily was in her glory; it was the first large dinner-party since Eleanor had gone, and though she pitied herself for having the trouble of entertaining the people, she really enjoyed the feeling that she now appeared as the mistress of New Court, with her cousin, the Marquis, by her side, to show how highly she was connected. And everything went off just as could be wished. Lord Rotherwood talked intelligibly and sensibly, and Mr. Mohun's neighbour at dinner had a voice which he could hear. Lily's pleasure was not less than her sister's, though of a different kind. She delighted in thinking how well Emily did the honours, in watching the varied expression of Lord Rotherwood's animated countenance, in imagining Claude's forehead to be finer than that of any one else, and in thinking how people must admire Reginald's tall, active figure, and very handsome face. She was asked to play, and did tolerably well, but was too shy to sing, nor, indeed, was Reginald encouraging. 'What is the use of your singing, Lily? If it was like Miss Weston's, now—'

Reginald had taken a great fancy to Miss Weston; he stood by her all the evening, and afterwards let her talk to him, and then began to chatter himself, at last becoming so confidential as to impart to her the grand object of his ambition, which was to be taller than Claude!

The next morning Lord Rotherwood left Beechcroft, somewhat to Emily's relief; for though she was very proud of him, and much enjoyed the dignity of being seen to talk familiarly with him, yet, when no strangers were present, and he became no more than an ordinary cousin, she was worried by his incessant activity, and desire to see, know, and do everything as fast and as thoroughly as possible. She could not see the use of such vehemence; she liked to take things in a moderate way, and as Claude said, much preferred the passive to the active voice. Claude, on the contrary, was ashamed of his constitutional indolence, looked on it as a temptation, and struggled against it, almost envying his cousin his unabated eagerness and untiring energy, and liking to be with him, because no one else so effectually roused him from his habitual languor. His indolence was, however, so much the effect of ill health, that exertion was sometimes scarcely in his power, especially in hot weather, and by the time his brothers' studies were finished each day, he was unfit for anything but to lie on the grass under the plane-tree.

The days glided on, and the holidays came to an end; Maurice spent them in adding to his collection of insects, which, with Jane's assistance, he arranged very neatly; and Reginald and Phyllis performed several exploits, more agreeable to themselves than satisfactory to the more rational part of the New Court community. At the same time, Reginald's devotion to Miss Weston increased; he never moved from her side when she sang, did not fail to be of the party when she walked with his sisters, offered her one of his own puppies, named his little ship 'Alethea,' and was even tolerably civil to Marianne.

At length the day of departure came; the boys returned to school, Claude joined Lord Rotherwood, and the New Court was again in a state of tranquillity.

CHAPTER XI
DANCING

'Prescribe us not our duties.'

'Well, Phyllis,' said her father, as he passed through the hall to mount his horse, 'how do you like the prospect of Monsieur le Roi's instructions?'

'Not at all, papa,' answered Phyllis, running out to the hall door to pat the horse, and give it a piece of bread.

'Take care you turn out your toes,' said Mr. Mohun. 'You must learn to dance like a dragon before Cousin Rotherwood's birthday next year.'

'Papa, how do dragons dance?'

'That is a question I must decide at my leisure,' said Mr. Mohun, mounting. 'Stand out of the way, Phyl, or you will feel how horses dance.'

Away he rode, while Phyllis turned with unwilling steps to the nursery, to be dressed for her first dancing lesson; Marianne Weston was to learn with her, and this was some consolation, but Phyllis could not share in the satisfaction Adeline felt in the arrival of Monsieur le Roi. Jane was also a pupil, but Lily, whose recollections of her own dancing days were not agreeable, absented herself entirely from the dancing-room, even though Alethea Weston had come with her sister.

Poor Phyllis danced as awkwardly as was expected, but Adeline seemed likely to be a pupil in whom a master might rejoice; Marianne was very attentive and not ungraceful, but Alethea soon saw reason to regret the arrangement that had been made, for she perceived that Jane considered the master a fair subject for derision, and her 'nods and becks, and wreathed smiles,' called up corresponding looks in Marianne's face.

'Oh Brownie, you are a naughty thing!' said Emily, as soon as M. le Roi had departed.

'He really was irresistible!' said Jane.

'I suppose ridicule is one of the disagreeables to which a dancing-master makes up his mind,' said Alethea.

'Yes,' said Jane, 'one can have no compunction in quizzing that species.'

'I do not think I can quite say that, Jane,' said Miss Weston.

'This man especially lays himself open to ridicule,' said Jane; 'do you know, Alethea, that he is an Englishman, and his name is King, only he calls himself Le Roi, and speaks broken English!'

Though Alethea joined in the general laugh, she did not feel quite satisfied; she feared that if not checked in time, Jane would proceed to actual impertinence, and that Marianne would be tempted to follow her example, but she did not like to interfere, and only advised Marianne to be on her guard, hoping that Emily would also speak seriously to her sister.

On the next occasion, however, Jane ventured still farther; her grimaces were almost irresistible, and she had a most comical manner of imitating the master's attitudes when his eye was not upon her, and putting on a demure countenance when he turned towards her, which sorely tried Marianne.

'What shall I do, Alethea?' said the little girl, as the sisters walked home together; 'I do not know how to help laughing, if Jane will be so very funny.'

'I am afraid we must ask mamma to let us give up the dancing,' replied Alethea; 'the temptation is almost too strong, and I do not think she would wish to expose you to it.'

'But, Alethea, why do not you speak to Jane?' asked Marianne; 'no one seems to tell her it is wrong; Miss Mohun was almost laughing.'

'I do not think Jane would consider that I ought to find fault with her,' said Alethea.

'But you would not scold her,' urged Marianne; 'only put her in mind that it is not right, not kind; that Monsieur le Roi is in authority over her for the time.'

'I will speak to mamma,' said Alethea, 'perhaps it will be better next time.'

And it was better, for Mr. Mohun happening to be at home, was dragged into the dancing-room by Emily and Ada. Once, when she thought he was looking another way, Jane tried to raise a smile, but a stern 'Jane, what are you thinking of?' recalled her to order, and when the lesson was over her father spoke gravely to her, telling her that he thought few things more disgusting in a young lady than impertinence towards her teachers; and then added, 'Miss Weston, I hope you keep strict watch over these giddy young things.'

Awed by her father, Jane behaved tolerably well at that time and the next, and Miss Weston hoped her interference would not be needed, but as if to make up for this restraint, her conduct a fortnight after was quite beyond bearing. She used every means to make Marianne laugh, and at last went so far as to pretend to think that M. le Roi had not understood what she said in English, and to translate it into French. Poor Marianne looked imploringly at her sister, and Alethea hoped that Emily would interpose, but Emily was turning away her head to conceal a laugh, and Miss Weston was obliged to give Jane a very grave look, which she perfectly understood, though she pretended not to see it. When the exercise was over Miss Weston made her a sign to approach, and said, 'Jane, do you think your papa would have liked—'

'What do you mean?' said Jane, 'I have not been laughing.'

'You know what I mean,' said Alethea, 'and pray do not be displeased if I ask you not to make it difficult for Marianne to behave properly.'

Jane drew up her head and went back to her place. She played no more tricks that day, but as soon as the guests were gone, began telling Lilias how Miss Weston had been meddling and scolding her.

'And well you must have deserved it,' said Lily.

'I do not say that Jenny was right,' said Emily, 'but I think Miss Weston might allow me to correct my own sister in my own house.'

'You correct Jane!' cried Lily, and Jane laughed.

'I only mean,' said Emily, 'that it was not very polite, and papa says the closest friendship is no reason for dispensing with the rules of politeness.'

'Certainly not,' said Lily, 'the rules of politeness are rules of love, and it was in love that Alethea spoke; she sees how sadly we are left to ourselves, and is kind enough to speak a word in season.'

'Perhaps,' said Jane, 'since it was in love that she spoke, you would like to have her for our reprover for ever, and I can assure you more unlikely things have happened. I have heard it from one who can judge.'

'Let me hear no more of this,' said Emily, 'it is preposterous and ridiculous, and very disrespectful to papa.'

Jane for once, rather shocked at her own words, went back to what had been said just before.

'Then, perhaps, you would like to have Eleanor back again?'

'I am sure you want some one to put you in mind of your duty,' said Lily.

'Eleanor and duty!' cried Emily; 'you who thought so much of the power of love!'

'Of Emily and love, she would say, if it sounded well,' said Jane.

'I cannot see what true love you or Jane are showing now,' said Lily, 'it is no kindness to encourage her pertness, or to throw away a friendly reproof because it offends your pride.'

'Nobody reproved me,' replied Emily; 'besides, I know love will prevail; for my sake Jane will not expose herself and me to a stranger's interference.'

'If you depend upon that, I wish you joy,' said Lilias, as she left the room.

'What a weathercock Lily is!' cried Jane, 'she has fallen in love with Alethea Weston, and echoes all she says.'

'Not considering her own inconsistency,' said Emily.

'That Alethea Weston,' exclaimed Jane, in an angry tone;—but Emily, beginning to recover some sense of propriety, said, 'Jenny, you know you were very ill-bred, and you made it difficult for the little ones to behave well.'

'Not our own little ones,' said Jane; 'honest Phyl did not understand the joke, and Ada was thinking of her attitudes; one comfort is, that I shall be confirmed in three weeks' time, and then people cannot treat me as a mere child—little as I am.'

'Oh! Jane,' said Emily, 'I do not like to hear you talk of confirmation in that light way.'

'No, no,' said Jane, 'I do not mean it—of course I do not mean it—don't look shocked—it was only by the bye—and another by the bye, Emily, you know I must have a cap and white ribbons, and I am afraid I must make it myself.'

'Ay, that is the worst of having Esther,' said Emily, 'she and Hannah have no notion of anything but the plainest work; I am sure if I had thought of all the trouble of that kind which having a young girl would entail, I would never have consented to Esther's coming.'

'That was entirely Lily's scheme,' said Jane.

'Yes; it is impossible to resist Lily, she is so eager and anxious, and it would have vexed her very much if I had opposed her, and that I cannot bear; besides, Esther is a very nice girl, and will learn.'

'There is Robert talking to papa on the green,' said Jane; 'what a deep conference; what can it be about?'

If Jane had heard that conversation she might have perceived that she could not wilfully offend, even in what she thought a trifling matter, without making it evident, even to others, that there was something very wrong about her. At that moment the Rector was saying to his uncle, 'I am in doubt about Jane, I cannot but fear she is not in a satisfactory state for confirmation, and I wished to ask you what you think?'

'Act just as you would with any of the village girls,' said Mr. Mohun.

'I should be very sorry to do otherwise,' said Mr. Devereux; 'but I thought you might like, since every one knows that she is a candidate, that she should not be at home at the time of the confirmation, if it is necessary to refuse her.'

'No,' said Mr. Mohun, 'I should not wish to shield her from the disgrace. It may be useful to her, and besides, it will establish your character for impartiality. I have not been satisfied with all I saw of little Jane for some time past, and I am afraid that much passes amongst my poor girls which never comes to my knowledge. Her pertness especially is probably restrained in my presence.'

'It is not so much the pertness that I complain of,' said Mr. Devereux, 'for that might be merely exuberance of spirits, but there is a sort of habitual irreverence, which makes one dread to bring her nearer to sacred tings.'

'I know what you mean,' said Mr. Mohun, 'and I think the pertness is a branch of it, more noticed because more inconvenient to others.'

'Yes,' said Mr. Devereux, 'I think the fault I speak of is most evident; when there is occasion to reprove her, I am always baffled by a kind of levity which makes every warning glance aside.'

'Then I should decidedly say refuse her,' said Mr. Mohun. 'It would be a warning that she could not disregard, and the best chance of improving her.'

'Yet,' said Mr. Devereux, 'if she is eager for confirmation, and regards it in its proper light, it is hard to say whether it is right to deny it to her; it may give her the depth and earnestness which she needs.'

'Poor child,' said Mr. Mohun, 'she has great disadvantages; I am quite sure our present system is not fit for her. Things shall be placed on a different footing, and in another year or two I hope she may be fitter for confirmation. However, before you finally decide, I should wish to have some conversation with her, and speak to you again.

'That is just what I wish,' said Mr. Devereux.

CHAPTER XII
THE FEVER

'Jane borrowed maxims from a doubting school,
And took for truth the test of ridicule.'

The question of Jane's confirmation was decided in an unexpected manner; for the day after Mr. Mohun's conversation with his nephew she was attacked by a headache and sore throat, spent a feverish night, and in the morning was so unwell that a medical man was sent for from Raynham. On his arrival he pronounced that she was suffering from scarlet fever, and Emily began to feel the approach of the same complaint.

Phyllis and Adeline were shut up in the drawing-room, and a system of quarantine established, which was happily brought to a conclusion by a note from Mrs. Weston, who kindly begged that they might be sent to her at Broomhill, and Mr. Mohun gladly availing himself of the offer, the little girls set off, so well pleased to make a visit alone, as almost to forget the occasion of it. Mrs. Weston had extended her invitation to Lilias, but she begged to be allowed to remain with her sisters, and Mr. Mohun thought that she had been already so much exposed to the infection that it was useless for her to take any precautions.

She was therefore declared head nurse; and it was well that she had an energetic spirit, and so sweet a temper, that she was ready to sympathise with all Emily's petulant complaints, and even to find fault with herself for not being in two places at once. Two of the maids were ill, and the whole care of Emily and Jane devolved upon her, with only the assistance of Esther.

Emily was not very seriously ill, but Jane's fever was very high, and Lily thought that her father was more anxious than he chose to appear. Of Jane's own thoughts little could be guessed; she was often delirious, and at all times speaking was so painful that she said as little as possible.

Lily's troubles seemed at their height one Sunday afternoon, while her father was at church. She had been reading the Psalms and Lessons to Emily, and she then rose to return to Jane.

'Do not go,' entreated Emily.

'I will send Esther.'

'Esther is of no use.'

'And therefore I do not like to leave her so long alone with Jane. Pray spare me a little smile.'

'Then come back soon.'

Lily was glad to escape with no more objections. She found Jane complaining of thirst, but to swallow gave her great pain, and she required so much attendance for some little time, that Emily's bell was twice rung before Esther could be spared to go to her.

She soon came back, saying, 'Miss Mohun wants you directly, Miss Lilias.'

'Tell her I will come presently,' said Lily, who had one hand pressed on Jane's burning temples, while the other was sprinkling her with ether.

'Stay,' said Jane, faintly, and Esther left the room.

Jane drew her breath with so much difficulty that a dreadful terror seized upon Lily, lest she should be suffocated. She raised her head, and supported her till Esther could bring more pillows. Esther brought a message from Emily to hasten her return; but Jane could not be left, and the grateful look she gave her as she arranged the pillows repaid her for all her toils. After a little time Jane became more comfortable, and said in a whisper, 'Dear Lily, I wish I was not so troublesome.'

Back came Esther at this moment, saying, 'Miss Emily says she is worse, and wants you directly, Miss Lilias.'

Lily hurried away to Emily's room, and found what might well have tried her temper. Emily was flushed indeed, and feverish, but her breathing was smooth and even, and her hand and pulse cool and slow, compared with the parched burning hands, and throbbings, too quick to count, which Lily had just been watching.

'Well, my dear Emily, I am sorry you do not feel better; what can I do for you?'

'How can I be better while I am left so long, and Esther not coming when I ring? What would happen if I were to faint away?'

'Indeed, I am very sorry,' said Lily; 'but when you rang, poor Jenny could spare neither of us.'

'How is poor Jenny?' said Emily.

'Her throat is very bad, but she is quite sensible now, and wishes to have me there. What did you want, Emily?'

'Oh! I wish you would draw the curtain, the light hurts me; that will do—no—now it is worse, pray put it as it was before. Oh! Lily, if you knew how ill I am you would not leave me.'

'Can I do anything for you—will you have some coffee?'

'Oh! no, it has a bad taste, I am sure it is carelessly made.'

'Shall I make you some fresh, with the spirit lamp?'

'No, I am tired of it. I wonder if I might have some tamarinds?'

'I will ask as soon as papa comes from church.'

'Is he gone to church? how could he go when we are all so ill?'

'Perhaps he was doing us more good at church than he could at home. You will be glad to hear, Emily, that he has sent for Rachel to come and help us.'

'Oh! has he? but she lives so far off, and gets her letters so seldom, I don't reckon at all upon her coming. If she could come directly it would be a comfort.'

'It would, indeed,' said Lily; 'she would know what to do for Jane.'

'Lily, where is the ether? You are always taking it away.'

'In Jane's room; I will fetch it.'

'No, no, if you once get into Jane's room I shall never see you back again.'

Now Emily knew that Jane was very ill, and Lily's pale cheeks, heavy eyes, and failing voice, might have reminded her that two sick persons were a heavy charge upon a girl of seventeen, without the addition of her caprices and fretfulness. And how was it that the kind-hearted, affectionate Emily never thought of all this? It was because she had been giving way to selfishness for nineteen years; and now the contemplation of her own sufferings was quite enough to hide from her that others had much to bear; and illness, instead of teaching her patience and consideration, only made her more exacting and querulous.

To Lily's unspeakable relief, Miss Weston accompanied Mr. Mohun from church, and offered to share her attendance. No one knew what it cost Alethea to come into the midst of a scene which constantly reminded her of the sisters she had lost, but she did not shrink from it, and was glad that her parents saw no objection to her offering to share Lily's toils. Her experience was most valuable, and relieved Lilias of the fear that was continually haunting her, lest her ignorance might lead to some fatal mistake. The next day brought Rachel, and both patients began to mend. Jane's recovery was quicker than Emily's, for her constitution was not so languid, and having no pleasure in the importance of being an invalid, she was willing to exert herself, and make the best of everything, while Emily did not much like to be told that she was better, and thought it cruel to hint that exertion would benefit her. Both were convalescent before the fever attacked Lily, who was severely ill, but not alarmingly so, and her gentleness and patience made Alethea delight in having the care of her. Lily was full of gratitude to her kind friend, and felt quite happy when Alethea chanced one day to call her by the name of Emma; she almost hoped she was taking the place of that sister, and the thought cheered her through many languid hours, and gave double value to all Alethea's kindness. She did not feel disposed to repine at an illness which brought out such affection from her friend, and still more from her father, who, when he came to see her, would say things which gave her a thrill of pleasure whenever she thought of them.

It happened one day that Jane, having finished her book, looked round for some other occupation; she knew that Miss Weston had walked to Broomhill;

Rachael was with Lilias, and there was no amusement at hand. At last she recollected that her papa had said in the morning, that he hoped to see her and Emily in the schoolroom in the course of the day, and hoping to meet her sister, she resolved to try and get there. The room had been Mr. Mohun's sitting-room since the beginning of their illness, and it looked so very comfortable that she was glad she had come, though she was so tired she wondered how she should get back again. Emily was not there, so she lay down on the sofa and took up a little book from the table. The title was *Susan Harvey, or Confirmation*, and she read it with more interest as she remembered with a pang that this was the day of the confirmation, to which she had been invited; she soon found herself shedding tears over the book, she who had never yet been known to cry at any story, however affecting. She had not finished when Mr. Devereux came in to look for Mr. Mohun, and finding her there, was going away as soon as he had congratulated her on having left her room, but she begged him to stay, and began asking questions about the confirmation.

'Were there many people?'

'Three hundred.'

'Did the Stoney Bridge people make a disturbance?'

'No.'

'How many of our people?'

'Twenty-seven.'

'Did all the girls wear caps?'

'Most of them.'

Jane was rather surprised at the shortness of her cousin's answers, but she went on, as he stood before the fire, apparently in deep thought.

'Was Miss Burnet confirmed? She is the dullest girl I ever knew, and she is older than I am. Was she confused?'

'She was.'

'Did you give Mary Wright a ticket?'

'No.'

'Then, of course, you did not give one to Ned Long. I thought you would never succeed in making him remember which is the ninth commandment.'

'I did not refuse him.'

'Indeed! did he improve in a portentous manner?'

'Not particularly.'

'Well, you must have been more merciful than I expected.'

'Indeed!'

'Robert, you must have lost the use of your tongue, for want of us to talk to. I shall be affronted if you go into a brown study the first day of seeing me.'

He smiled in a constrained manner, and after a few minutes said, 'I have been considering whether this is a fit time to tell you what will give you pain. You must tell me if you can bear it.'

'About Lily, or the little ones?'

'No, no! only about yourself. Your father wished me to speak to you, but I would not have done so on this first meeting, but what you have just been saying makes me think this is the best occasion.'

'Let me know; I do not like suspense,' said Jane, sharply.

'I think it right to tell you, Jane, that neither your father nor I thought it would be desirable for you to be confirmed at this time.'

'Do you really mean it?' said Jane.

'Look back on the past year, and say if you sincerely think you are fit for confirmation.'

'As to that,' said Jane, 'the best people are always saying that they are not fit for these things.'

'None can call themselves worthy of them; but I think the conscience of some would bear them witness that they had profited so far by their present means of grace as to give grounds for hoping that they would derive benefit from further assistance.'

'Well, I suppose I must be very bad, since you see it,' said Jane, in a manner rather more subdued; 'but I did not think myself worse than other people.'

'Is a Christian called, only to be no worse than others?'

'Oh no! I see, I mean—pray tell me my great fault. Pertness, I suppose—love of gossip?'

'There must be a deeper root of evil, of which these are but the visible effects, Jane.'

'What do you mean, Robert?' said Jane, now seeming really impressed.

'I think, Jane, that the greatest and most dangerous fault of your character is want of reverence. I think it is want of reverence which makes you press forward to that for which you confess yourself unfit; it is want of reverence for holiness which makes you not care to attain it; want of reverence for the Holy Word that makes you treat it as a mere lesson; and in smaller matters your pertness is want of reverence for your superiors; you would not be ready to believe and to say the worst of others, if you reverenced what good there may be in them. Take care that your want of reverence is not in reality want of faith.'

Jane's spirits were weak and subdued. It was a great shock to her to hear that she was not thought worthy of confirmation; her faults had never been called by so hard a name; she was in part humbled, and in part grieved, and what she thought harshness in her cousin; she turned away her face, and did not speak. He continued, 'Jane, you must not think me unkind, your father desired me to talk to you, and, indeed, the time of recovery from sickness is too precious to be trifled away.'

Jane wept bitterly. Presently he said, 'It grieves me to have been obliged to speak harshly to you, you must forgive me if I have talked too much to you, Jane.'

Jane tried to speak, but sobs prevented her, and she gave way to a violent fit of crying. Her cousin feared he had been unwise in saying so much, and had weakened the effect of his own words. He would have been glad to see tears of repentance, but he was afraid that she was weeping over fancied unkindness, and that he might have done what might be hurtful to her in her weak state. He said a few kind words, and tried to console her, but this change of tone rather added to her distress, and she became hysterical. He was much vexed and alarmed, and, ringing the bell, hastened to call assistance. He found Esther, and sent her to Jane, and on returning to the schoolroom with some water, he found her lying exhausted on the sofa; he therefore went in search of his uncle, who was overlooking some farming work, and many were the apologies made, and many the assurances he received, that it would be better for her in the end, as the impression would be more lasting.

Jane was scarcely conscious of her cousin's departure, or of Esther's arrival, but after drinking some water, and lying still for a few moments, she exclaimed, 'Oh, Robert! oh, Esther! the confirmation!' and gasped and sobbed again. Esther thought she had guessed the cause of her tears, and tried to comfort her.

'Ah! Miss Jane, there will be another confirmation some day; it was a sad thing you were too ill, to be sure, but—'

'Oh! if I had—if he would not say—if he had thought me fit.'

Esther was amazed, and asked if she should call Miss Weston, who was now with Lilias.

'No, no!' cried Jane, nearly relapsing into hysterics. 'She shall not see me in this state.'

Esther hardly knew what to do, but she tried to soothe and comfort her by following what was evidently the feeling predominating in Jane's mind, as indicated by her broken sentences, and said, 'It was a pity, to be sure, that Mr. Devereux came and talked so long, he could not know of your being so very weak, Miss Jane.'

'Yes,' said Jane, faintly, 'I could have borne it better if he had waited a few days.'

'Yes, Miss, when you had not been so very ill. Mr. Devereux is a very good gentleman, but they do say he is very sharp.'

'He means to be kind,' said Jane, 'but I do not think he has much consideration, always.'

'Yes, Miss Jane, that is just what Mrs. White said, when—'

Esther's speech was cut short by the entrance of Miss Weston. Jane started up, dashed off her tears, and tried to look as usual, but the paleness of her face, and the redness of her eyes, made this impossible, and she was obliged to lie down again. Esther left the room, and Miss Weston did not feel intimate enough with Jane to ask any questions; she gave her some *sal volatile*, talked kindly to her of her weakness, and offered to read to her; all the time leaving an opening for confidence, if Jane wished to relieve her mind. The book which lay near her accounted, as she thought, for her agitation, and she blamed herself for having judged her harshly as deficient in feeling, now that she found her so much distressed, because illness had prevented her confirmation. Under this impression she honoured her reserve, while she thought with more affection of Lily's open heart. Jane, who never took, or expected others to take, the most favourable view of people's motives, thought Alethea knew the cause of her distress, and disliked her the more, as having witnessed her humiliation.

Such was Jane's love of gossip that the next time she was alone with Esther she asked for the history of Mrs. White, thus teaching her maid disrespect to her pastor, indirectly complaining of his unkindness, and going far to annul the effect of what she had learnt at school. Perhaps during her hysterics Jane's conduct was not under control, but subsequent silence was in her power, and could she be free from blame if Esther's faults gained greater ascendency?

The next day Mr. Mohun attempted to speak to Jane, but being both frightened and unhappy, she found it very easy and natural, as well as very convenient, to fall into hysterics again, and her father was obliged to desist, regretting that, at the only time she was subdued enough to listen to reproof, she was too weak to bear it without injury. Rachel, who was nearly as despotic among the young ladies as she had been in former times in the nursery, now insisted on Emily's going into the schoolroom, and when there, she made rapid progress. Alethea was amused to see how Jane's decided will and lively spirit would induce Emily to make exertions, which no persuasions of hers could make her think other than impossible.

A few days more, and they were nearly well again; and Lilias so far recovered as to be able to spare her kind friend, who returned home with a double portion of Lily's love, and of deep gratitude from Mr. Mohun; but these feelings were scarcely expressed in words. Emily gave her some graceful thanks, and Jane disliked her more than ever.

It was rather a dreary time that now commenced with the young ladies; they were tired of seeing the same faces continually, and dispirited by hearing that the fever was spreading in the village. The autumn was far advanced, the weather was damp and gloomy, and the sisters sat round the fire shivering with cold, feeling the large room dreary and deserted, missing the merry voices of the children, and much tormented by want of occupation. They could not go out, their hands were not steady enough to draw, they felt every letter which they had to write a heavy burden; neither Emily nor Lily could like needlework; they could have no music, for the piano at the other end of the room seemed to be in an Arctic Region, and they did little but read novels and childish stories, and play at chess or backgammon. Jane was the best off. Mrs. Weston sent her a little sock, with a request that she would make out the way in which it was knit, in a complicated feathery pattern, and in puzzling over her cotton, taking stitches up and letting them down, she made the time pass a little less heavily with her than with her sisters.

CHAPTER XIII
A CURIOSITY MAP

'Keek into the draw-well,
        Janet, Janet,
There ye'll see your bonny sell,
        My jo Janet.'

It was at this time that Lady Rotherwood and her daughter arrived at Devereux Castle, and Mr. Mohun was obliged to go to meet her there, leaving his three daughters to spend a long winter evening by themselves, in their doleful and dismal way, as Lily called it.

The evening had closed in, but they did not ring for candles, lest they should make it seem longer; and Jane was just beginning to laugh at Emily for the deplorable state of her frock and collar, tumbled with lying on the sofa, when the three girls all started at the unexpected sound of a ring at the front door.

With a rapid and joyful suspicion who it might be, Emily and Lilias sprang to the door, Jane thrust the poker into the fire, in a desperate attempt to produce a flame, drove an arm-chair off the hearth-rug, whisked an old shawl out of sight, and flew after them into the hall, just as the deep tones of a well-known voice were heard greeting old Joseph.

'William!' cried the girls. 'Oh! is it you? Are you not afraid of the scarlet fever?'

'No, who has it?'

'We have had it, but we are quite well now. How cold you are!'

'But where is my father?'

'Gone to Hetherington with Robert, to meet Aunt Rotherwood. Come into the drawing-room.'

Here Emily glided off to perform a hurried toilette.

'And the little ones?'

'At Broomhill. Mrs. Weston was so kind as to take them out of the way of the infection,' said Lily.

'Oh! William, those Westons!'

'Westons, what Westons? Not those I knew at Brighton?'

'The very same,' said Lily. 'They have taken the house at Broomhill. Oh! they have been so very kind, I do not know what would have become of us without Alethea.'

'Why did you not tell me they were living here? And you like them?'

'Like them! No one can tell the comfort Alethea has been. She came to us and nursed us, and has been my great support.'

'And Phyllis and Ada are with them?'

'Yes, they have been at Broomhill these six weeks, and more.'

Here Emily came in and told William that his room was ready, and Rachel on the stairs wishing to see the Captain.

'How well he looks!' cried Lily, as he closed the door; 'it is quite refreshing to see any one looking so strong and bright.'

'And more like Sir Maurice than ever,' said Emily.

'Ah! but Claude is more like,' said Lily, 'because he is pale.'

'Well,' said Jane, 'do let us in the meantime make the room look more fit to be seen before he comes down.'

The alacrity which had long been wanting to Lilias and Jane had suddenly returned, and they succeeded in making the room look surprisingly comfortable, compared with its former desolate aspect, before William came down, and renewed his inquiries after all the family.

'And how is my father's deafness?' was one of his questions.

'Worse,' said Emily. 'I am afraid all the younger ones will learn to vociferate. He hears no one well but ourselves.'

'Oh! and Alethea Weston,' said Lily. 'Her voice is so clear and distinct, that she hardly ever raises it to make him hear. And have you ever heard her sing?'

'Yes, she sings very well. I cannot think why you never told me they were living here.'

'Because you never honour us with your correspondence,' said Emily; 'if you had vouchsafed to write to your sisters you could not have escaped hearing of the Westons.'

'And has Mr. Weston given up the law?'

'No, he only came home in the vacation,' said Emily. 'Did you know they had lost two daughters?'

'I saw it in the paper. Emma and Lucy were nice girls, but not equal to Miss Weston. What a shock to Mrs. Weston!'

'Yes, she quite lost her health, and the doctors said she must move into the country directly. Mrs. Carrington, who is some distant connection, told them of this place, and they took it rather hastily.'

'Do they like it?'

'Oh yes, very much!' said Emily. 'Mrs. Weston is very fond of the garden, and drives about in the pony-carriage, and it is quite pleasant to see how she admires the views.'

'And,' added Lily, 'Alethea walks with us, and sings with me, and teaches at school, and knows all the poor people.'

'I must go and see those children to-morrow,' said William.

The evening passed very pleasantly; and perhaps, in truth, Captain Mohun and his sisters were surprised to find each other so agreeable; for, in the eyes of the young ladies, he was by far the most awful person in the family.

When he had been last at home Harry's recent death had thrown a gloom over the whole family, and he had especially missed him. Himself quick, sensible, clever, and active, he was intolerant of opposite qualities, and the principal effect of that visit to Beechcroft was to make all the younger ones afraid of him, to discourage poor Claude, and to give to himself a gloomy remembrance of that home which had lost its principal charms in his mother and Harry.

He had now come home rather from a sense of duty than an expectation of pleasure, and he was quite surprised to find how much more attractive the New Court had become. Emily and Lilias were now conversible and intelligent companions, better suited to him than Eleanor had ever been, and he had himself in these four years acquired a degree of gentleness and consideration which prevented him from appearing so unapproachable as in days of old. This was especially the case with regard to Claude, whose sensitive and rather timid nature had in his childhood suffered much from William's boyish attempts to make him manly, and as he grew older, had almost felt himself despised; but now William appreciated his noble qualities, and was anxious to make amends for his former unkindness.

Claude came home from Oxford, not actually ill, but in the ailing condition in which he often was, just weak enough to give his sisters a fair excuse for waiting upon him, and petting him all day long. About the same time Phyllis and Adeline came back from Broomhill, and there was great joy at the New Court at the news that Mrs. Hawkesworth was the happy mother of a little boy.

Claude was much pleased by being asked by Eleanor to be godfather to his little nephew, whose name was to be Henry. Perhaps he hoped, what Lilias was quite sure of, that Eleanor did not think him unworthy to stand in Harry's place.

The choice of the other sponsors did not meet with universal approbation. Emily thought it rather hard that Mr. Hawkesworth's sister, Mrs. Ridley, should have been chosen before herself, and both she and Ada would have greatly preferred either Lord Rotherwood, Mr. Devereux, or William, to Mr. Ridley, while Phyllis had wanderings of her own how Claude could be godfather without being present at the christening.

One evening Claude was writing his answer to Eleanor, sitting at the sofa table where a small lamp was burning. Jane, attracted by its bright and soft radiance, came and sat down opposite to him with her work.

'What a silence!' said Lily, after about a quarter of an hour.

'What made you start, Jane?' said William.

'Did I?' said Jane.

'My speaking, I suppose,' said Lily, 'breaking the awful spell of silence.'

'How red you look, Jane. What is the matter?' said William.

'Do I?' asked Jane, becoming still redder.

'It is holding your face down over that baby's hood,' said Emily, 'you will sacrifice the colour of your nose to your nephew.'

Claude now asked Jane for the sealing-wax, folded up his letter, sealed it, put on a stamp, and as Jane was leaving the room at bedtime, said, 'Jenny, my dear, as you go by, just put that letter in the post-bag.'

Jane obeyed, and left the room. Claude soon after took the letter out of the bag, went to Emily's door, listened to ascertain that Jane was not there, and then knocked and was admitted.

'I could not help coming,' said he, 'to tell you of the trap in which Brownie has been caught.'

'Ah!' said Lily, 'I fancied I saw her peeping slyly at your letter.'

'Just so,' said Claude, 'and I hope she has experienced the truth of an old proverb.'

'Oh! tell us what you have said,' cried the sisters.

Claude read, 'Jane desires me to say that a hood for the baby shall be sent in the course of a week, and she hopes that it may be worn at the christening. I should rather say I hope it may be lost in the transit, for assuredly the head that it covers must be infected with something far worse than the scarlet fever—the fever of curiosity, the last quality which I should like my godson to possess. My only consolation is, that he will see the full deformity of the vice, as, poor little fellow, he becomes acquainted with "that worst of plagues, a prying maiden aunt." If Jane was simply curious, I should not complain, but her love of investigation is not directed to what ought to be known, but rather to find out some wretched subject for petty scandal, to blacken every action, and to add to the weight of every misdeed, and all for the sake of detailing her discoveries in exchange for similar information with Mrs. Appleton, or some equally suitable confidante.'

'Is that all?' said Lily.

'And enough, too, I hope,' said Claude.

'It ought to cure her!' cried Emily.

'Cure her!' said Claude, 'no such thing; cures are not wrought in this way; this is only a joke, and to keep it up, I will tell you a piece of news, which Jane must have spied out in my letter, as I had just written it when I saw her eyes in a suspicious direction. It was settled that Messieurs Maurice and Redgie are to go for two hours a day, three times a week, to Mr. Stevens, during the holidays.'

'The new Stoney Bridge curate?' said Emily.

'I am very glad you are not to be bored by them,' said Lily, 'but how they will dislike it!'

'It is very hard upon them,' said Claude, 'and I tried to prevent it, but the Baron was quite determined. Now I will begin to talk about this plan, and see whether Jenny betrays any knowledge of it.'

'Oh! it will be rare!' cried Lily; 'but do not speak of it before the Baron or William.'

'Let it be at luncheon,' said Emily, 'you know they never appear. Do you mean to send the letter?'

'Not that part of it,' said Claude, 'you see I can tear off the last page, and it is only to add a new conclusion. Good-night.'

Jane had certainly not spent the evening in an agreeable manner; she had not taken her seat at Claude's table with any evil designs towards his letter, but his writing was clear and legible, and her eye caught the word 'Maurice;' she wished to know what Claude could be saying about him, and having once begun, she could not leave off, especially when she saw her own name. When aware of the compliments he was paying her, she looked at him, but his eyes were fixed on his pen, and no smile, no significant expression betrayed that he was aware of her observations; and even when he gave her the letter to put into the post-bag he looked quite innocent and unconcerned. On the other hand, she did not like to think that he had been sending such a character of her to Eleanor in sober sadness; it was impossible to find out whether he had sent the letter; she could not venture to beg him to keep it back, she could only trust to his good-nature.

At luncheon, as they had agreed, Lily began by asking where her papa and William were gone? Claude answered, 'To Stoney Bridge, to call upon Mr. Stevens; they mean to ask him to dine one day next week, to be introduced to his pupils.'

'Is he an Oxford or Cambridge man?' asked Lily.

'Oxford,' exclaimed Jane, quite forgetting whence she had derived her information, 'he is a fellow of—'

'Indeed?' said Lily; 'how do you know that?'

'Why, we have all been talking of him lately,' said Jane.

'Not I,' said Emily, 'why should he interest us?'

'Because he is to tutor the boys,' said Jane.

'When did you hear that he is to tutor the boys?' asked Lily.

'When you did, I suppose,' said Jane, blushing.

'You did, did you?' said Claude. 'I feel convinced, if so, that you must really be what you are so often called, a changeling. I heard it, or rather read it first at Oxford, where the Baron desired me to make inquiries about him. You were, doubtless, looking over my shoulder at the moment. This is quite a discovery. We shall have to perform a brewery of egg-shells this evening, and put the elf to flight with a red-hot poker, and what a different sister Jane we shall recover, instead of this little mischief-making sprite, so quiet, so reserved, never intruding her opinion, showing constant deference to all her superiors—yes, and to her inferiors, shutting her eyes to the faults of others, and when they come before her, trying to shield the offender from those who regard them as merely exciting news.'

Claude's speech had become much more serious than he intended, and he felt quite guilty when he had finished, so that it was not at all an undesirable interruption when Phyllis and Adeline asked for the story of the brewery of egg-shells.

Emily and Lilias kindly avoided looking at Jane, who, after fidgeting on her chair and turning very red, succeeded in regaining outward composure. She resolved to let the matter die away, and think no more about it.

When Mr. Mohun and William came home, they brought the news that Lady Rotherwood had invited the whole party to dinner.

'I am very glad we are allowed to see them,' said Emily, 'I am quite tired of being shut up.'

'If it was not for the Westons we might as well live in Nova Zembla,' said Jane.

'I am glad you damsels should know a little more of Florence,' said Mrs. Mohun.

'Yes,' said Claude, 'cousins were made to be friends.'

'In that case one ought to be able to choose them,' said William.

'And know them,' said Emily. 'We have not seen Florence since she was eleven years old.'

'Cousin or not,' said Lilias, 'Florence can hardly be so much my friend as Alethea.'

'Right, Lily,' said William, 'stand up for old friends against all the cousins in the universe.'

'Has Alethea a right to be called an old friend?' said Emily; 'does three quarters of a year make friendship venerable?'

'No one can deny that she is a tried friend,' said Lilias.

'But pray, good people,' said Claude, 'what called forth those vows of eternal constancy? why was my innocent general observation construed into an attack upon Miss Weston?'

'Because there is something invidious in your tone,' said Lily.

'What kind of girl is that Florence?' asked William.

'Oh! a nice, lively, pleasant girl,' said Claude.

'I cannot make out what her pursuits are,' said Lily; 'Rotherwood never talks of her reading anything.'

'She has been governessed and crammed till she is half sick of all reading,' said Claude, 'of all study—ay, and all accomplishments.'

'So that is the friend you recommend, Lily!' said William.

'Well, Claude, that is what I call a great shame,' said Emily.

'Stay,' said Claude, 'you have heard but half my story, I say that this is the reaction. Florence has no lack of sense, and if you young ladies are wise, you may help her to find the use of it.'

Claude's further opinion did not transpire, as dinner was announced, and nothing more was said about Lady Florence till the girls had an opportunity of judging for themselves. She had a good deal of her brother's vivacity, with gentleness and grace, which made her very engaging, and her perfect recollection of the New Court, and of childish days, charmed her cousins. Lady Rotherwood was very kind and affectionate, and held out hopes of many future meetings. The next day Maurice and Reginald came home from school, bringing a better character for diligence than usual, on which they founded hopes that the holidays would be left to their own disposal. They were by no means pleased with the arrangement made with Mr. Stevens and most unwillingly did they undertake the expedition to Stony Bridge, performing the journey in a very unsociable manner. Maurice was no horseman, and chose to jog on foot through three miles of lane, while Reginald's pony cantered merrily along, its master's head being intent upon the various winter sports in which William and Lord Rotherwood allowed him to share. Little did Maurice care for such diversions; he was, as Adeline said, studying another 'apology.' This time it was phrenology, for which the cropped heads of Lilias and Jane afforded unusual facility. There was, however, but a limited supply of heads willing to be fingered, and Maurice returned to the most abiding of his tastes, and in an empty room at the Old Court laboured assiduously to find the secret of perpetual motion.

A few days before Christmas Rachel Harvey again took leave of Beechcroft, with a promise that she would make them another visit when Eleanor came home. Before she went she gave Emily a useful caution, telling her it was not right to trust her keys out of her own possession. It was what Miss Mohun never would have done, she had never once committed them even to Rachel.

'With due deference to Eleanor,' said Emily, with her winning smile, 'we must allow that that was being over cautious.'

Rachel smiled, but her lecture was not averted by the compliment.

'It might have been very well since you have known me, Miss Emily, but I do not know what would have come of it, if I had been too much trusted when I was a giddy young thing like Esther; that girl comes of a bad lot, and if anything is to be made of her, it is by keeping temptation out of her way, and not letting her be with that mother of hers.'

Rachel had rather injured the effect of her advice by behaving too like a mistress during her visit; Emily had more than once wished that all servants were not privileged people, and she was more offended than convinced by the remonstrance.

CHAPTER XIV
CHRISTMAS

'Slee, sla, slud,
  Stuck in the mud,
O! it is pretty to wade through a flood,
  Come, wheel round,
  The dirt we have found,
Would he an estate at a farthing a pound.'

Lily's illness interrupted her teaching at the village school for many weeks, and she was in no great haste to resume it. Alethea Weston seemed to enjoy doing all that was required, and Lily left it in her hands, glad to shut her eyes as much as possible to the disheartening state the parish had been in ever since her former indiscretion.

The approach of Christmas, however, made it necessary for her to exert herself a little more, and her interest in parish matters revived as she distributed the clothing-club goods, and in private conference with each good dame, learnt the wants of her family. But it was sad to miss several names struck out of the list for non-attendance at church; and when Mrs. Eden came for her child's clothing, Lily remarked that the articles she chose were unlike those of former years, the cheapest and coarsest she could find.

St. Thomas's day was marked by the custom, called at Beechcroft 'gooding.' Each mother of a family came to all the principal houses in the parish to receive sixpence, towards providing a Christmas dinner, and it was Lily's business to dispense this dole at the New Court. With a long list of names and a heap of silver before her, she sat at the oaken table by the open chimney in the hall, returning a nod or a smiling greeting to the thanks of the women as they came, one by one, to receive the little silver coins, and warm themselves by the glowing wood fire.

Pleasant as the task was at first, it ended painfully. Agnes Eden appeared, in order to claim the double portion allotted to her mother, as a widow. This was the first time that Mrs. Eden had asked for the gooding-money, and Lily knew that it was a sign that she must be in great distress. Agnes made her a little courtesy, and crept away again as soon as she had received her shilling; but Mrs. Grey, who was Mrs. Eden's neighbour, had not quite settled her penny-club affairs, and remained a little longer. An unassuming and lightly-principled person was Mrs. Grey, and Lily enjoyed a talk with her, while she was waiting for the purple stuff frock which Jane was measuring off for Kezia. They spoke of the children, and of a few other little matters, and presently something was said about Mrs. Eden; Lily asked if the blacksmith helped her.

'Oh! no, Miss Lilias, he will do nothing for her while she sends her child to school and to church. He will not speak to her even. Not a bit of butter, nor a morsel of bacon, has been in her house since Michaelmas, and what she would have done if it was not for Mr. Devereux and Mrs. Weston, I cannot think.'

Lilias, much shocked by this account of the distress into which she and Jane had been the means of bringing the widow, reported it to her father and to the Rector;

entreating the former to excuse her rent, which he willingly promised to do, and also desired his daughters to give her a blanket, and tell her to come to dine house whenever any broth was to be given away. Mr. Devereux, who already knew of her troubles, and allowed her a small sum weekly, now told his cousins how much the Greys had assisted her. Andrew Grey had dug up and housed her winter's store of potatoes, he had sought work for her, and little Agnes often shared the meals of his children. The Greys had a large family, very young, so that all that they did for her was the fruit of self-denial. Innumerable were the kindnesses which they performed unknown to any but the widow and her child. More, by a hundred times, did they assist her, than the thoughtless girls who had occasioned her sufferings, though Lily was not the only one who felt that nothing was too much for them to do. Nothing, perhaps, would have been too much, except to bear her in mind and steadily aid her in little things; but Lily took no account of little things, talked away her feelings, and thus all her grand resolutions produced almost nothing. Lord Rotherwood sent Mrs. Eden a sovereign, the girls newly clothed little Agnes, Phyllis sometimes carried her the scraps of her dinner, Mrs. Eden once came to work at the New Court, and a few messes of broth were given to her, but in general she was forgotten, and when remembered, indolence or carelessness too often prevented the Miss Mohuns from helping her. In Emily's favourite phrase, each individual thing was 'not worth while.'

When Lilias did think it 'worth while,' she would do a great deal upon impulse, sometimes with more zeal than discretion, as she proved by an expedition which she took on Christmas Eve. Mr. Mohun did not allow the poor of the village to depend entirely on the gooding for their Christmas dinner, but on the 24th of December a large mess of excellent beef broth was prepared at the New Court, and distributed to all his own labourers, and the most respectable of the other cottagers.

In the course of the afternoon Lily found that one portion had not been given out. It was that which was intended for the Martins, a poor old rheumatic couple, who lived at South End, the most distant part of the parish. Neither of them could walk as far as the New Court, and most of their neighbours had followed Farmer Gage, and had therefore been excluded from the distribution, so that there was no one to send. Lily, therefore, resolved herself to carry the broth to them, if she could find an escort, which was not an easy matter, as the frost had that morning broken up, and a good deal of snow and rain had been falling in the course of the day. In the hall she met Reginald, just turned out of Maurice's workshop, and much at a loss for employment.

'Redgie,' said she, 'you can do me a great kindness.'

'If it is not a bore,' returned Reginald.

'I only want you to walk with me to South End.'

'Eh?' said Reginald; 'I thought the little Misses were too delicate to put their dear little proboscises outside the door.'

'That is the reason I ask you; I do not think Emily or Jane would like it, and it is too far for Claude. Those poor old Martins have not got their broth, and there is no one to fetch it for them.'

'Then do not be half an hour putting on your things.'

'Thank you; and do not run off, and make me spend an hour in hunting for you, and then say that I made you wait.'

'I will wait fast enough. You are not so bad as Emily,' said Reginald, while Lily ran upstairs to equip herself. When she came down, she was glad to find her escort employed in singeing the end of the tail of the old rocking-horse at the fire in the hall, so that she was not obliged to seek him in the drawing-room, where her plans would probably have met with opposition. She had, however, objections to answer from an unexpected quarter. Reginald was much displeased when she took possession of the pitcher of broth.

'I will not walk with such a thing as that,' said he, 'it makes you look like one of the dirty girls in the village.'

'Then you ought, like the courteous Rinaldo, to carry it for me,' said Lily.

'I touch the nasty thing! Faugh! Throw it into the gutter, Lily.'

He made an attempt to dispose of it in that manner, which it required all Lily's strength to withstand, as well as an imploring 'Now, Redgie, think of the poor old people. Remember, you have promised.'

'Promised! I never promised to walk with a greasy old pitcher. What am I to do if we meet Miss Weston?'

Lily contrived to overcome Reginald's refined notions sufficiently to make him allow her to carry the pitcher; and when he had whistled up two of the dogs, they proceeded merrily along the road, dirty and wet though it was. Their walk was not entirely without adventures; first, they had to turn back in the path by the river side, which would have saved them half a mile, but was now flooded. Then, as they were passing through a long lane, which led them by Edward Gage's farm, a great dog rushed out of the yard, and fell upon the little terrier, Viper. Old Neptune flew to the rescue, and to the great alarm of Lily, Reginald ran up with a stick; happily, however, a labourer at the same time came out with a pitchfork, and beat off the enemy. These two delays, together with Reginald's propensity for cutting sticks, and for breaking ice, made it quite late when they arrived at South End. When there, they found that a kind neighbour had brought the old people their broth in the morning, and intended to go for her own when she came home from her work in the evening. It was not often that Lily went to South End; the old people were delighted to see her, and detained her for some time by a long story about their daughter at service, while Reginald looked the picture of impatience, drumming on his knee, switching the leg of the table, and tickling Neptune's ears. When they left the cottage it was much later and darker than they had expected; but Lily was unwilling again to encounter the perils of the lane, and consulted her brother whether there was not some other way. He gave notice of a cut across some fields, which would take them into the turnpike road, and Lily agreeing, they climbed over a gate into a pathless turnip field. Reginald strode along first, calling to the dogs, while Lily followed, abstaining from dwelling on the awkward circumstance that every step she took led her farther from home, and rejoicing that it was so dark that she could not see the mud which plastered the edge of her petticoats. After plodding through three very long fields, they found themselves shut in by a high hedge and tall ditch.

'That fool of a farmer!' cried Reginald.

'What is to be done?' said Lily, disconsolately.

'There is the road,' said Reginald. 'How do you propose to get into it?'

'There was a gap here last summer,' said the boy.

'Very likely! Come back; try the next field; it must have a gate somewhere.'

Back they went, after seeing the carrier's cart from Raynham pass by.

'Redgie, it must be half-past five! We shall never be in time. Aunt Rotherwood coming too!'

After a desperate plunge through a swamp of ice, water, and mud, they found themselves at a gate, and safely entered the turnpike road.

'How it rains!' said Lily. 'One comfort is that it is too dark for any one to see us.'

'Not very dark, either,' said Reginald; 'I believe there is a moon if one could see it. Ha! here comes some one on horseback. It is a gray horse; it is William.'

'Come to look for us,' said Lily. 'Oh, Redgie!'

'Coming home from Raynham,' said Reginald. 'Do not fancy yourself so important, Lily. William, is that you?'

'Reginald!' exclaimed William, suddenly checking his horse. 'Lily, what is all this?'

'We set out to South End, to take the broth to the old Martins, and we found the meadows flooded, which made us late; but we shall soon be at home,' said Lily, in a make-the-best-of-it tone.

'Soon? You are a mile and a half from home now, and do you know how late it is?'

'Half-past five,' said Lily.

'Six, at least; how could you be so absurd?' William rode quickly on; Reginald laughed, and they plodded on; at length a tall dark figure was seen coming towards them, and Lily started, as it addressed her, 'Now what is the meaning of all this?'

'Oh, William, have you come to meet us? Thank you; I am sorry—'

'How were you to come through the village in the dark, without some one to take care of you?'

'I am taking care of her,' said Reginald, affronted.

'Make haste; my aunt is come. How could you make the people at home so anxious?'

William gave Lily his arm, and on finding she was both tired and wet, again scolded her, walked so fast that she was out of breath, then complained of her folly, and blamed Reginald. It was very unpleasant, and yet she was very much obliged to him, and exceedingly sorry he had taken so much trouble.

They came home at about seven o'clock. Jane met them in the hall, full of her own and Lady Rotherwood's wonderings; she hurried Lily upstairs, and—skilful, quick, and ready—she helped her to dress in a very short time. As they ran down Reginald overtook them, and they entered the drawing-room as the dinner-bell was ringing. William did not appear for some time, and his apologies were not such as to smooth matters for his sister.

Perhaps it was for this very reason that Mr. Mohun allowed Lily to escape with no more than a jesting reproof. Lord Rotherwood wished to make his cousin's hardihood and enterprise an example to his sister, and, in his droll exaggerating way, represented such walks as every-day occurrences. This was just the contrary to what Emily wished her aunt to believe, and Claude was much diverted with the struggle between her politeness to Lord Rotherwood and her desire to maintain the credit of the family.

Lady Florence, though liking Lilias, thought this walk extravagant. Emily feared Lilias had lost her aunt's good opinion, and prepared herself for some hints about a governess. It was untoward; but in the course of the evening she was a little comforted by a proposal from Lady Rotherwood to take her and Lilias to a ball at Raynham, which was to take place in January; and as soon as the gentlemen appeared, they submitted the invitation to their father, while Lady Rotherwood pressed William to accompany them, and he was refusing.

'What are soldiers intended for but to dance!' said Lord Rotherwood.

'I never dance,' said William, with a grave emphasis.

'I am out of the scrape,' said the Marquis. 'I shall be gone before it takes place; I reserve all my dancing for July 30th. Well, young ladies, is the Baron propitious?'

'He says he will consider of it,' said Emily.

'Oh then, he will let you go,' said Florence, 'people never consider when they mean no.'

'No, Florence,' said her brother, 'Uncle Mohun's "consider of it" is equivalent to Le Roi's "avisera."'

'What is he saying?' asked Lily, turning to listen. 'Oh, that my wig is in no ball-going condition.'

'A wreath would hide all deficiencies,' said Florence; 'I am determined to have you both.'

'I give small hopes of both,' said Claude; 'you will only have Emily.'

'Why do you think so, Claude?' cried both Florence and Lilias.

'From my own observation,' Claude answered, gravely.

'I am very angry with the Baron,' said Lord Rotherwood; 'he is grown inhospitable: he will not let me come here to-morrow—the first Christmas these five years that I have missed paying my respects to the New Court sirloin and turkey. It is too bad—and the Westons dining here too.'

'Cousin Turkey-cock, well may you be in a passion,' muttered Claude, as if in soliloquy.

Lord Rotherwood and Lilias both caught the sound, and laughed, but Emily, unwilling that Florence should see what liberties they took with her brother, asked quickly why he was not to come.

'I think we are much obliged to him,' said Florence, 'it would be too bad to leave mamma and me to spend our Christmas alone, when we came to the castle on purpose to oblige him.'

'Ay, and he says he will not let me come here, because I ought to give the Hetherington people ocular demonstration that I go to church,' said Lord Rotherwood.

'Very right, as Eleanor would say,' observed Claude.

'Very likely; but I don't care for the Hetherington folks; they do not know how to make the holly in the church fit to be seen, and they will not sing the good old Christmas carols. Andrew Grey is worth all the Hetherington choir put together.'

'Possibly; but how are they to mend, if their Marquis contents himself with despising them?' said Claude.

'That is too bad, Claude. When you heard how submissively I listened to the Baron, and know I mean to abide by what he said, you ought to condole with me a little, if you have not the grace to lament my absence on your own account. Why, I thought myself as regular a part of the feast as the mince-pies, and almost as necessary.'

Here a request for some music put an end to his lamentations. Lilias was vexed by the uncertainty about the ball, and was, besides, too tired to play with spirit. She saw that Emily was annoyed, and she felt ready to cry before the evening was over; but still she was proud of her exploit, and when, after the party was gone, Emily began to represent to her the estimate that her aunt was likely to form of her character, she replied, 'If she thinks the worse of me for carrying the broth to those poor old people, I am sure I do not wish for her good opinion.'

Mr. Mohun was not propitious when the question of Lily's going to the ball was pressed upon him. He said that he thought her too young for gaieties, and, besides, that late hours never agreed with her, and he advised her to wait for the 30th of July.

Lilias knew that it was useless to say any more. She was much disappointed, and at the same time provoked with herself for caring about such a matter. Her temper was out of order on Christmas Day; and while she wondered why she could not enjoy the festival as formerly, with thoughts fitted to the day, she did not examine herself sufficiently to find out the real cause of her uncomfortable feelings.

The clear frost was only cold; the bright sunshine did not rejoice her; the holly and the mistletoe seemed ill arranged; and none of the pleasant sights of the day could give her such blitheness as once she had known.

She was almost angry when she saw that the Westons had left off their mourning, declaring that they did not look like themselves; and her vexation came to a height when she found that Alethea actually intended to go to the ball with Mrs. Carrington. The excited manner in which she spoke of it convinced Mr. Mohun that he had acted wisely in not allowing her to go, since the very idea seemed to turn her head.

CHAPTER XV
MINOR MISFORTUNES

'Loving she is, and tractable though wild.'

In a day or two Lady Rotherwood and her daughter called at the New Court. On this occasion Lilias was employed in as rational and lady-like a manner as could be desired—in practising her music in the drawing-room; Emily was reading, and Ada threading beads.

Lady Rotherwood greeted her nieces very affectionately, gave a double caress to Adeline, stroked her pretty curls, admired her beadwork, talked to her about her doll, and then proceeded to invite the whole family to a Twelfth-Day party, given for their especial benefit. The little Carringtons and the Weston girls were also to be asked. Emily and Lilias were eagerly expressing their delight when suddenly a trampling, like a charge of horse, was heard in the hall; the door was thrown back, and in rushed Reginald and Phyllis, shouting, 'Such fun!—the pigs are in the garden!'

At the sight of their aunt they stopped short, looking aghast, and certainly those who beheld them partook of their consternation. Reginald was hot and gloveless; his shoes far from clean; his brown curls hanging in great disorder from his Scotch cap; his handkerchief loose; his jacket dusty—but this was no great matter, since, as Emily said, he was 'only a boy.' His bright open smile, the rough, yet gentleman-like courtesy of his advance to the Marchioness, his comical roguish glance at Emily, to see if she was very angry, and to defy her if she were, and his speedy exit, all greatly amused Lady Florence, and made up for what there might have been of the wild schoolboy in his entrance.

Poor Phyllis had neither the excuse of being a schoolboy nor the good-humoured fearlessness that freed her brother from embarrassment, and she stood stock-still, awkward and dismayed, not daring to advance; longing to join in the pig-chase, yet afraid to run away, her eyes stretched wide open, her hair streaming into them, her bonnet awry, her tippet powdered with seeds of hay, her gloves torn and soiled, the colour of her brown holland apron scarcely discernible through its various stains, her frock tucked up, her stockings covered with mud, and without shoes, which she had taken off at the door.

'Phyllis,' said Emily, 'what are you thinking of? What makes you such a figure? Come and speak to Aunt Rotherwood.'

Phyllis drew off her left-hand glove, and held out her hand, making a few sidelong steps towards her aunt, who gave her a rather reluctant kiss. Lily bent her bonnet into shape, and pulled down her frock, while Florence laughed, patted her cheek, and asked what she had been doing.

'Helping Redgie to chop turnips,' was the answer.

Afraid of some further exposure, Emily hastily sent her away to be made fit to be seen, and Lady Rotherwood went on caressing Ada and talking of something else. Emily had no opportunity of explaining that this was not Phyllis's usual condition, and she was afraid that Lady Rotherwood would never believe that it was accidental. She was much annoyed, especially as the catastrophe only served to divert Mr. Mohun and Claude. Of all the family William and Adeline alone took her view of the case. Ada lectured Phyllis on her 'naughtiness,' and plumed herself on her aunt's evident preference, but William was not equally sympathetic. He was indeed as fastidious as Emily herself, and as much annoyed by such misadventures; but he maintained that she was to blame for them, saying that the state of things was not such as it should be, and that the exposure might be advantageous if it put her on her guard in future.

It appeared as if poor Phyllis was to be punished for the vexation which she had caused, for in the course of her adventures with Reginald she caught a cold, which threatened to prevent her from being of the party on Twelfth-Day. She had a cough, which did not give her by any means as much inconvenience as the noise it occasioned did to other people. Every morning and every evening she anxiously asked her sisters whether they thought she would be allowed to go. Another of the party seemed likely to fail. On the 5th of January Claude came down to breakfast later even than usual; but he had no occasion to make excuses, for his heavy eyes, the dark lines under them, his pale cheeks, and the very sit of his hair, were sure signs that he had a violent headache. He soon betook himself to the sofa in the drawing-room, attended by Lily, with pillows, cushions, ether, and lavender. Late in the afternoon the pain diminished a little, and he fell asleep, to the great joy of his sister, who sat watching him, scarcely daring to move.

Suddenly a frightful scream and loud crash was heard in the room above them. Claude started up, and Lily, exclaiming, 'Those tiresome children!' hurried to the room whence the noise had come.

Reginald, Phyllis, and Ada, all stood there laughing. Reginald and Phyllis had been climbing to the top of a great wardrobe, by means of a ladder of chairs and tables. While Phyllis was descending her brother had made some demonstration that startled her, and she fell with all the chairs over her, but without hurting herself.

'You naughty troublesome child,' cried Lily, in no gentle tone. 'How often have you been told to leave off such boyish tricks! And you choose the very place for disturbing poor Claude, with his bad headache, making it worse than ever.'

Phyllis tried to speak, but only succeeded in giving a dismal howl. She went on screaming, sobbing, and roaring so loud that she could not hear Lily's attempts to quiet her. The next minute Claude appeared, looking half distracted. Reginald ran off, and as he dashed out of the room, came full against William, who caught hold of him, calling out to know what was the matter.

'Only Phyllis screaming,' said Lily. 'Oh, Claude, I am very sorry!'

'Is that all?' said Claude. 'I thought some one was half killed!'

He sank into a chair, pressing his hand on his temples, and looking very faint. William supported him, and Lily stood by, repeating, 'I am very sorry—it was all my fault—my scolding—'

'Hush,' said William, 'you have done mischief enough. Go away, children.'

Phyllis had already gone, and the next moment thrust into Lily's hand the first of the medicaments which she had found in the drawing-room. The faintness soon went off, but Claude thought he had better not struggle against the headache any longer, but go to bed, in hopes of being better the next day. William went with him to his room, and Lilias lingered on the stairs, very humble, and very wretched. William soon came forth again, and asked the meaning of the uproar.

'It was all my fault,' said she; 'I was vexed at Claude's being waked, and that made me speak sharply to Phyllis, and set her roaring.'

'I do not know which is the most inconsiderate of you,' said William.

'You cannot blame me more than I deserve,' said Lily. 'May I go to poor Claude?'

'I suppose so; but I do not see what good you are to do. Quiet is the only thing for him.'

Lily, however, went, and Claude gave her to understand that he liked her to stay with him. She arranged his blinds and curtains comfortably, and then sat down to watch him. William went to the drawing-room to write a letter. Just as he had sat down he heard a strange noise, a sound of sobbing, which seemed to come from the corner where the library steps stood. Looking behind them, he beheld Phyllis curled up, her head on her knees, crying bitterly.

'You there! Come out. What is the matter now?'

'I am so very sorry,' sighed she.

'Well, leave off crying.' She would willingly have obeyed, but her sobs were beyond her own control; and he went on, 'If you are sorry, there is no more to be said. I hope it will be a lesson to you another time. You are quite old enough to have more consideration for other people.'

'I am very sorry,' again said Phyllis, in a mournful note.

'Be sorry, only do not roar. You make that noise from habit, I am convinced, and you may break yourself off it if you choose.'

Phyllis crept out of the room, and in a few minutes more the door was softly opened by Emily, returning from her walk.

'I thought Claude was here. Is he gone to bed? Is his head worse?'

'Yes, the children have been doing their best to distract him. Emily, I want to know why it is that those children are for ever in mischief and yelling in all parts of the house.'

'I wish I could help it,' said Emily, with a sigh; 'they are very troublesome.'

'There must be great mismanagement,' said her brother.

'Oh, William! Why do you think so?'

'Other children do not go on in this way, and it was not so in Eleanor's time.'

'It is only Phyllis,' said Emily.

'Phyllis or not, it ought not to be. What will that child grow up, if you let her be always running wild with the boys?'

'Consider, William, that you see us at a disadvantage; we are all unsettled by this illness, and the children have been from home.'

'As if they learnt all these wild tricks at Broomhill! That excuse will not do, Emily.'

'And then they are always worse in the holidays,' pleaded Emily.

'Yes, there are reasons to be found for everything that goes wrong; but if you were wise you would look deeper. Now, Emily, I do not wish to be hard upon you, for I know you are in a very difficult position, and very young for such a charge, but I am sure you might manage better. I do not think you use your energies. There is no activity, nor regularity, nor method, about this household. I believe that my father sees that this is the case, but it is not his habit to find fault with little things. You may think that, therefore, I need not interfere, but—'

'Oh, William! I am glad—'

'But remember that comfort is made up of little things. And, Emily, when you consider how much my father has suffered, and how desolate his home must be at the best, I think you will be inclined to exert yourself to prevent him from being anxious about the children or harassed by your negligence.'

'Indeed, William,' returned Emily, with many tears, 'it is my most earnest wish to make him comfortable. Thank you for what you have said. Now that I am stronger, I hope to do more, and I will really do my best.'

At this moment Emily was sincere; but the good impulse of one instant was not likely to endure against long cherished habits of selfish apathy.

Claude did not appear again till the middle of the next day. His headache was nearly gone, but he was so languid that he gave up all thoughts of Devereux Castle that evening. Lord Rotherwood, who always seemed to know what was going on at Beechcroft, came to inquire for him, and very unwillingly allowed that it would be better for him to stay at home. Lilias wished to remain with him; but this her cousin would not permit, saying that he could not consent to lose three of the party, and Florence would be disappointed in all her plans. Neither would Claude hear of keeping her at home, and she was obliged to satisfy herself with putting his arm-chair in his favourite corner by the fire, with the little table before it, supplied with books, newspaper, inkstand, paper-knife, and all the new periodicals, and he declared that he should enjoy the height of luxury.

Phyllis considered it to be entirely her fault that he could not go, and was too much grieved on that account to have many regrets to spare for herself. She enjoyed seeing Adeline dressed, and hearing Esther's admiration of her. And having seen the party set off, she made her way into the drawing-room, opening the door as gently as possible, just wide enough to admit her little person, then shutting it as if she was afraid of hurting it, she crept across the room on tiptoe. She started when Claude looked up and said, 'Why, Phyl, I have not seen you to-day.'

'Good morning,' she mumbled, advancing in her sidelong way.

Claude suspected that she had been more blamed the day before than the occasion called for, and wishing to make amends he kissed her, and said something good-natured about spending the evening together.

Phyllis, a little reassured, went to her own occupations. She took out a large heavy volume, laid it on the window-seat, and began to read. Claude was interested in his own book, and did not look up till the light failed him. He then, closing his book, gave a long yawn, and looked round for his little companion, almost thinking, from the stillness of the room, that she must have gone to seek for amusement in the nursery.

She was, however, still kneeling against the window-seat, her elbows planted on the great folio, and her head between her hands, reading intently.

'Little Madam,' said he, 'what great book have you got there?'

'*As You Like It*,' said Phyllis.

'What! are you promoted to reading Shakspeare?'

'I have not read any but this,' said Phyllis. 'Ada and I have often looked at the pictures, and I liked the poor wounded stag coming down to the water so much, that I read about it, and then I went on. Was it wrong, Claude? no one ever told me not.'

'You are welcome to read it,' said Claude, 'but not now—it is too dark. Come and sit in the great chair on the other side of the fire, and be sociable. And what do you think of '*As You Like It*?''

'I like it very much,' answered Phyllis, 'only I cannot think why *Jacks* did not go to the poor stag, and try to cure it, when he saw its tears running into the water.'

To save the character of *Jacks*, Claude gravely suggested the difficulty of catching the stag, and then asked Phyllis her opinion of the heroines.

'Oh! it was very funny about Rosalind dressing like a man, and then being ready to cry like a girl when she was tired, and then pretending to pretend to be herself; and Celia, it was very kind of her to go away with Rosalind; but I should have liked her better if she had stayed at home, and persuaded her father to let Rosalind stay too. I am sure she would if she had been like Ada. Then it is so nice about Old Adam and Orlando. Do not you think so, Claude? It is just what I am sure Wat Greenwood would do for Redgie, if he was to be turned out like Orlando.'

'It is just what Wat Greenwood's ancestor did for Sir Maurice Mohun,' said Claude.

'Yes, Dame Greenwood tells us that story.'

'Well, Phyl, I think you show very good taste in liking the scene between Orlando and Adam.'

'I am glad you like it, too, Claude. But I will tell you what I like best,' exclaimed the little girl, springing up, 'I do like it, when Orlando killed the lioness and the snake,—and saved Oliver; how glad he must have been.'

'Glad to have done good to his enemy,' said Claude; 'yes, indeed.'

'His enemy! he was his brother, you know. I meant it must be so very nice to save anybody—don't you think so, Claude?'

'Certainly.'

'Claude, do you know there is nothing I wish so much as to save somebody's life. It was very nice to save the dragon-fly; and it is very nice to let flies out of spiders' webs, only they always have their legs and wings torn, and look miserable; and it was very nice to put the poor little thrushes back into their nest when they tumbled out, and then to see their mother come to feed them; and it was very pleasant to help the poor goose that had put its head through the pales, and could not get it back. Mrs. Harrington said it would have been strangled if I had not helped it. That was very nice, but how delightful it would be to save some real human person's life.'

Claude did not laugh at the odd medley in her speech, but answered, 'Well, those little things train you in readiness and kindness.'

'Will they?' said Phyllis, pressing on to express what had long been her earnest wish. 'If I could but save some one, I should not mind being killed myself—I think not—I hope it is not naughty to say so. I believe there is something in the Bible about it, about laying down one's life for one's friend.'

'There is, Phyl, and I quite agree with you; it must be a great blessing to have saved some one.'

'And little girls have sometimes done it, Claude. I know a story of one who saved her little brother from drowning, and another waked the people when the house was on fire. And when I was at Broomhill, Marianne showed me a story of a young lady who helped to save the Prince, that Prince Charlie that Miss Weston sings about. I wish the Prince of Wales would get into some misfortune—I should like to save him.'

'I do not quite echo that loyal wish,' said Claude.

'Well, but, Claude, Redgie wishes for a rebellion, like Sir Maurice's, for he says all the boys at his school would be one regiment, in green velvet coats, and white feathers in their hats.'

'Indeed! and Redgie to be Field Marshal?'

'No, he is to be Sir Reginald Mohun, a Knight of the Garter, and to ask the Queen to give William back the title of Baron of Beechcroft, and make papa a Duke.'

'Well done! he is to take good care of the interests of the family.'

'But it is not that that I should care about,' said Phyllis. 'I should like it better for the feeling in one's own self; I think all that fuss would rather spoil it—don't you, Claude?'

'Indeed, I do; but Phyllis, if you only wish for that feeling, you need not look for dangers or rebellions to gain it.'

'Oh! you mean the feeling that very good people indeed have—people like Harry—but that I shall never be.'

'I hope you mean to try, though.'

'I do try; I wish I was as good as Ada, but I am so naughty and so noisy that I do not know what to do. Every day when I say my prayers I think about being quiet, and not idling at my lessons, and sometimes I do stop in time, and behave better, but sometimes I forget, and I do not mind what I am about, and my voice gets loud, and I let the things tumble down and make a noise, and so it was yesterday.' Here she looked much disposed to cry.

'No, no, we will not have any crying this evening,' said Claude. 'I do not think you did me much mischief, my head ached just as much before.'

'That was a thing I wanted to ask you about: William says my crying loud is all habit, and that I must cure myself of it. How does he mean? Ought I to cry every day to practise doing it without roaring?'

'Do you like to begin,' said Claude, laughing; 'shall I beat you or pinch you?'

'Oh! it would make your head bad again,' said Phyllis; 'but I wish you would tell me what he means. When I cry I only think about what makes me unhappy.'

'Try never to cry,' said Claude; 'I assure you it is not pleasant to hear you, even when I have no headache. If you wish to do anything right, you must learn self-control, and it will be a good beginning to check yourself when you are going to cry. Do not look melancholy now. Here comes the tea. Let me see how you will perform as tea-maker.'

'I wish the evening would not go away so fast!'

'And what are we to do after tea? You are queen of the evening.'

'If you would but tell me a story, Claude.'

They lingered long over the tea-table, talking and laughing, and when they had finished, Phyllis discovered with surprise that it was nearly bedtime. The promised story was not omitted, however, and Phyllis, sitting on a little footstool at her brother's feet, looked up eagerly for it.

'Well, Phyl, I will tell you a true history that I heard from an officer who had served in the Peninsular War—the war in Spain, you know.'

'Yes, with the French, who killed their king. Lily told me.'

'And the Portuguese were helping us. Just after we had taken the town of Ciudad Rodrigo, some of the Portuguese soldiers went to find lodgings for themselves, and, entering a magazine of gunpowder, made a fire on the floor to dress their food. A most dangerous thing—do you know why?'

'The book would be burnt,' said Phyllis.

'What book, you wise child?'

'The Magazine; I thought a magazine was one of the paper books that Maurice is always reading.'

'Oh!' said Claude, laughing, 'a magazine is a store, and as many different things are stored in those books, they are called magazines. A powder magazine is a store of barrels of gunpowder. Now do you see why it was dangerous to light a fire?'

'It blows up,' said Phyllis; 'that was the reason why Robinson Crusoe was afraid of the lightning.'

'Right, Phyl, and therefore a candle is never allowed to be carried into a powder magazine, and even nailed shoes are never worn there, lest they should strike fire. One spark, lighting on a grain of gunpowder, scattered on the floor, might communicate with the rest, make it all explode, and spread destruction everywhere. Think in what fearful peril these reckless men had placed, not only themselves, but the whole town, and the army. An English officer chanced to discover them, and what do you think he did?'

'Told all the people to run away.'

'How could he have told every one, soldiers, inhabitants, and all? where could they have gone? No, he raised no alarm, but he ordered the Portuguese out of the building, and with the help of an English sergeant, he carried out, piece by piece, all the wood which they had set on fire. Now, imagine what that must have been. An explosion might happen at any moment, yet they had to walk steadily, slowly, and with the utmost caution, in and out of this place several times, lest one spark might fly back.'

'Then they were saved?' cried Phyllis, breathlessly; 'and what became of them afterwards?'

'They were both killed in battle, the officer, I believe, in Badajoz, and the sergeant sometime afterwards.'

Phyllis gave a deep sigh, and sat silent for some minutes. Next, Claude began a droll Irish fairy-tale, which he told with spirit and humour, such as some people would have scorned to exert for the amusement of a mere child. Phyllis laughed, and was so happy, that when suddenly they heard the sound of wheels, she started up, wondering what brought the others home so soon, and was still more surprised when Claude told her it was past ten.

'Oh dear! what will papa and Emily say to me for being up still? But I will stay now, it would not be fair to pretend to be gone to bed.'

'Well said, honest Phyl; now for the news from the castle.'

'Why, Claude,' said his eldest brother, entering, 'you are alive again.'

'I doubt whether your evening could have been pleasanter than ours,' said Claude.

'Phyl,' cried Ada, 'do you know, Mary Carrington's governess thought I was Florence's sister.'

'You look so bright, Claude,' said Jane, 'I think you must have taken Cinderella's friend with the pumpkin to enliven you.'

'My fairy was certainly sister to a Brownie,' said Claude, stroking Phyllis's hair.

'Claude,' again began Ada, 'Miss Car—'

'I wish Cinderella's fairy may be forthcoming the day of the ball,' said Lily, disconsolately.

'And William is going after all,' said Emily.

'Indeed! has the great Captain relented?'

'Yes. Is it not good of him? Aunt Rotherwood is so much pleased that he consents to go entirely to oblige her.'

'Sensible of his condescension,' said Claude. 'By the bye, what makes the Baron look so mischievous?'

'Mischievous!' said Emily, looking round with a start, 'he is looking very comical, and so he has been all the evening.'

'What? You thought mischievous was meant in Hannah's sense, when she complains of Master Reginald being very mischie-vi-ous.'

Ada now succeeded in saying, 'The Carringtons' governess called me Lady Ada.'

'How could she bring herself to utter so horrid a sound?' said Claude.

'Ada is more cock-a-hoop than ever now,' said Reginald; 'she does not think Miss Weston good enough to speak to.'

'But, Claude, she really did, she thought I was Florence's sister, and she said I was just like her.'

'I wish you would hold your tongue, or go to bed,' said William, 'I have heard nothing but this nonsense all the way home.'

While William was sending off Ada to bed, and Phyllis was departing with her, Lily told Claude that the Captain had been most agreeable. 'I feared,' said she, 'that he would be too grand for this party, but he was particularly entertaining; Rotherwood was quite eclipsed.'

'Rotherwood wants Claude to set him off,' said Mr. Mohun. 'Now, young ladies, reserve the rest of your adventures for the morning.'

Adeline had full satisfaction in recounting the governess's mistake to the maids, and in hearing from Esther that it was no wonder, 'for that she looked more like a born lady than Lady Florence herself!'

Lilias's fit of petulance about the ball had returned more strongly than ever; she partly excused herself to her own mind, by fancying she disliked the thought of the lonely evening she was to spend more than that of losing the pleasure of the ball. Mr. Mohun would be absent, conducting Maurice to a new school, and Claude and Reginald would also be gone.

Her temper was affected in various ways; she wondered that William and Emily could like to go—she had thought that Miss Weston was wiser. Her daily occupations were irksome—she was cross to Phyllis.

It made her very angry to be accused by the young brothers of making a fuss, and Claude's silence was equally offensive. It was upon principle that he said nothing. He knew it was nothing but a transient attack of silliness, of which she was herself ashamed; but he was sorry to leave her in that condition, and feared Lady Rotherwood's coming into the neighbourhood was doing her harm, as certainly as it was spoiling Ada. The ball day arrived, and it was marked by a great burst of fretfulness on the part of poor Lilias, occasioned by so small a matter as the being asked by Emily to write a letter to Eleanor. Emily was dressing to go to dine at Devereux Castle when she made the request.

'What have I to say? I never could write a letter in my life, at least not to the Duenna—there is no news.'

'About the boys going to school,' Emily suggested.

'As if she did not know all about them as well as I can tell her. She does not care for my news, I see no one to hear gossip from. I thought you undertook all the formal correspondence, Emily?'

'Do you call a letter to your sister formal correspondence!'

'Everything is formal with her. All I can say is, that you and William are going to the ball, and she will say that is very silly.'

'Eleanor once went to this Raynham ball; it was her first and last,' said Emily.

'Yes, not long before they went to Italy; it will only make her melancholy to speak of it—I declare I cannot write.'

'And I have no time,' said Emily, 'and you know how vexed she is if she does not get her letter every Saturday.'

'All for the sake of punctuality, nothing else,' said Lily. 'I rather like to disappoint fidgety people—don't you, Emily?'

'Well,' said Emily, 'only papa does not like that she should be disappointed.'

'You might have written, if you had not dawdled away all the morning.'

This was true, and it therefore stung Emily, who complained that Lily was very unkind. Lily defended herself sharply, and the dispute was growing vehement, when William happily cut it short by a summons to Emily to make haste.

When they were gone Lily had time for reflection. Good-temper was so common a virtue, and generally cost her so little effort, that she took no pains to cultivate it, but she now felt she had lost all claim to be considered amiable under disappointment. It was too late to bear the privation with a good grace. She was heartily ashamed of having been so cross about a trifle, and ashamed of being discontented at Emily's having a pleasure in which she could not share. Would this have been the case a year ago? She was afraid to ask herself the question, and without going deep enough into the history of her own mind to make her sorrow and shame profitable, she tried to satisfy herself with a superficial compensation, by making herself particularly agreeable to her three younger sisters, and by writing a very long and entertaining letter to Eleanor.

She met Emily with a cheerful face the next day, and listened with pleasure to her history of the ball; and when Mr. Mohun returned home he saw that the cloud had passed away. But, alas! Lilias neglected to take the only means of preventing its recurrence.

The next week William departed. Before he went he gave his sisters great pleasure by desiring them to write to him, and not to let him fall into his ancient state of ignorance respecting the affairs of Beechcroft.

'Mind,' was his farewell speech, 'I expect you to keep me *au courant du jour*. I will not be in the dark about your best friends and neighbours when I come home next July.'

CHAPTER XVI
VANITY AND VEXATION

'And still I have to tell the same sad tale
Of wasted energies, and idle dreams.'

Devereux Castle now became the great resort of the Miss Mohuns. They were always sure of a welcome there. Lady Rotherwood liked to patronise them, and Florence was glad of their society.

This was quite according to the wishes of Emily, who now had nothing left to desire, but that the style of dress suitable, in her opinion, to the granddaughter of the Marquis of Rotherwood, was more in accordance with the purse of the daughter of the Esquire of Beechcroft. It was no part of Emily's character to care for dress. She was at once too indolent and too sensible; she saw the vulgarity of finery, and only aimed at simplicity and elegance. During their girlhood Emily and Lilias had had no more concern with their clothes than with their food; Eleanor had carefully taught them plain needlework, and they had assisted in making more than one set of shirts; but they had nothing to do with the choice or fashion of their own apparel. They were always dressed alike, and in as plain and childish a manner as they could be, consistently with their station. On Eleanor's marriage a suitable allowance was given to each of them, in order that they might provide their own clothes, and until Rachel left them they easily kept themselves in very good trim. When Esther came Lily cheerfully took the trouble of her own small decorations, considering it as her payment for the pleasure of having Esther in the house. Emily, however, neglected the useful 'stitch in time,' till even 'nine' were unavailing. She soon found herself compelled to buy new ready-made articles, and expected Lilias to do the same. But Lilias demurred, for she was too wise to think it necessary to ruin herself in company with Emily, and thus the two sisters were no longer dressed alike. A constant fear tormented Emily lest she should disgrace Lady Rotherwood, or be considered by some stranger as merely a poor relation of the great people, and not as the daughter of the gentleman of the oldest family in the county. She was, therefore, anxious to be perfectly fashionable, and not to wear the same things too often, and in her disinterested desire to maintain the dignity of the family the allowance which she received at Christmas melted away in her hands.

Lily, though exempt from this folly, was not in a satisfactory state of mind. She was drawn off from her duties by a kind of spell. It was not that she liked Florence's society better than her home pursuits.

Florence was indeed a very sweet-tempered and engaging creature; but her mind was not equal to that of Lilias, and there was none of the pleasure of relying upon her, and looking up to her, which Lilias had learnt to enjoy in the company of her brother Claude, and of Alethea Weston. It was only that Lily's own mind had been turned away from her former occupations, and that she did not like to resume them. She had often promised herself to return to her really useful studies, and her positive duties, as soon as her brothers were gone; but day after day passed and nothing was done, though her visits to the cottages and her lessons to Phyllis were often neglected. Her calls at Devereux Castle took up many afternoons. Florence continually lent her amusing books, her aunt took great interest in her music, and she spent much time in practising. The mornings were cold and dark, and she could not rise early, and thus her time slipped away, she knew not how, uselessly and unsatisfactorily. The three younger ones were left more to themselves, and to the maids. Jane sought for amusement in village gossip, and the little ones, finding the nursery more agreeable than the deserted drawing-room, made Esther their companion.

Mr. Mohun had, at this time, an unusual quantity of business on his hands; he saw that the girls were not going on well, but he had reasons for not interfering at present, and he looked forward to Eleanor's visit as the conclusion of their trial.

'I cannot think,' said Marianne Weston one day to her sister, 'why Mr. Mohun comes here so often.'

Alethea told her he had some business with their mamma, and she thought no more of the matter, till she was one day questioned by Jane. She was rather afraid of Jane, who, as she thought, disliked her, and wished to turn her into ridicule; so it was with no satisfaction that she found herself separated from the others in the course of a walk, and submitted to a cross-examination.

Jane asked, in a mysterious manner, who had been at Broomhill that morning.

'Mr. Mohun,' said Marianne.

'What did he go there for?' said Jane.

'Alethea says he has some business with mamma.'

'Then you did not hear what it was?'

'I was not in the room.'

'Are you never there when he comes?'

'Sometimes.'

'And is Alethea there?'

'Oh yes!'

'His business must be with her too. Cannot you guess it?'

'No,' said Marianne, looking amazed.

'How can you be so slow?'

'I am not sure that I would guess if I could,' said Marianne, 'for I do not think they wish me to know.'

'Oh! nonsense, it is fine fun to find out secrets,' said Jane. 'You will know it at last, you may be sure, so there can be no harm in making it out beforehand, so as to have the pleasure of triumph when the wise people vouchsafe to admit you into their confidence; I am sure I know it all.'

'Then please do not tell me, Jane, I ought not to hear it.'

'Little Mrs. Propriety,' said Jane, 'you are already assuming all the dignity of my Aunt Marianne, and William's Aunt Marianne—oh! and of little Henry's Great-aunt Marianne. Now,' she added, laughing, 'can you guess the secret?'

Marianne stood still in amazement for a moment, and then exclaimed, 'Jane, Jane! you do not mean it, you are only trying to tease me.'

'I am quite serious,' said Jane. 'You will see that I am right.'

Here they were interrupted, and as soon as she returned from her walk Marianne, perplexed and amazed, went to her mother, and told her all that Jane had said.

'How can she be so silly?' said Mrs. Weston.

'Then it is all nonsense, as I thought,' said Marianne, joyfully. 'I should not like Alethea to marry an old man.'

'Mr. Mohun is very unlikely to make himself ridiculous,' said Mrs. Weston. 'Do not say anything of it to Alethea; it would only make her uncomfortable.'

'If it had been Captain Mohun, now—' Marianne stopped, and blushed, finding her speech unanswered.

A few days after, Mr. Mohun overtook Marianne and her mother, as he was riding home from Raynham, and dismounting, led his horse, and walked on with them. Either not perceiving Marianne, or not caring whether she heard him, he said,

'Has Miss Weston received the letter she expected?'

'No,' said Mrs. Weston, 'she thinks, as there is no answer, the family must be gone abroad, and very probably they have taken Miss Aylmer with them; but she has written to another friend to ask about them.'

'From all I hear,' said Mr. Mohun, 'I should prefer waiting to hear from her, before we make further inquiries; we shall not be ready before midsummer, as I should wish my eldest daughter to assist me in making this important decision.'

'In that case,' said Mrs. Weston, 'there will be plenty of time to communicate with her. I can see some of the friends of the family when I go to London, for we must not leave Mr. Weston in solitude another spring.'

'Perhaps I shall see you there,' said Mr. Mohun. 'I have some business in London, and I think I shall meet the Hawkesworths there in May or June.'

After a little more conversation Mr. Mohun took his leave, and as soon as he had ridden on, Marianne said, 'Oh! mamma, I could not help hearing.'

'My dear,' said Mrs. Weston, 'I know you may be trusted; but I should not have told you, as you may find such a secret embarrassing when you are with your young friends.'

'And so they are to have a governess?'

'Yes; and we are trying to find Miss Aylmer for them.'

'Miss Aylmer! I am glad of it; how much Phyllis and Ada will like her!'

'Yes, it will be very good for them; I wish I knew the Grants' direction.'

'Well, I hope Jane will not question me any more; it will be very difficult to manage, now I know the truth.'

But poor Marianne was not to escape. Jane was on the watch to find her alone, and as soon as an opportunity offered, she began:—

'Well, auntie, any discoveries?'

'Indeed, Jane, it is not right to fancy Mr. Mohun can do anything so absurd.'

'That is as people may think,' said Jane.

'I wish you would not talk in that way,' said Marianne.

'Now, Marianne,' pursued the tormentor, 'if you can explain the mystery I will believe you, otherwise I know what to think.'

'I am certain you are wrong, Jane; but I can tell you no more.'

'Very well, my good aunt, I am satisfied.'

Jane really almost persuaded herself that she was right, as she perceived that her father was always promoting intercourse with the Westons, and took pleasure in conversing with Alethea. She twisted everything into a confirmation of her idea; while the prospect of having Miss Weston for a stepmother increased her former dislike; but she kept her suspicions to herself for the present, triumphing in the idea that, when the time came, she could bring Marianne as a witness of her penetration.

The intercourse between the elder Miss Mohuns and Miss Weston was, however, not so frequent as formerly; and Alethea herself could not but remark that, while Mr. Mohun seemed to desire to become more intimate, his daughters were more backward in making appointments with her. This was chiefly remarkable in Emily and Jane. Lilias was the same in openness, earnestness, and affection; but there was either a languor about her spirits or they were too much excited, and her talk was more of novels, and less of poor children than formerly. The constant visits to Devereux Castle prevented Emily and Lilias from being as often as before at church, and thus they lost many walks and talks that they used to enjoy in the way home. Marianne began to grow indignant, especially on one occasion, when Emily and Lily went out for a drive with Lady Rotherwood, forgetting that they had engaged to take a walk with the Westons that afternoon.

'It is really a great deal too bad,' said she to Alethea; 'it is exactly what we have read of in books about grandeur making people cast off their old friends.'

'Do not be unfair, Marianne,' said Alethea. 'Lady Florence has a better right to—'

'Better right!' exclaimed Marianne. 'What, because she is a marquis's daughter?'

'Because she is their cousin.'

'I do not believe Lilias really cares for her half as much as for you,' said Marianne. 'It is all because they are fine people.'

'Nay, Marianne, if our cousins were to come into this neighbourhood, we should not be as dependent on the Mohuns as we now feel.'

'I hope we should not break our engagements with them.'

'Perhaps they could not help it. When their aunt came to fetch them, knowing how seldom they can have the carriage, it would have been scarcely civil to say that they had rather take a walk with people they can see any day.'

'Last year Lilias would have let Emily go by herself,' said Marianne. 'Alethea, they are all different since that Lady Rotherwood came—all except Phyl. Ada is a great deal more conceited than she was when she was staying here; she pulls out her curls, and looks in the glass much more, and she is always talking about some one having taken her for Lady Florence's sister. And, Alethea, just fancy, she does not like me to go through a gate before her, because she says she has precedence!'

Alethea was much amused, but she would not let Marianne condemn the whole family for Ada's folly. 'It will all come right,' said she, 'let us be patient and good-humoured, and nothing can be really wrong.'

Though Alethea made the best of it to her sister, she could not but feel hurt, and would have been much more so if her temper had been jealous or sentimental. Almost in spite of herself she had bestowed upon Lilias no small share of her affection, and she would have been more pained by her neglect if she had not partaken of that spirit which 'thinketh no evil, but beareth all things, believeth all things, hopeth all things, and endureth all things.'

Lilias was not satisfied with either herself, her home, her sisters, or her school; she was far from being the fresh, happy creature that she had been the year before. She had seen the fallacy of her principle of love, but in her self-willed adherence to it she had lost the strong sense and habit of duty which had once ruled her; and in a vague and restless frame of mind, she merely sought from day to day for pleasure and idle occupation. Lent came, but she was not roused, she was only more uncomfortable when she saw the Rector, or Alethea, or went to church. Alethea's unfailing gentleness she felt almost as a rebuke; and Mr. Devereux, though always kind and good-natured, had ceased to speak to her of those small village matters in which she used to be prime counsellor.

The school became a burthen instead of a delight, and her attendance there a fatigue. On going in one Sunday morning, very late, she found Alethea teaching her class as well as her own. With a look of vexation she inquired, as she took her place, if it was so very late, and on the way to church she said again, 'I thought I was quite in time; I do not like to hurry the children—the distant ones have not time to come. It was only half-past nine.'

'Oh, Lilias,' said Marianne, 'it was twenty minutes to ten, I know, for I had just looked at the clock.'

'That clock is always too fast,' said Lily.

The next Sunday was very cold, and Lilias did not feel at all disposed to leave the fire when the others prepared to go to the afternoon school.

'Is it time?' said she. 'I was chilled at church, and my feet are still like ice; I will follow you in five minutes.'

Alethea went, and Lilias lingered by the fire. Mrs. Weston once asked her if she knew how late it was; but still she waited, until she was startled by the sound of the bell for evening service. As she went to church with Mrs. Weston and Emily she met Jane, who told her that her class had been unemployed all the afternoon.

'I would have taken them,' said she, 'but that Robert does not like me to teach the great girls, and I do think Alethea might have heard them.'

'It is very provoking,' said Lily, pettishly; 'I thought I might depend—' She turned and saw Miss Weston close to her. 'Oh, Alethea!' said she, 'I thought you would have heard those girls.'

'I thought you were coming,' said Alethea.

'So I was, but I am sure the bell rang too early. I do wish you had taken them, Alethea.'

'I am sorry you are vexed,' said Alethea, simply.

'What makes you think I am vexed? I only thought you liked hearing my class.'

They were by this time at the church door, and as they entered Alethea blamed herself for feeling grieved, and Lily awoke to a sense of her unreasonableness. She longed to tell Alethea how sorry she felt, but she had no opportunity, and she resolved to go to Broomhill the next day to make her confession. In the night, however, snow began to fall, and the morning showed the February scene of thawing snow and pouring rain. Going out was impossible, both on that day and the next. Wednesday dawned fair and bright; but just after breakfast Lily received a little note, with the intelligence that Mr. Weston had arrived at Broomhill on Monday evening, and with his wife and daughters was to set off that very day to make a visit to some friends on the way to London. Had not the weather been so bad, Alethea said she should have come to take leave of her New Court friends on Tuesday, but she could now only send this note to tell them how sorry she was to go without seeing them, and to beg Emily to send back a piece of music which she had lent to her. The messenger was Faith Longley, who was to accompany them, and who now was going home to take leave of her mother, and would call again for the music in a quarter of an hour. Lily ran to ask her when they were to go. 'At eleven,' was the answer; and Lily telling her she need not call again, as she herself would bring the music, went to look for it. High and low did she seek, and so did Jane, but it was not to be found in any nook, likely or unlikely; and when at last Lily, in despair, gave up the attempt to find it, it was already a quarter to eleven. Emily sent many apologies and civil messages, and Lily set out at a rapid pace to walk to Broomhill by the road, for the thaw had rendered the fields impassable. Fast as she walked, she was too late. She had the mortification of seeing the carriage turn out at the gates, and take the Raynham road; she was not even seen, nor had she a wave of the hand, or a smile to comfort her.

Almost crying with vexation, she walked home, and sat down to write to Alethea, but, alas! she did not know where to direct a letter. Bitterly did she repent of the burst of ill-temper which had stained her last meeting with her friend, and she was scarcely comforted even by the long and affectionate letter which she received a week after their departure. Kindness from her was now forgiveness; never did she so strongly feel Florence's inferiority; and she wondered at herself for having sought her society so much as to neglect her patient and superior friend. She became careless and indifferent to Florence, and yet she went on in her former course, following Emily, and fancying that nothing at Beechcroft could interest her in the absence of her dear Alethea Weston.

CHAPTER XVII
LITTLE AGNES

'O guide us when our faithless hearts
  From Thee would start aloof,
Where patience her sweet skill imparts,
  Beneath some cottage roof.'

Palm Sunday brought Lily many regrets. It was the day of the school prize giving, and she reflected with shame, how much less she knew about the children than last year, and how little they owed to her; she feared to think of the approach of Easter Day, a dread which she had never felt before, and which she knew to be a very bad sign; but her regret was not repentance—she talked, and laughed, and tried to feel at ease. Agnes Eden's happy face was the most pleasant sight on that day. The little girl received a Bible, and as it was given to her her pale face was coloured with bright pink, her blue eyes lighted up, her smile was radiant with the beauty of innocence, but Lily could not look at her without self-reproach. She resolved to make up for her former neglect by double kindness, and determined that, at any rate, Passion Week should be properly spent—she would not once miss going to church.

But on Monday, when Emily proposed to ride to Devereux Castle, she assented, only saying that they would return for evening service. She took care to remind her sister when it was time to set out homewards; but Emily was, as usual, so long in taking her leave that it was too late to think of going to church when they set off.

About two miles from Beechcroft Lily saw a little figure in a gray cloak trudging steadily along the road, and as she came nearer she recognised Kezia Grey. She stopped and asked the child what brought her so far from home.

'I am going for the doctor, Miss,' said the child.

'Is your mother worse?' asked Lily.

'Mother is pretty well,' said Kezia; 'but it is for Agnes Eden, Miss—she is terrible bad.'

'Poor little Agnes!' exclaimed Lily. 'Why, she was at school yesterday.'

'Yes, Miss, but she was taken bad last night.'

After a moment's consultation between the sisters, Kezia was told that she might return home, and the servant who accompanied the Miss Mohuns was sent to Raynham for the doctor. The next afternoon Lily was just setting out to inquire for Agnes when Lord Rotherwood arrived at the New Court with his sister. He wanted to show Florence some of his favourite haunts at Beechcroft, and had brought her to join his cousins in their walk. A very pleasant expedition they made, but it led them so far from home that the church bell was heard pealing over the woods far in the distance. Lily could not go to Mrs. Eden's cottage, because she did not know the nature of Agnes's complaint, and her aunt could not bear that Florence should go into any house where there was illness. In the course of the walk, however, she met Kezia, on her way to the New Court, to ask for a blister for Agnes, the doctor having advised Mrs. Eden to apply to the Miss Mohuns for one, as it was wanted quickly, and it was too far to send to Raynham. Lily promised to send the blister as soon as possible, and desired the little messenger to return home, where she was much wanted, to help her mother, who had a baby of less than a week old.

Alas! in the mirth and amusement of the evening Lily entirely forgot the blister, until just as she went to bed, when she made one of her feeble resolutions to take it, or send it early in the morning. She only awoke just in time to be ready for breakfast, went downstairs without one thought of the sick child, and never recollected her, until at church, just before the Litany, she heard these words: 'The prayers of the congregation are desired for Agnes Eden.'

She felt as if she had been shot, and scarcely knew where she was for several moments. On coming out of church, she stood almost in a dream, while Emily and Jane were talking to the Rector, who told them how very ill the child was, and how little hope there was of her recovery. He took leave of them, and Lily walked home, scarcely hearing the soothing words with which Emily strove to comfort her. The meaning passed away mournfully; Lily sat over the fire without speaking, and without attempting to do anything. In the afternoon rain came on; but Lily, too unhappy not to be restless, put on her bonnet and cloak, and went out.

She walked quickly up the hill, and entered the field where the cottage stood. There she paused. She did not dare to knock at the cottage door; she could not bear to speak to Mrs. Eden; she dreaded the sight of Mrs. Grey or Kezia, and she gazed wistfully at the house, longing, yet fearing, to know what was passing within it. She wandered up and down the field, and at last was trying to make up her mind to return home, when she heard footsteps behind her, and turning, saw Mr. Devereux advancing along the path at the other end of the field.

'Have you been to inquire for Agnes?' said he.

'I could not. I long to know, but I cannot bear to ask, I cannot venture in.'

'Do you like to go in with me?' said her cousin. 'I do not think you will see anything dreadful.'

'Thank you,' said Lily, 'I would give anything to know about her.'

'How you tremble! but you need not be afraid.'

He knocked at the door, but there was no answer; he opened it, and going to the foot of the stairs, gently called Mrs. Eden, who came down calm and quiet as ever, though very pale.

'How is she?'

'No better, sir, thank you, light-headed still.'

'Oh! Mrs. Eden, I am so sorry,' sobbed Lily. 'Oh! can you forgive me?'

'Pray do not take on so, Miss,' said Mrs. Eden. 'You have always been a very kind friend to her, Miss Lilias. Do not take on so, Miss. If it is His will, nothing could have made any difference.'

Lily was going to speak again, but Mr. Devereux stopped her, saying, 'We must not keep Mrs. Eden from her, Lily.'

'Thank you, sir, her aunt is with her,' said Mrs. Eden, 'and no one is any good there now, she does not know any one. Will you walk up and see her, sir? will you walk up, Miss Lilias?'

Lily silently followed her cousin up the narrow stairs to the upper room, where, in the white-curtained bed, lay the little child, tossing about and moaning, her cheeks flushed with fever, and her blue eyes wide open, but unconscious. A woman, whom Lily did not at first perceive to be Mrs. Naylor, rose and courtsied on their entrance. Agnes's new Bible was beside her, and her mother told them that she was not easy if it was out of sight for an instant.

At this moment Agnes called out, 'Mother,' and Mrs. Eden bent down to her, but she only repeated, 'Mother' two or three times, and then began talking:

'Kissy, I want my bag—where is my thimble—no, not that I can't remember—my catechism-book—my godfathers and godmothers in my baptism, wherein I was made a member—my Christian name—my name, it is my Christian name; no, that is not it—

"It is a name by which I am
  Writ in the hook of life,
And here below a charm to keep,
  Unharmed by sin and strife;
As often as my name I hear,
  I hear my Saviour's voice."'

Then she began the Creed, but, breaking off, exclaimed, 'Where is my Bible, mother, I shall read it to-morrow—read that pretty verse about "I am the good Shepherd—the Lord is my Shepherd, therefore can I lack nothing—yea, though I walk through the valley of the shadow of death, I will fear no evil, for Thou art within me."

"I now am of that little flock
  Which Christ doth call His own,
For all His sheep He knows by name,
  And He of them is known."'

'Let us call upon your good Shepherd, Agnes,' said the pastor, and the child turned her face towards him as if she understood him. Kneeling down, he repeated the Lord's Prayer, and the feeble voice followed his. He then read the prayer for a sick child, and left the room, for he saw that Lily would be quite overcome if she remained there any longer. Mrs. Eden followed them downstairs, and again stung poor Lily to the heart by thanks for all her kindness.

They then left the house of mourning; Lily trembled violently, and clung to her cousin's arm for support. Her tears streamed fast, but her sobs were checked by awe at Mrs. Eden's calmness. She felt as if she had been among the angels.

'How pale you are!' said her cousin, 'I would not have taken you there if I thought it would overset you so much. Come into Mrs. Grey's, and sit down and recover a little.'

'No, no, do not let me see any one,' said Lily. 'Oh! that dear child! Robert, let me tell you the worst, for your kindness is more than I can bear. I promised Agnes a blister and forgot it!'

She could say no more for some minutes, but her cousin did not speak. Recovering her voice, she added, 'Only speak to me, Robert.'

'I am very sorry for you,' answered he, in a kind tone.

'But tell me, what shall I do?'

'What to do, you ask,' said the Rector; 'I am not sure that I know what you mean. If your neglect has added to her sufferings, you cannot remove them; and I would not add to your sorrow unless you wished me to do so for your good.'

'I do not see how I could be more unhappy than I am now,' said Lily.

'I think if you wish to turn your grief to good account you must go a little deeper than this omission.'

'You mean that it is a result of general carelessness,' said Lily; 'I know I have been in an odd idle way for some time; I have often resolved, but I seem to have no power over myself.'

'May I ask you one question, Lily? How have you been spending this Lent?'

'Robert, you are right,' cried Lily; 'you may well ask. I know I have not gone to church properly, but how could you guess the terrible way in which I have been indulging myself, and excusing myself every unpleasant duty that came in my way? That was the very reason of this dreadful neglect; well do I deserve to be miserable at Easter, the proper time for joy. Oh! how different it will be.'

'It will be, I hope, an Easter marked by repentance and amendment,' said the Rector.

'No, Robert, do not begin to be kind to me yet, you do not know how very bad I have been,' said Lily; 'it all began from just after Eleanor's wedding. A mad notion came into my head and laid hold of me. I fancied Eleanor stern, and cold, and unlovable; I was ingratitude itself. I made a foolish theory, that regard for duty makes people cold and stern, and that feeling, which I confused with Christian love, was all that was worth having, and the more Claude tried to cure me, the more obstinate I grew; I drew Emily over to my side, and we set our follies above everything. Justified ourselves for idling, neglecting the children, indulging ourselves, calling it love, and so it was, self-love. So my temper has been spoiling, and my mind getting worse and worse, ever since we lost Eleanor. At last different things showed me the fallacy of my principle, but then I do believe I was beyond my own management. I felt wrong, and could not mend, and went on recklessly. You know but too well what mischief I have done in the village, but you can never know what harm I have done at home. I have seen more and more that I was going on badly, but a sleep, a spell was upon me.'

'Perhaps the pain you now feel may be the means of breaking the spell.'

'But is it not enough to drive me mad to think that improvement in me should be bought at such a price—the widow's only child?'

'You forget that the loss is a blessing to her.'

'Still I may pray that my punishment may not be through them,' said Lily.

'Surely,' was the answer, 'it is grievous to see that dear child cut off; and her patient mother left desolate—yet how much more grievous it would be to see that spotless innocence defiled.'

'If it was to fall on any one,' said Lilias, 'I should be thankful that it is on one so fit to die.'

The church bell began to ring, and they quickened their steps in silence. Presently Lily said, 'Tell me of something to do, Robert, something that may be a pledge that my sorrow is not a passing shower, something unnecessary, but disagreeable, which may keep me in remembrance that my Lent was not one of self-denial.'

'You must be able to find more opportunities of self-denial than I can devise,' said her cousin.

'Of course,' said Lily; 'but some one thing, some punishment.'

'I will answer you to-morrow,' said Mr. Devereux.

'One thing more,' said Lily, looking down; 'after this great fall, ought I to come to next Sunday's feast? I would turn away if you thought fit.'

'Lily, you can best judge,' said the Rector, kindly. 'I should think that you were now in a humble, contrite frame, and therefore better prepared than when self-confident.'

'How many times! how shall I think of them! but I will,' said Lily; 'and Robert, will you think of me when you say the Absolution now and next Sunday at the altar?'

They were by this time at the church-porch. As Mr. Devereux uncovered his head, he turned to Lilias, and said in a low tone, 'God bless you, Lilias, and grant you true repentance and pardon.'

Early the next morning the toll of the passing-bell informed Lily that the little lamb had been gathered into the heavenly fold.

When she took her place in church she found in her Prayer-book a slip of paper in the handwriting of her cousin. It was thus: 'You had better find out in which duty you have most failed, and let the fulfilment of that be your proof of self-denial. R. D.'

Afterwards Lily learnt that Agnes had been sensible for a short time before her peaceful death. She had spoken much of her baptism, had begged to be buried next to a little sister of Kezia's, and asked her mother to give her new Bible to Kezia.

It was not till Sunday that Lilias felt as if she could ever be comforted. Her heart was indeed ready to break as she walked at the head of the school children behind the white-covered coffin, and she felt as if she did not deserve to dwell upon the child's present happiness; but afterwards she was relieved by joining in prayer for the pardon of our sins and negligences, and she felt as if she was forgiven, at least by man, when she joined with Mrs. Eden in the appointed feast of Easter Day.

Mrs. Naylor was at church on that and several following Sundays; but though her husband now showed every kindness to his sister, he still obstinately refused to be reconciled to Mr. Devereux.

For many weeks poor little Kezia looked very unhappy. Her blithe smiles were gone, her eyes filled with tears whenever she was reminded of her friend, she walked to school alone, she did not join the sports of the other children, but she kept close to the side of Mrs. Eden, and seemed to have no pleasure but with her, or in nursing her little sister, who, two Sundays after the funeral, was christened by the name of Agnes.

It was agreed by Mr. Mohun and Lilias that the grave of the little girl should be marked by a stone cross, thus inscribed:—

'Agnes Eden,

April 8th, 1846,

Aged 7 years.

"He shall gather the lambs in His arms."'

CHAPTER XVIII
DOUBLE, DOUBLE TOIL AND TROUBLE

'Truly the tender mercies of the weak,
As of the wicked, are but cruel.'

And how did Lilias show that she had been truly benefited by her sorrows? Did she fall back into her habits of self-indulgence, or did she run into ill-directed activity, selfish as her indolence, because only gratifying the passion of the moment?

Those who lived with her saw but little change; kind-hearted and generous she had ever been, and many had been her good impulses, so that while she daily became more steady in well-doing, and exerting herself on principle, no one remarked it, and no one entered into the struggles which it cost her to tame her impetuosity, or force herself to do what was disagreeable to herself, and might offend Emily.

However, Emily could forgive a great deal when she found that Lily was ready to take any part of the business of the household and schoolroom, which she chose to impose upon her, without the least objection, yet to leave her to assume as much of the credit of managing as she chose—to have no will or way of her own, and to help her to keep her wardrobe in order.

The schoolroom was just now more of a labour than had ever been the case, at least to one who, like Lilias, if she did a thing at all, would not be satisfied with half doing it. Phyllis was not altered, except that she cried less, and had in a great measure cured herself of dawdling habits and tricks, by her honest efforts to obey well-remembered orders of Eleanor's; but still her slowness and dulness were trying to her teachers, and Lily had often to reproach herself for being angry with her 'when she was doing her best.'

But Adeline was Lily's principal trouble; there was a change in her, for which her sister could not account. Last year, when Eleanor left them, Ada was a sweet-tempered, affectionate child, docile, gentle, and, excepting a little occasional affectation and carelessness, very free from faults; but now her attention could hardly be commanded for five minutes together; she had lost the habit of ready and implicit obedience, was petulant when reproved, and was far more eager to attract notice from strangers—more conceited, and, therefore, more affected, and, worse than all, Lily sometimes thought she perceived a little slyness, though she was never able to prove any one instance completely to herself, much less to bring one before her father. Thus, if Ada had done any mischief, she would indeed confess it on being examined; but when asked why she had not told of it directly, would say she had forgotten; she would avail herself of Phyllis's assistance in her lessons without acknowledging it, and Lilias found it was by no means safe to leave the Key to the French Exercises alone in the room with her.

Emily's mismanagement had fostered Ada's carelessness and inattention. Lady Rotherwood's injudicious caresses helped to make her more affected; other faults had grown up for want of sufficient control, but this last was principally Esther's work. Esther had done well at school; she liked learning, was stimulated by notice, was really attached to Lilias, and tried to deserve her goodwill; but her training at school and at home were so different, that her conduct was, even at the best, far too much of eye-service, and she had very little idea of real truth and sincerity.

On first coming to the New Court she flattered the children, because she did not know how to talk to them otherwise, and afterwards, because she found that Miss Ada's affections were to be gained by praise. Then, in her ignorant good-nature, she had no scruples about concealing mischief which the children had done, or procuring for Ada little forbidden indulgences on her promise of secrecy, a promise which Phyllis would not give, thus putting a stop to all those in which she would have participated. It was no wonder that Ada, sometimes helping Esther to deceive, sometimes deceived by her, should have learnt the same kind of cunning, and ceased to think it a matter of course to be true and just in all her dealings.

But how was it that Phyllis remained the same 'honest Phyl' that she had ever been, not one word savouring of aught but strict truth having ever crossed her lips, her thoughts and deeds full of guileless simplicity? She met with the same temptations, the same neglect, the same bad example, as her sister; why had they no effect upon her? In the first place, flattery could not touch her, it was like water on a duck's back, she did not know that it was flattery, but so thoroughly humble was her mind that no words of Esther's would make her believe herself beautiful, agreeable, or clever. Yet she never found out that Esther over-praised her sister; she admired Ada so much that she never suspected that any commendation of her was more than she deserved. Again, Phyllis never thought of making herself appear to advantage, and her humility saved her from the habit of concealing small faults, for which she expected no punishment; and, when seriously to blame, punishment seemed so natural a consequence, that she never thought of avoiding it, otherwise than by expressing sorrow for her fault. She was uninfected by Esther's deceit, though she never suspected any want of truth; her singleness of mind was a shield from all evil; she knew she was no favourite in the nursery, but she never expected to be liked as much as Ada, her pride and glory. In the meantime Emily went on contriving opportunities and excuses for spending her time at Devereux Castle, letting everything fall into Lily's hands, everything that she had so eagerly undertaken little more than a year ago. And now all was confusion; the excellent order in which Eleanor had left the household affairs was quite destroyed. Attention to the storeroom was one of the ways in which Lilias thought that she could best follow the advice of Mr. Devereux, since Eleanor had always taught that great exactness in this point was most necessary.

Great disorder now, however, prevailed there, and she found that her only chance of rectifying it was to measure everything she found there, and to beg Emily to allow her to keep the key; for, when several persons went to the storeroom, no one ever knew what was given out, and she was sure that the sweet things diminished much faster than they ought to do; but her sister treated the proposal as an attempt to deprive her of her dignity, and she was silenced.

She was up almost with the light, to despatch whatever household affairs could be settled without Emily, before the time came for the children's lessons; many hours were spent on these, while she was continually harassed by Phyllis's dulness, Ada's inattention, and the interruption of work to do for Emily, and often was she baffled by interference from Jane or Emily. She was conscious of her unfitness to teach the children, and often saw that her impatience, ignorance, and inefficiency, were doing mischief; but much as this pained her, she could not speak to her father without compromising her sister, and to argue with Emily herself was quite in vain. Emily had taken up the principle of love, and defended herself with it on every occasion, so that poor Lily was continually punished by having her past follies quoted against herself.

Each day Emily grew more selfish and indolent; now that Lily was willing to supply all that she neglected, and to do all that she asked, she proved how tyrannical the weak can be.

The whole of her quarter's allowance was spent in dress, and Lily soon found that the only chance of keeping her out of debt was to spend her own time and labour in her behalf; and what an exertion of patience and kindness this required can hardly be imagined. Emily did indeed reward her skill with affectionate thanks and kind praises, but she interfered with her sleep and exercise, by her want of consideration, and hardened herself more and more in her apathetic selfishness.

Some weeks after Easter Lilias was arranging some books on a shelf in the schoolroom, when she met with a crumpled piece of music-paper, squeezed in behind the books. It proved to be Miss Weston's lost song, creased, torn, dust-stained, and spoiled; she carried it to Emily, who decided that nothing could be done but to copy it for Alethea, and apologise for the disaster. Framing apologies was more in Emily's way than copying music; and the former task, therefore, devolved upon Lily, and occupied her all one afternoon, when she ought to have been seeking a cure for the headache in the fresh air. It was no cure to find the name of Emma Weston in the corner, and to perceive how great and irreparable the loss of the paper was to her friend. The thought of all her wrongs towards Alethea, caused more than one large tear to fall, to blot the heads of her crotchets and quavers, and thus give her all her work to do over again.

The letter that she wrote was so melancholy and repentant, that it gave great pain to her kind friend, who thought illness alone could account for the dejection apparent in the general tone of all her expressions. In answer, she sent a very affectionate consoling letter, begging Lily to think no more of the matter; and though she had too much regard for truth to say that she had not been grieved by the loss of Emma's writing, she added that Lily's distress gave her far more pain, and that her copy would have great value in her eyes.

The beginning of June now arrived, and brought with it the time for the return of Claude and Lord Rotherwood.

The Marquis's carriage met him at Raynham, and he set down Claude at New Court, on his way to Hetherington, just coming in to exchange a hurried greeting with the young ladies.

Their attention was principally taken up by their brother.

'Claude, how well you look! How fat you are!' was their exclamation.

'Is not he?' said Lord Rotherwood. 'I am quite proud of him. Not one headache since he went. He will have no excuse for not dancing the polka.'

'I do not return the compliment to you, Lily,' said Claude, looking anxiously at his sister. 'What is the matter with you? Have you been ill?'

'Oh, no! not at all!' said Lily, smiling.

'I am sure there is enough to make any one ill,' said Emily, in her deplorable tone; 'I thought this poor parish had had its share of illness, with the scarlet fever, and now it has turned to a horrible typhus fever.'

'Indeed!' said Claude. 'Where? Who?'

'Oh! the Naylors, and the Rays, and the Walls. John Ray died this morning, and they do not think that Tom Naylor will live.'

'Well,' interrupted Lord Rotherwood, 'I shall not stop to hear any more of this chapter of accidents. I am off, but mind, remember the 30th, and do not any of you frighten yourselves into the fever.'

He went, and Lily now spoke. 'There is one thing in all this, Claude, that is matter of joy, Tom Naylor has sent for Robert.'

'Then, Lily, I do most heartily congratulate you.'

'I hope things may go better,' said Lily, with tears in her eyes. 'The poor baby is with its grandmother. Mrs. Naylor is ill too, and every one is so afraid of the fever that nobody goes near them but Robert, and Mrs. Eden, and old Dame Martin. Robert says Naylor is in a satisfactory frame—determined on having the baby christened—but, oh! I am afraid the christening is to be bought by something terrible.'

'I do not think those fevers are often very infectious,' said Claude.

'So papa says,' replied Emily; 'but Robert looks very ill. He is wearing himself out with sitting up. Making himself nurse as well as everything else.'

This was very distressing, but still Claude scarcely thought it accounted for the change that had taken place in Lilias. Her cheek was pale, her eye heavy, her voice had lost its merry tone; Claude knew that she had had much to grieve her, but he was as yet far from suspecting how she was overworked and harassed. He spoke of Eleanor's return, and she did not brighten; she smiled sadly at his attempts to cheer her, and he became more and more anxious about her. He was not long in discovering what was the matter.

The second day after his return Robert told them at the churchyard gate that Tom Naylor was beginning to mend, and this seemed to be a great comfort to Lily, who walked home with a blither step than usual. Claude betook himself to the study, and saw no more of his sisters till two o'clock, when Lily appeared, with the languid, dejected look which she had lately worn, and seemed to find it quite an effort to keep the tears out of her eyes. Ada and Phyllis were in very high spirits, because they were going to Raynham with Emily and Jane, and at every speech of Ada's Lily looked more grieved. After the Raynham party were gone Claude began to look for Lily. He found her in her room, an evening dress spread on the bed, a roll of ribbon in one hand, and with the other supporting her forehead, while tears were slowly rolling down her cheeks.

'Lily, my dear, what is the matter?'

'Oh! nothing, nothing, Claude,' said she, quickly.

'Nothing! no, that is not true. Tell me, Lily. You have been disconsolate ever since I came home, and I will not let it go on so. No answer? Then am I to suppose that these new pearlins are the cause of her sorrow? Come, Lily, be like yourself, and speak. More tears! Here, drink this water, be yourself again, or I shall be angry and vexed. Now then, that is right: make an effort, and tell me.'

'There is nothing to tell,' said Lily; 'only you are very kind—I do not know what is the matter with me—only I have been very foolish of late—and everything makes me cry.'

'My poor child, I knew you had not been well. They do not know how to take care of you, Lily, and I shall take you in hand. I am going to order the horses, and we will have a gallop over the Downs, and put a little colour into your cheeks.'

'No, no, thank you, Claude, I cannot come, indeed I cannot, I have this work, which must be done to-day.'

'At work at your finery instead of coming out! You must be altered, indeed, Lily.'

'It is not for myself,' said Lily, 'but I promised Emily she should have it ready to wear to-morrow.'

'Emily, oh? So she is making a slave of you?'

'No, no, it was a voluntary promise. She does not care about it, only she would be disappointed, and I have promised.'

'I hate promises!' said Claude. 'Well, what must be, must be, so I will resign myself to this promise of yours, only do not make such another. Well, but that was not all; you were not crying about that fine green thing, were you?'

'Oh, no!' said Lily, smiling, as now she could smile again.

'What then? I will know, Lily.'

'I was only vexed at something about the children.'

'Then what was it?'

'It was only that Ada was idle at her lessons; I told her to learn a verb as a punishment, she went to Emily, and, somehow or other, Emily did not find out the exact facts, excused her, and took her to Raynham. I was vexed, because I am sure it does Ada harm, and Emily did not understand what I said afterwards; I am sure she thought me unjust.'

'How came she not to be present?'

'Emily does not often sit in the schoolroom in the morning, since she has been about that large drawing.'

'So you are governess as well as ladies'-maid, are you, Lily? What else? Housekeeper, I suppose, as I see you have all the weekly bills on your desk. Why, Lily, this is perfectly philanthropic of you. You are exemplifying the rule of love in a majestic manner. Crying again! Water lily once more?'

Lily looked up, and smiled; 'Claude, how can you talk of that old, silly, nay, wicked nonsense of my principle. I was wise above what was written, and I have my punishment in the wreck which my "frenzy of spirit and folly of tongue" have wrought. The unchristened child, Agnes's death, the confusion of this house, all are owing to my hateful principle. I see the folly of it now, but Emily has taken it up, and acts upon it in everything. I do struggle against it a little; but I cannot blame any one, I can do no good, it is all owing to me. We have betrayed papa's confidence; if he does not see it now it will all come upon him when Eleanor comes home, and what is to become of us? How it will grieve him to see that we cannot be trusted!'

'Poor Lily!' said Claude. 'It is a bad prospect, but I think you see the worst side of it. You are not well, and, therefore, doleful. This, Lily, I can tell you, that the Baron always considered Emily's government as a kind of experiment, and so perhaps he will not be so grievously disappointed as you expect. Besides, I have a strong suspicion that Emily's own nature has quite as much to do with her present conduct as your principle, which, after all, did not live very long.'

'Just long enough to unsettle me, and make it more difficult for me to get any way right,' said Lily. 'Oh! dear, what would I give to force backward the wheels of time!'

'But as you cannot, you had better try to brighten up your energies. Come, you know I cannot tell you not to look back, but I can tell you not to look forward. Nay,

I do tell you literally, to look forward, out of the window, instead of back into this hot room. Do not you think the plane-tree there looks very inviting? Suppose we transport Emily's drapery there, and I want to refresh my memory with Spenser; I do not think I have touched him since plane-tree time last year.'

'I believe Spenser and the plane-tree are inseparably woven together in your mind,' said Lily.

'Yes, ever since the time when I first met with the book. I remember well roving over the bookcase, and meeting with it, and taking it out there, for fear Eleanor should see me and tell mama. Phyl, with *As You Like It*, put me much in mind of myself with that.'

Claude talked in this manner, while Lily, listening with a smile, prepared her work. He read, and she listened. It was such a treat as she had not enjoyed for a long time, for she had begun to think that all her pleasant reading days were past. Her work prospered, and her face was bright when her sisters came home.

But, alas! Emily was not pleased with her performance; she said that she intended something quite different, and by manner, rather than by words, indicated that she should not be satisfied unless Lily completely altered it. It was to be worn at the castle the next evening, and Lily knew she should have no time for it in the course of the day. Accordingly, at half-past twelve, as Claude was going up to bed, he saw a light under his sister's door, and knocked to ask the cause. Lily was still at work upon the trimming, and very angry he was, particularly when she begged him to take care not to disturb Emily. At last, by threatening to awake her, for the express purpose of giving her a scolding, he made Lily promise to go to bed immediately, a promise which she, poor weary creature, was very glad to make.

Claude now resolved to tell his father the state of things, for he well knew that though it was easy to obtain a general promise from Emily, it was likely to be of little effect in preventing her from spurring her willing horse to death.

The next morning he rose in time to join his father in the survey which he usually took of his fields before breakfast, and immediately beginning on the subject on which he was anxious, he gave a full account of his sister's proceedings. 'In short,' said he, 'Emily and Ada torment poor Lily every hour of her life; she bears it all as a sort of penance, and how it is to end I cannot tell.'

'Unless,' said Mr. Mohun, smiling, 'as Rotherwood would say, Jupiter will interfere. Well, Jupiter has begun to take measures, and has asked Mrs. Weston to look out for a governess. Eh! Claude?' he continued, after a pause, 'you set up your eyebrows, do you? You think it will be a bore. Very likely, but there is nothing else to be done. Jane is under no control, Phyllis running wild, Ada worse managed than any child of my acquaintance—'

'And poor Lily wearing herself to a shadow, in vain attempts to mend matters,' said Claude.

'If Lily was the eldest, things would be very different,' said Mr. Mohun.

'Or even if she had been as wise last year as she is now,' said Claude, 'she would have kept Emily in order then, but now it is too late.'

'This year is, on many accounts, much to be regretted,' said Mr. Mohun, 'but I think it has brought out Lily's character.'

'And a very fine character it is,' said Claude.

'Very. She has been, and is, more childish than Eleanor ever was, but she is her superior in most points. She has been your pupil, Claude, and she does you credit.'

'Thereby hangs a tale which does me no credit,' muttered Claude, as he remembered how foolishly he had roused her spirit of contradiction, besides the original mischief of naming Eleanor the duenna; 'but we will not enter into that now. I see this governess is their best chance. Have you heard of one?'

'Of several; but the only one who seems likely to suit us is out of reach for the present, and I do not regret it, for I shall not decide till Eleanor comes.'

'Emily will not be much pleased,' said Claude. 'It has long been her great dread that Aunt Rotherwood should recommend one.'

'Ay, Emily's objections and your aunt's recommendations are what I would gladly avoid,' said Mr. Mohun.

'But Lily!' said Claude, returning to the subject on which he was most anxious. 'She is already what Ada calls a monotony, and there will be nothing left of her by the time Eleanor comes, if matters go on in their present fashion.'

'I have a plan for her. A little change will set her to rights, and we will take her to London when we go next week to meet Eleanor. She deserves a little extra pleasure; you must take her under your protection, and lionise her well.'

'Trust me for that,' said Claude. 'It is the best news I have heard for a long time.'

'Well, I am glad that one of my remedies meets with your approbation,' said his father, smiling. 'For the other, you are much inclined to pronounce the cure as bad as the disease.'

'Not for Lily,' said Claude, laughing.

'And,' said Mr. Mohun, 'I think I can promise you that a remedy will be found for all the other grievances by Michaelmas.'

Claude looked surprised, but as Mr. Mohun explained no further, only observing upon the potatoes, through which they were walking, he only said, 'Then it is next week that you go to London.'

'There is much to do, both for Rotherwood and for Eleanor; I shall go as soon as I can, but I do not think it will be while this fever is so prevalent. I had rather not be from home—I do not like Robert's looks.'

CHAPTER XIX
THE RECTOR'S ILLNESS

'Thou drooping sick man, bless the guide
That checked, or turned thy headstrong youth.'

The thought of her brother's kindness, and the effect of his consolation, made Lilias awake that morning in more cheerful spirits; but it was not long before grief and anxiety again took possession of her.

The first sound that she heard on opening the schoolroom window was the tolling of the church bell, giving notice of the death of another of those to whom she felt bound by the ties of neighbourhood.

At church she saw that Mr. Devereux was looking more ill than he yet had done, and it was plainly with very great exertion that he succeeded in finishing the service. The Mohun party waited, as usual, to speak to him afterwards, for since his attendance upon Naylor had begun he had not thought it safe to come to the New Court as usual, lest he should bring the infection to them. He was very pale, and walked wearily, but he spoke cheerfully, as he told them that Naylor was now quite out of danger.

'Then I hope you did not stay there all last night,' said Mr. Mohun.

'No, I did not, I was so tired when I came back from poor John Ray's funeral, that I thought I would take a holiday, and sleep at home.'

'I am afraid you have not profited by your night's rest,' said Emily, 'you look as if you had a horrible headache.'

'Now,' said Mr. Mohun, 'I prescribe for you that you go home and lie down. I am going to Raynham, and I will tell your friend there that you want help for the evening service. Do not think of moving again to-day. I shall send Claude home with you to see that you obey my prescription.'

Claude went home with his cousin, and his sisters saw him no more till late in the day, when he came to tell them that Mr. Mohun had brought back Dr. Leslie from Raynham with him, that Dr. Leslie had seen Mr. Devereux, and had pronounced that he had certainly caught the fever.

Lily had made up her mind to this for some time, but still it seemed almost as great a blow as if it had come without any preparation. The next day was the first Sunday that Mr. Devereux had not read the service since he had been Rector of Beechcroft. The villagers looked sadly at the stranger who appeared in his place, and many tears were shed when the prayers of the congregation were desired for Robert Devereux, and Thomas and Martha Naylor. It was announced that the daily service would be discontinued for the present, and Lily felt as if all the blessings which she had misused were to be taken from her.

For some time Mr. Devereux continued very ill, and Dr. Leslie gave little hope of his improvement. Mr. Mohun and Claude were his constant attendants—an additional cause of anxiety to the Miss Mohuns. Emily was listless and melancholy, talking in a maundering, dismal way, not calculated to brace her spirits or those of her sisters. Jane was not without serious thoughts, but whether they would benefit her depended on herself; for, as we have seen by the events of the autumn, sorrow and suffering do not necessarily produce good effects, though some effects they always produce.

Thus it was with Lilias. Grief and anxiety aided her in subduing her will and learning resignation. She did not neglect her daily duties, but was more exact in their fulfilment; and low as her spirits had been before, she now had an inward spring which enabled her to be the support of the rest. She was useful to her father, always ready to talk to Claude, or walk with him in the intervals when he was sent out of the sickroom to rest and breathe the fresh air. She was cheerful and patient with Emily, and devoid of petulance when annoyed by the spirits of the younger ones rising higher than accorded with the sad and anxious hearts of their elders. Her most painful feeling was, that it was possible that she might be punished through her cousin, as she had already been through Agnes; that her follies might have brought this distress upon every one, and that this was the price at which the child's baptism was to be bought. Yet Lily would not have changed her present thoughts for any of her varying frames of mind since that fatal Whitsuntide. Better feelings were springing up within her than she had then known; the church service and Sunday were infinitely more to her, and she was beginning to obtain peace of mind independent of external things.

She could not help rejoicing to see how many evidences of affection to the Rector were called forth by this illness; presents of fruit poured in from all quarters, from Lord Rotherwood's choice hothouse grapes, to poor little Kezia Grey's wood-strawberries; inquiries were continual, and the stillness of the village was wonderful. There was no cricket on the hill, no talking in the street, no hallooing in the hay-field, and no burst of noise when the children were let out of school. Many of the people were themselves in grief for the loss of their own relations; and when on Sunday the Miss Mohuns saw how many were dressed in black, they thought with a pang how soon they themselves might be mourning for one whose influence they had crippled, and whose plans they had thwarted during the three short years of his ministry.

During this time it was hard to say whether Lord Rotherwood was more of a comfort or a torment. He was attached to his cousin with all the ardour of his affectionate disposition, and not one day passed without his appearing at Beechcroft. At first it was always in the parlour at the parsonage that he took up his station, and waited till he could find some means of getting at Claude or his uncle, to hear the last report from them, and if possible to make Claude come out for a walk or ride with him. And once Mr. Mohun caught him standing just outside Mr. Devereux's door, waiting for an opportunity to make an entrance. He could not, or would not see why Mr. Mohun should allow Claude to run the risk of infection rather than himself, and thus he kept his mother in continual anxiety, and even his uncle could not feel by any means certain that he would not do something imprudent. At last a promise was extracted from him that he would not again enter the parsonage, but he would not gratify Lady Rotherwood so far as to abstain from going to Beechcroft, a place which she began to regard with horror. He now was almost constantly at the New Court, talking over the reports, and quite provoking Emily by never desponding, and never choosing to perceive how bad things really were. Every day which was worse than the last was supposed to be the crisis, and every restless sleep that they heard of he interpreted into the beginning of recovery. At last, however, after ten days of suspense, the report began to improve, and Claude came to the New Court with a more cheerful face, to say that his cousin was munch better. The world seemed immediately to grow brighter, people went about with joyful looks, Lord Rotherwood declared that from the first he had known all would be well, and Lily began to hope that now she had been spared so heavy a punishment, it was a kind of earnest that other things would mend, that she had suffered enough. The future no longer hung before her in such dark colours as before Mr. Devereux's illness, though still the New Court was in no satisfactory state, and still she had reason to expect that her father and Eleanor would be disappointed and grieved. Thankfulness that Mr. Devereux was recovering, and that Claude had escaped the infection, made her once more hopeful and cheerful; she let the morrow take thought for the things of itself, rejoicing that it was not her business to make arrangements.

CHAPTER XX
THE LITTLE NEPHEW

'You must be father, mother, both,
  And uncle, all in one.'

Mr. Mohun had much business to transact in London which he could not leave undone, and as soon as his nephew began to recover he thought of setting off to meet Mr. and Mrs. Hawkesworth, who had already been a week at Lady Rotherwood's house in Grosvenor Square, which she had lent to them for the occasion. Claude had intended to stay at home, as his cousin was not yet well enough to leave the room; but just at this time a college friend of the Rector's, hearing of his illness, wrote to propose to come and stay with him for a month or six weeks, and help him in serving his church. Mr. Devereux was particularly glad to accept this kind offer, as it left him no longer dependent on Mr. Stephens and the Raynham curates, and set Claude at liberty for the London expedition. All was settled in the short space of one day. The very next they were to set off, and in great haste; Lily did all she could for the regulation of the house, packed up her goods, and received the commissions of her sisters.

Ada gave her six shillings, with orders to buy either a doll or a book—the former if Eleanor did not say it was silly; and Phyllis put into her hands a weighty crown piece, begging for as many things as it could buy. Jane's wants and wishes were moderate and sensible, and she gave Lily the money for them. With Emily there was more difficulty. All Lily's efforts had not availed to prevent her from contracting two debts at Raynham. More than four pounds she owed to Lily, and this she offered to pay her, giving her at the same time a list of commissions sufficient to swallow up double her quarter's allowance. Lily, though really in want of the money for her own use, thought the debts at Raynham so serious, that she begged Emily to let her wait for payment till it was convenient, and to pay the shoemaker and dressmaker immediately.

Emily thanked her, and promised to do so as soon as she could go to Raynham, and Lily next attempted to reduce her list of London commissions to something more reasonable. In part she succeeded, but it remained a matter of speculation how all the necessary articles which she had to buy for herself, and all Emily's various orders, were to come out of her own means, reduced as they were by former loans.

The next day Lilias was on her way to London; feeling, as she left Beechcroft, that it was a great relief that the schoolroom and storeroom could not follow her.

She was sorry that she should miss seeing Alethea Weston, who was to come home the next day, but she left various messages for her, and an affectionate note, and had received a promise from her sisters that the copy of the music should be given to her the first day that they saw her. Her journey afforded her much amusement, and it was not till towards the end of the day that she had much time for thinking, when, her companions being sleepily inclined, she was left to her own meditations and to a dull country. She began to revolve her own feelings towards Eleanor, and as she remembered the contempt and ingratitude she had once expressed, she shrank from the meeting with shame and dread, and knew that she should feel reproached by Eleanor's wonted calmness of manner. And as she mused upon all that Eleanor had endured, and all that she had done, such a reverence for suffering and sacrifice took possession of her mind that she was ready to look up to her sister with awe. She began to recollect old reproofs, and found herself sitting more upright, and examining the sit of the folds of her dress with some uneasiness at the thought of Eleanor's preciseness. In the midst of her meditations her two companions were roused by the slackening speed of the train, and starting up, informed her that they were arriving at their journey's end. The next minute she heard her father consigning her and the umbrellas to Mr. Hawkesworth's care, and all was bewilderment till she found herself in the hall of her aunt's house, receiving as warm and affectionate a greeting from Eleanor as Emily herself could have bestowed.

'And the baby, Eleanor?'

'Asleep, but you shall see him; and how is Ada? and all of them? why, Claude, how well you look! Papa, let me help you to take off your greatcoat—you are cold—will you have a fire?'

Never had Lily heard Eleanor say so much in a breath, or seen her eye so bright, or her smile so ready, yet, when she entered the drawing-room, she saw that Mrs. Hawkesworth was still the Eleanor of old. In contrast with the splendid furniture of the apartments, a pile of shirts was on the table, Eleanor's well-known work-basket on the floor, and the ceaseless knitting close at hand.

Much news was exchanged in the few minutes that elapsed before Eleanor carried off her sister to her room, indulging her by the way with a peep at little Harry, and one kiss to his round red cheek as he lay asleep in his little bed. It was not Eleanor's fault that she did not entirely dress Lily, and unpack her wardrobe; but Lilias liked to show that she could manage for herself; and Eleanor's praise of her neat arrangements gave her as much pleasure as in days of yore.

The evening passed very happily. Eleanor's heart was open, she was full of enjoyment at meeting those she loved, and the two sisters sat long together in the twilight, talking over numerous subjects, all ending in Beechcroft or the baby.

Yet when Lily awoke the next morning her awe of Eleanor began to return, and she felt like a child just returned to school. She was, however, mistaken; Eleanor assumed no authority, she treated Lily as her equal, and thus made her feel more like a woman than she had ever done before. Lily thought either that Eleanor was much altered, or that in her folly she must have fancied her far more cold and grave than she really was. She had, however, no time for studying her character; shopping and sight-seeing filled up most of her time, and the remainder was spent in resting, and in playing with little Henry.

One evening, when Mr. Mohun and Claude were dining out, Lilias was left alone with Mr. and Mrs. Hawkesworth. Lily was very tired, but she worked steadily at marking Eleanor's pocket-handkerchiefs, until her sister, seeing how weary she was, made her lie down on the sofa.

'Here is a gentleman who is tired too,' said Eleanor, dancing the baby; 'we will carry you off, sir, and leave Aunt Lily to go to sleep.'

'Aunt Lily is not so tired as that,' said Lily; 'pray keep him.'

'It is quite bedtime,' said Eleanor, in her decided tone, and she carried him off.

Lilias took up the knitting which she had laid down, and began to study the stitches. 'I should like this feathery pattern,' said she, '(if it did not remind me so much of the fever); but, by the bye, Frank, have you completed Master Henry's outfit? I looked forward to helping to choose his pretty little things, but I see no preparation but of stockings.'

'Why, Lily, did not you know that he was to stay in England?'

'To stay in England? No, I never thought of that—how sorry you must be.'

At this moment Eleanor returned, and Mr. Hawkesworth told her he had been surprised to find Lily did not know their intentions with regard to the baby.

'If we had any certain intentions we should have told her,' said Eleanor; 'I did not wish to speak to her about it till we had made up our minds.'

'Well, I know no use in mysteries,' said Mr. Hawkesworth, 'especially when Lily may help us to decide.'

'On his going or staying?' exclaimed Lily, eagerly looking to Mr. Hawkesworth, who was evidently more disposed to speak than his wife.

'Not on his going or staying—I am sorry to say that point was settled long ago—but where we shall leave him.'

Lily's heart beat high, but she did not speak.

'The truth is,' proceeded Mr. Hawkesworth, 'that this young gentleman has, as perhaps you know, a grandpapa, a grandmamma, and also six or seven aunts. With his grandmamma he cannot be left, for sundry reasons, unnecessary to mention. Now, one of his aunts is a staid matronly lady, and his godmother besides, and in all respects the person to take charge of him,—only she lives in a small house in a town, and has plenty of babies of her own, without being troubled with other people's.

Master Henry's other five aunts live in one great house, in a delightful country, with nothing to do but make much of him all day long, yet it is averred that these said aunts are a parcel of giddy young colts, amongst whom, if Henry escapes being demolished as a baby he will infallibly be spoilt as he grows up. Now, how are we to decide?'

'You have heard the true state of the case, Lily,' said Mrs. Hawkesworth. 'I did not wish to harass papa by speaking to him till something was settled; you are certainly old enough to have an opinion.'

'Yes, Lily,' said Frank; 'do you think that the hospitable New Court will open to receive our poor deserted child, and that these said aunts are not wild colts but discreet damsels?'

Playful as Mr. Hawkesworth's manner was, Lily saw the earnestness that was veiled under it: she felt the solemnity of Eleanor's appeal, and knew that this was no time to let herself be swayed by her wishes. There was a silence. At last, after a great struggle, Lily's better judgment gained the mastery, and raising her head, she said, 'Oh! Frank, do not ask me—I wish—but, Eleanor, when you see how much harm we have done, how utterly we have failed—'

Lily's newly-acquired habits of self-command enabled her to subdue a violent fit of sobbing, which she felt impending, but her tears flowed quietly down her cheeks.

'Remember,' said Frank, 'those who mistrust themselves are the most trustworthy.'

'No, Frank, it is not only the feeling of the greatness of the charge, it is the knowledge that we are not fit for it—that our own faults have forfeited such happiness.'

Again Lily was choked with tears.

'Well,' said Frank, 'we shall judge at Beechcroft. At all events, one of those aunts is to be respected.'

Eleanor added her 'Very right.'

This kindness on the part of her brother-in-law, which Lily felt to be undeserved, caused her tears to flow faster, and Eleanor, seeing her quite overcome, led her out of the room, helped her to undress, and put her to bed, with tenderness such as Lily had never experienced from her, excepting in illness.

In spite of bitter regrets, when she thought of the happiness it would have been to keep her little nephew, and of importunate and disappointing hopes that Mrs. Ridley would find it impossible to receive him, Lily felt that she had done right, and had made a real sacrifice for duty's sake. No more was said on the subject, and Lily was very grateful to Eleanor for making no inquiries, which she could not have answered without blaming Emily.

Sight-seeing prospered very well under Claude's guidance, and Lily's wonder and delight was a constant source of amusement to her friends. Her shopping was more of a care than a pleasure, for, in spite of the handsome equipments which Mr. Mohun presented to all his daughters, it was impossible to contract Emily's requirements within the limits of what ought to be her expenditure, and the different views of her brother and sister were rather troublesome in this matter. Claude hated the search for ladies' finery, and if drawn into it, insisted on always taking her to the grandest and most expensive shops; while, on the other hand, though Eleanor liked to hunt up cheap things and good bargains, she had such rigid ideas about plainness of dress, that there was little chance that what she approved would satisfy Emily.

CHAPTER XXI
CHARITY BEGINS AT HOME

'Suddenly, a mighty jerk
A mighty mischief did.'

In the meantime Emily and Jane went on very prosperously at home, looking forward to the return of the rest of the party on Saturday, the 17th of July. In this, however, they were doomed to disappointment, for neither Mr. Mohun nor Mr. Hawkesworth could wind up their affairs so as to return before the 24th. Maurice's holidays commenced on Monday the 19th, and Claude offered to go home on the same day, and meet him, but in a general council it was determined to the contrary. Claude was wanted to stay for a concert on Thursday, and both Mr. Mohun and Eleanor thought Maurice, without Reginald, would not be formidable for a few days.

At first he seemed to justify this opinion. He did not appear to have any peculiar pursuit, unless such might be called a very earnest attempt to make Phyllis desist from her favourite preface of 'I'll tell you what,' and to reform her habit of saying, 'Please for,' instead of 'If you please.' He walked with the sisters, carried messages for Mr. Devereux, performed some neat little bits of carpentry, and was very useful and agreeable.

On Wednesday afternoon Lord Rotherwood and Florence called, their heads the more full of the 30th because the Marquis had not once thought of it while Mr. Devereux was ill. Among the intended diversions fireworks were mentioned, and from that moment rockets, wheels, and serpents, commenced a wild career through Maurice's brain. Through the whole evening he searched for books on what he was pleased to call the art of pyrotechnics, studied them all Wednesday, and the next morning announced his intention of making some fireworks on a new plan.

'No, you must not,' said Emily, 'you will be sure to do mischief.'

'I am going to ask Wat for some powder,' was Maurice's reply, and he walked off.

'Stop him, Jane, stop him,' cried Emily. 'Nothing can be so dangerous. Tell him how angry papa would be.'

Though Jane highly esteemed her brother's discretion, she did not much like the idea of his touching powder, and she ran after him to suggest that he had better wait till papa's return.

'Then Redgie will be at home,' said Maurice, 'and I could not be answerable for the consequence of such a careless fellow touching powder.'

This great proof of caution quite satisfied Jane, but not so Wat Greenwood, who proved himself a faithful servant by refusing to let Master Maurice have one grain of gunpowder without express leave from the squire. Maurice then had recourse to Jane, and his power over her was such as to triumph over strong sense and weak notions of obedience, so that she was prevailed upon to supply him with the means of making the dangerous and forbidden purchase.

Emily was both annoyed and alarmed when she found that the gunpowder was actually in the house, and she even thought of sending a note to the parsonage to beg Mr. Devereux to speak to Maurice; but Jane had gone over to the enemy, and Emily never could do anything unsupported. Besides, she neither liked to affront Maurice nor to confess herself unable to keep him in order; and she, therefore, tried to put the whole matter out of her head, in the thoughts of an expedition to Raynham, which she was about to make in the manner she best liked, with Jane in the close carriage, and the horses reluctantly spared from their farm work.

As they were turning the corner of the lane they overtook Phyllis and Adeline on their way to the school with some work, and Emily stopped the carriage, to desire them to send off a letter which she had left on the chimney-piece in the schoolroom. Then proceeding to Raynham, they made their visits, paid Emily's debts, performed their commissions, and met the carriage again at the bookseller's shop, at the end of about two hours.

'Look here, Emily!' exclaimed Jane. 'Read this! can it be Mrs. Aylmer?'

'The truly charitable,' said Emily, contemptuously. 'Mrs. Aylmer is above—'

'But read. It says "unbeneficed clergyman and deceased nobleman," and who can that be but Uncle Rotherwood and Mr. Aylmer.'

'Well, let us see,' said Emily, 'those things are always amusing.'

It was an appeal to the 'truly charitable,' from the friends of the widow of an unbeneficed clergyman of the diocese, one of whose sons had, it was said, by the kindness of a deceased nobleman, received the promise of an appointment in India, of which he was unable to avail himself for want of the funds needful for his outfit. This appeal was, it added, made without the knowledge of the afflicted lady, but further particulars might be learnt by application to E. F., No. 5 West Street, Raynham.

'E. F. is plainly that bustling, little, old Miss Fitchett, who wrote to papa for some subscription,' said Emily. 'You know she is a regular beggar, always doing these kind of things, but I can never believe that Mrs. Aylmer would consent to appear in this manner.'

'Ah! but it says without her knowledge,' said Jane. 'Don't you remember Rotherwood's lamenting that they were forgotten?'

'Yes, it is shocking,' said Emily; 'the clergyman that married papa and mamma!'

'Ask Mr. Adam what he knows,' said Jane.

Emily accordingly applied to the bookseller, and learnt that Mrs. Aylmer was indeed the person intended. 'Something must be done,' said she, returning to Jane. 'Our name will be a help.'

'Speak to Aunt Rotherwood,' said Jane. 'Or suppose we apply to Miss Fitchett, we should have time to drive that way.'

'I am sure I shall not go to Miss Fitchett,' said Emily, 'she only longs for an excuse to visit us. What can you be thinking of? Lend me your pencil, Jenny, if you please.'

And Emily wrote down, 'Miss Mohun, £5,' and handed to the bookseller all that she possessed towards paying her just debts to Lilias. While she was writing, Jane had turned towards the window, and suddenly exclaiming, 'There is Ben! Oh! that gunpowder!' darted out of the shop. She had seen the groom on horseback, and the next moment she was asking breathlessly, 'Is it Maurice?'

'No, Miss Jane; but Miss Ada is badly burnt, and Master Maurice sent me to fetch Mr. Saunders.'

'How did it happen?'

'I can't say, Miss; the schoolroom has been on fire, and Master Maurice said the young ladies had got at the gunpowder.'

Emily had just arrived at the door, looking dreadfully pale, and followed by numerous kind offers of salts and glasses of water; but Jane, perceiving that at least she had strength to get into the carriage, refused them all, helped her in, and with instant decision, desired to be driven to the surgeon's. Emily obeyed like a child, and threw herself back in the carriage without a word; Jane trembled like an aspen leaf; but her higher spirit took the lead, and very sensibly she managed, stopping at Mr. Saunders's door to offer to take him to Beechcroft, and getting a glass of sal-volatile for Emily while they were waiting for him. His presence was a great relief, for Emily's natural courtesy made her exert herself, and thus warded off much that would have been very distressing.

In the meantime we will return to Beechcroft, where Emily's request respecting her letter had occasioned some discussion between the little girls, as they returned from a walk with Marianne. Phyllis thought that Emily meant them to wafer the letter, since they were under strict orders never to touch fire or candle; but Ada argued that they were to seal it, and that permission to light a candle was implied in the order. At last, Phyllis hoped the matter might be settled by asking Maurice to seal the letter, and meeting him at the front door, she began, in fortunately, with 'Please, Maurice—'

'I never listen to anything beginning with please,' said Maurice, who was in a great hurry, 'only don't touch my powder.'

Away he went, deaf to all his sister's shouts of 'Maurice, Maurice,' and they went in, Ada not sorry to be unheard, as she was bent on the grand exploit of lighting a lucifer match, but Phyllis still pleading for the wafer. They found the schoolroom strewed with Maurice's preparations for fireworks, and Emily's letter on the chimney-piece.

'Let us take the letter downstairs, and put on a wafer,' said Phyllis. 'Won't you come, Ada?'

'No, the stamps are here, and so are the matches, I can do it easily.'

'But Ada, Ada, it would be naughty. Only wait, and I will show you such a pretty wafer that I know of in the drawing-room. I will run and fetch it.'

Phyllis went, and Ada stood a few moments in doubt, looking at the letter. The recollection of duty was not strong enough to balance the temptation, and she took up a match and drew it along the sandpaper. It did not light—a second pull, and the flame appeared more suddenly than she had expected, while at the same moment the lock of the door turned, and fancying it was Maurice, she started, and dropped the match. Phyllis opened the door, heard a loud explosion and a scream, saw a bright flash and a cloud of smoke. She started back, but the next moment again opened the door, and ran forward. Hannah rushed in at the same time, and caught up Ada, who had fallen to the ground. A light in the midst of the smoke made Phyllis turn, and she beheld the papers on the table on fire. Maurice's powder-horn was in the midst, but the flames had not yet reached it, and, mindful of Claude's story, she sprung forward, caught it up, and dashed it through the window; she felt the glow of the fire upon her cheek, and stood still as if stunned, till Hannah carried Ada out of the room, and screamed to her to come away, and call Joseph. The table was now one sheet of flame, and Phyllis flew to the pantry, where she gave the summons in almost inaudible tones. The servants hurried to the spot, and she was left alone and bewildered; she ran hither and thither in confusion, till she met Hannah, eagerly asking for Master Maurice, and saying that the surgeon must be instantly sent for, as Ada's face and neck were badly burnt. Phyllis ran down, calling Maurice, and at length met him at the front door, looking much frightened, and asking for Ada.

'Oh! Maurice, her face and neck are burnt, and badly. She does scream?'

'Did I not tell you not to meddle with the powder?' said Maurice.

'Indeed, I could not help it,' said Phyllis.

'Stuff and nonsense! It is very well that you have not killed Ada, and I think that would have made you sorry.'

Phyllis with difficulty mentioned Hannah's desire that a surgeon should be sent for: Maurice went to look for Ben, and she followed him. Then he began asking how she had done the mischief.

'I do not know,' said she, 'I do not much think I did it.'

'Mind, you can't humbug me. Did you not say that you touched the powder?'

'Yes, but—'

'No buts,' said Maurice, making the most of his brief authority. 'I hate false excuses. What were you doing when it exploded?'

'Coming into the room.'

'Oh! that accounts for it,' said Maurice, 'the slightest vibration causes an explosion of that sort of rocket, and of course it was your bouncing into the room! You have had a lesson against rushing about the house. Come, though, cheer up, Phyl, it is a bad business, but it might have been worse; you will know better next time. Don't cry, Phyl, I will explain to you all about the patent rocket.'

'But do you really think that I blew up Ada?'

'Blew up Ada! caused the powder to ignite. The inflammable matter—'

As he spoke he followed Phyllis to the nursery, and there was so much shocked, that he could no longer lord it over her, but shrinking back, shut himself up in his room, and bolted the door.

Nearly an hour passed away before the arrival of Emily, Jane, and Mr. Saunders. Phyllis ran down, and meeting them at the door, exclaimed, 'Oh! Emily, poor Ada! I am so sorry.'

The sisters hurried past her to the nursery, where Ada was lying on the bed, half undressed, and her face, neck, and arm such a spectacle that Emily turned away, ready to faint. Mr. Saunders was summoned, and Phyllis thrust out of the room. She sat down on the step of the stairs, resting her forehead on her knees, and trembling, listened to the sounds of voices, and the screams which now and then reached her ears. After a time she was startled by hearing herself called from the stairs *by below* a voice which she had not heard for many weeks, and springing up, saw Mr. Devereux leaning on the banisters. The great change in his appearance frightened her almost as much as the accident itself, and she stood looking at him without speaking. 'Phyllis,' said he, in a voice hoarse with agitation, 'what is it? tell me at once.'

She could not speak, and her wild and frightened air might well give him great alarm. She pointed to the nursery, and put her finger to her lips, and he, beckoning to her to follow him, went downstairs, and turning into the drawing-room, said, as he sank down upon the sofa, 'Now, Phyllis, what has happened?'

'The gunpowder—I made it go off, and it has burnt poor Ada's face! Mr. Saunders is there, and she screams—'

Phyllis finding herself ready to roar, left off speaking, and laying her head on the table, burst into an agony of crying, while Mr. Devereux was too much exhausted to address her; at last she exclaimed: 'I hear the nursery door; he is going!'

She flew to the door, and listened, and then called out, 'Emily, Jane, here is Cousin Robert!'

Jane came down, leaving Emily to finish hearing Mr. Saunders's directions. She was even more shocked at her cousin's looks than Phyllis had been, and though she tried to speak cheerfully, her manner scarcely agreed with her words. 'It is all well, Robert, I am sorry you have been so frightened. It is but a slight affair, though it looks so shocking. There is no danger. But, oh, Robert! you ought not to be here. What shall we do for you? you are quite knocked up.'

'Oh! no,' said Mr. Devereux, 'I am only a little out of breath. A terrible report came to me, and I set off to learn the truth. I should like to hear what Mr. Saunders says of her.'

'I will call him in here before he goes,' said Jane; 'how tired you are; you have not been out before.'

'Only to the gate to speak to Rotherwood yesterday, and prevent him from coming in,' said Mr. Devereux, 'but I have great designs for Sunday. They come home to-morrow, do not they?'

Jane was much relieved by hearing her cousin talk in this manner, and answered, 'Yes, and a dismal coming home it will be; it is too late to let them know.'

Mr. Saunders now entered, and gave a very favourable account of the patient, saying that even the scars would probably disappear in a few weeks. His gig had come from Raynham, and he offered to set Mr. Devereux down at the parsonage, a proposal which the latter was very glad to accept. Emily and Jane had leisure, when they were gone, to inquire into the manner of the accident. Phyllis answered that Maurice said that her banging the door had made the powder go off. Jane then asked where Maurice was, and Phyllis reporting that he was in his own room, she repaired thither, and knocked twice without receiving an answer. On her call, however, he opened the door; she saw that he had been in tears, and hastened to tell him Mr. Saunders's opinion. He fastened the door again as soon as she had entered. 'If I could have thought it!' sighed he. 'Fool that I was, not to lock the door!'

'Then you were not there? Phyllis says that she did it by banging the door. Is not that nonsense?'

'Not at all. Did I not read to you in the *Year Book of Facts* about the patent signal rockets, which explode with the least vibration, even when a carriage goes by? Now, mine was on the same principle. I was making an experiment on the ingredients; I did not expect to succeed the first time, and so I took no precautions. Well! Pyrotechnics are a dangerous science! Next time I study them it shall be at the workshop at the Old Court.'

Maurice was sincerely sorry for the consequence of his disobedience, and would have been much to be pitied had it not been for his secret satisfaction in the success of his art. He called his sister into the schoolroom to explain how it happened. The room was a dismal sight, blackened with smoke, and flooded with water, the table and part of the floor charred, a mass of burnt paper in the midst, and a stifling smell of fire. A pane of glass was shattered, and Maurice ran down to the lawn to see if he could find anything there to account for it. The next moment he returned, the powder-horn in his hand. 'See, Jenny, how fortunate that this was driven through the window with the force of the explosion. The whole place might have been blown to atoms with such a quantity as this.'

'Then what was it that blew up?' asked Jane.

'What I had put out for my rocket, about two ounces. If this half-pound had gone there is no saying what might have happened.'

'Now, Maurice,' said Jane, 'I must go back to Ada, and will you run down to the parsonage with a parcel, directed to Robert, that you will find in the hall?'

This was a device to occupy Maurice, who, as Jane saw, was so restless and unhappy that she did not like to leave him, much as she was wanted elsewhere. He went, but afraid to see his cousin, only left the parcel at the door. As he was going back he heard a shout, and looking round saw Lord Rotherwood mounted on Cedric, his most spirited horse, galloping up the lane. 'Maurice!' cried he, 'what is all this? they say the New Court is blown up, and you and half the girls killed, but I hope one part is as true as the other.'

'Nobody is hurt but Ada,' said Maurice, 'but her face is a good deal burnt.'

'Eh? then she won't be fit for the 30th, poor child! tell me how it was, make haste. I heard it from Mr. Burnet as I came down to dinner. We have a dozen people at dinner. I told him not to mention it to my mother, and rode off to hear the truth. Make haste, half the people were come when I set off.'

The horse's caperings so discomposed Maurice that he could scarcely collect his wits enough to answer: 'Some signal rocket on a new principle—detonating powder, composed of oxymuriate—Oh! Rotherwood, take care!'

'Speak sense, and go on.'

'Then Phyllis came in, banged the door, and the vibration caused the explosion,' said Maurice, scared into finishing promptly.

'Eh! banging the door? You had better not tell that story at school.'

'But, Rotherwood, the deton—Oh! that horse—you will be off!'

'Not half so dangerous as patent rockets. Is Emily satisfied with such stuff?'

'Don't you know that fulminating silver—'

'What does Robert Devereux say?'

'Really, Rotherwood, I could show you—'

'Show me? No; if rockets are so perilous I shall have nothing to do with them. Stand still, Cedric! Just tell me about Ada. Is there much harm done?'

'Her face is scorched a good deal, but they say it will soon be right.'

'I am glad—we will send to inquire to-morrow, but I cannot come—ha, ha! a new infernal machine. Good-bye, Friar Bacon.'

Away he went, and Maurice stood looking after him with complacent disdain. 'There they go, Cedric and Rotherwood, equally well provided with brains! What is the use of talking science to either?'

It was late when he reached the house, and his two sisters shortly came down to tea, with news that Adeline was asleep and Phyllis was going to bed. The accident was again talked over.

'Well,' said Emily, 'I do not understand it, but I suppose papa will.'

'The telling papa is a bad part of the affair, with William and Eleanor there too,' said Jane.

'I do not mean to speak to Phyllis about it again,' said Emily, 'it makes her cry so terribly.'

'It will come out fast enough,' sighed Maurice. 'Good-night.'

More than once in the course of the night did poor Phyllis wake and cry, and the next day was the most wretched she had ever spent; she was not allowed to stay in the nursery, and the schoolroom was uninhabitable, so she wandered listlessly about the garden, sometimes creeping down to the churchyard, where she looked up at the old tower, or pondered over the graves, and sometimes forgetting her troubles in converse with the dogs, in counting the rings in the inside of a foxglove flower, or in rescuing tadpoles stranded on the broad leaf of a water-lily.

Her sisters and brothers were not less forlorn. Emily sighed and lamented; Adeline was feverish and petulant; and Jane toiled in vain to please and soothe both, and to comfort Maurice; but with all her good-temper and good-nature she had not the spirit which alone could enable her to be a comfort to any one. Ada whined, fretted, and was disobedient, and from Maurice she met with nothing but rebuffs; he was silent and sullen, and spent most of the day in the workshop, slowly planing scraps of deal board, and watching with a careless eye the curled shavings float to the ground.

In the course of the afternoon Alethea and Marianne came to inquire after the patient. Jane came down to them and talked very fast, but when they asked for a further explanation of the cause of the accident, Jane declared that Maurice said it was impossible that any one who did not understand chemistry should know how it happened, and Alethea went away strongly reminded that it was no affair of hers.

Notes passed between the New Court and the vicarage, but Mr. Devereux was feeling the effect of his yesterday's exertion too much to repeat it, and no persuasion of the sisters could induce Maurice to visit him.

CHAPTER XXII
THE BARONIAL COURT

'Still in his eyes his soul revealing,
He dreams not, knows not of concealing,
Does all he does with single mind,
And thinks of others that are kind.'

The travellers were expected to arrive at about seven o'clock in the evening, and in accordance with a well-known taste of Eleanor's, Emily had ordered no dinner, but a substantial meal under the name of tea. When the sound of carriage wheels was heard, Jane was with Adeline, Maurice was in his retreat at the Old Court, and it was with no cheerful alacrity that Emily went alone into the hall. Phyllis was already at the front door, and the instant Mr. Mohun set foot on the threshold, her hand grasped his coat, and her shrill voice cried in his ear, 'Papa, I am very sorry I blew up the gunpowder and burnt Ada.'

'What, my dear? where is Ada?'

'In bed. I blew up the gunpowder and burnt her face,' repeated Phyllis.

'We have had an accident,' said Emily, 'but I hope it is nothing very serious, only poor Ada is a sad figure.'

In another moment Mr. Mohun and Eleanor were on the way to the nursery; Lilias was following, but she recollected that a general rush into a sickroom was not desirable, and therefore paused and came back to the hall. The worst was over with Phyllis when the confession had been made. She was in raptures at the sight of the baby, and was presently showing the nurse the way upstairs, but her brother William called her back: 'Phyllis, you have not spoken to any one.'

Phyllis turned, and came down slowly in her most ungainly manner, believing herself in too great disgrace to be noticed by anybody, and she was quite surprised and comforted to be greeted by her brothers and Lily just as usual.

'And how did you meet with this misfortune?' asked Mr. Hawkesworth.

'I banged the door, and made it go off,' said Phyllis.

'What can you mean?' said William, in a tone of surprise, which Phyllis took for anger, and she hid her face to stifle her sobs.

'No, no, do not frighten her,' said Claude's kind voice.

'Run and make friends with your nephew, Phyllis,' said Mr. Hawkesworth; 'do not greet us with crying.'

'First tell me what is become of Maurice,' said Claude, 'is he blown up too?'

'No, he is at the Old Court,' said Phyllis. 'Shall I tell him that you are come?'

'I will look for him,' said Claude, and out he went.

The others dispersed in different directions, and did not assemble again for nearly half an hour, when they all met in the drawing-room to drink tea; Claude and Maurice were the last to appear, and, on entering, the first thing the former said was, 'Where is Phyllis?'

'In the nursery,' said Jane; 'she has had her supper, and chooses to stay with Ada.'

'Has any one found out the history of the accident?' said William.

'I have vainly been trying to make sense of Maurice's account,' said Claude.

'Sense!' said William, 'there is none.'

'I am perfectly bewildered,' said Lily; 'every one has a different story, only consenting in making Phyllis the victim.'

'And,' added Claude, 'I strongly suspect she is not in fault.'

'Why should you doubt what she says herself?' said Eleanor.

'What does she say herself?' said William, 'nothing but that she shut the door, and what does that amount to?—Nothing.'

'She says she touched the powder,' interposed Jane.

'That is another matter,' said William; 'no one told me of her touching the powder. But why do you not ask her? She is publicly condemned without a hearing.'

'Who accuses her?' said Mr. Mohun.

'I can hardly tell,' said Emily; 'she met us, saying she was very sorry. Yes, she accuses herself. Every one has believed it to be her.'

'And why?'

There was a pause, but at last Emily said, 'How would you account for it otherwise?'

'I have not yet heard the circumstances. Maurice, I wish to hear your account. I will not now ask how you procured the powder. Whoever was the immediate cause of the accident, you are chiefly to blame. Where was the powder?'

Maurice gave his theory and his facts, ending with the powder-horn being driven out of the window upon the green.

'I hear,' said Mr. Mohun. 'But, Maurice, did you not say that Phyllis touched the powder? How do you reconcile that with this incomprehensible statement?'

'She might have done that before,' said Maurice.

'Now call Phyllis,' said his father.

'Is it not very formidable for her to be examined before such an assembly?' said Emily.

'The accusation has been public, and the investigation shall be the same,' said Mr. Mohun.

'Then you do not think she did it, papa?' cried Lily.

'Not by shutting the door,' said William.

Phyllis entered, and Mr. Mohun, holding out both hands to her, drew her towards him, and placing her with her back to the others, still retained her hands, while he said, 'Phyllis, do not be frightened, but tell me where you were when the powder exploded?'

'Coming into the room,' said Phyllis, in a trembling voice.

'Where had you been?'

'Fetching a wafer out of the drawing-room.'

'What was the wafer for?'

'To put on Emily's letter, which she told us to send.'

'And where was Ada?'

'In the schoolroom, reading the direction of the letter.'

'Tell me exactly what happened when you came back.'

'I opened the door, and there was a flash, and a bang, and a smoke, and Ada tumbled down.'

'I have one more question to ask. When did you touch the powder?'

'Then,' said Phyllis.

'When it had exploded? Take care what you say.'

'Was it naughty? I am very sorry,' said Phyllis, beginning to cry.

'What powder did you touch? I do not understand you, tell me quietly.'

'I touched the powder-horn. What went off was only a little in a paper on the table, and there was a great deal more. When the rocket blew up there was a great noise, and Ada and I both screamed, and Hannah ran in and took up Ada in her arms. Then I saw a great fire, and looked, and saw Emily's music-book, and all the papers blazing. So I thought if it got to the powder it would blow up again, and I laid hold of the horn and threw it out of the window. That is all I know, papa, only I hope you are not very angry with me.'

She looked into his face, not knowing how to interpret the unusual expression she saw there.

'Angry with you!' said he. 'No, my dear child, you have acted with great presence of mind. You have saved your sister and Hannah from great danger, and I am very sorry that you have been unjustly treated.'

He then gave his little daughter a kiss, and putting his hand on her head, added, 'Whoever caused the explosion, Phyllis is quite free from blame, and I wish every one to understand this, because she has been unjustly accused, without examination, and because she has borne it patiently, and without attempting to justify herself.'

'Very right,' observed Eleanor.

'Shake hands, Phyllis,' said William.

The others said more with their eyes than with their lips. Phyllis stood like one in a dream, and fixing her bewildered looks upon Claude, said, 'Did not I do it?'

'No, Phyllis, you had nothing to do with it,' was the general exclamation.

'Maurice said it was the door,' said Phyllis.

'Maurice talked nonsense,' said Claude; 'you were only foolish in believing him.'

Phyllis went up to Claude, and laid her head on his arm; Mr. Hawkesworth held out his hand to her, but she did not look up, and Claude withdrawing his arm, and raising her head, found that she was crying. Eleanor and Lilias both rose, and came towards her but Claude made them a sign, and led her away.

'What a fine story this will be for Reginald,' said William.

'And for Rotherwood,' said Mr. Mohun.

'I do not see how it happened,' said Eleanor.

'Of course Ada did it herself,' said William.

'Of course,' said Maurice. 'It was all from Emily's setting them to seal her letter, that is plain now.'

'Would not Ada have said so?' asked Eleanor.

Lily sighed at the thought of what Eleanor had yet to learn.

'Did you tell them to seal your letter, Emily?' said Mr. Mohun.

'I am sorry to say that I did tell them to send it,' said Emily, 'but I said nothing about sealing, as Jane remembers, and I forgot that Maurice's gunpowder was in the room.'

Eleanor shook her head sorrowfully, and looked down at her knitting, and Lily knew that her mind was made up respecting little Henry's dwelling-place.

It was some comfort to have raised no false expectations.

'Ada must not be frightened and agitated to-night,' said Mr. Mohun, 'but I hope you will talk to her to-morrow, Eleanor. Well, Claude, have you made Phyllis understand that she is acquitted?'

'Scarcely,' said Claude; 'she is so overcome and worn out, that I thought she had better go to bed, and wake in her proper senses to-morrow.'

'A very unconscious heroine,' said William. 'She is a wonder—I never thought her anything but an honest sort of romp.'

'I have long thought her a wonderful specimen of obedience,' said Mr. Mohun.

William and Claude now walked to the parsonage, and the council broke up; but it must not be supposed that this was the last that Emily and Maurice heard on the subject.

CHAPTER XXIII
JOYS AND SORROWS

'Complaint was heard on every part
Of something disarranged.'

The next day, Sunday, was one of the most marked in Lily's life. It was the first time she saw Mr. Devereux after his illness, and though Claude had told her he was going to church, it gave her a sudden thrill of joy to see him there once more, and perhaps she never felt more thankful than when his name was read before the Thanksgiving. After the service there was an exchange of greetings, but Lily spoke no word, she felt too happy and too awe-struck to say anything, and she walked back to the New Court in silence.

In the afternoon she had hopes that a blessing would be granted to her, for which at one time she had scarcely dared to hope; and she felt convinced that so it would be when she saw that Mr. Devereux wore his surplice, although, as in the morning, his friend read the service. After the Second Lesson there was a pause, and then Mr. Devereux left the chair by the altar, walked along the aisle, and took his stand on the step of the font. Lily's heart beat high as she saw who were gathering round him—Mrs. Eden, Andrew Grey, James Harrington, and Mrs. Naylor, who held in her arms a healthy, rosy-checked boy of a year old.

She could not have described the feelings which made her eyes overflow with tears, as she saw Mr. Devereux's thin hand sprinkle the drops over the brow of the child, and heard him say, 'Robert, I baptize thee'—words which she had heard in dreams, and then awakened to remember that the parish was at enmity with the pastor, the child unbaptized, and herself, in part, the cause.

The name of the little boy was an additional pledge of reconciliation, and at the same time it made her feel again what had been the price of his baptism. When she looked back upon the dreary feelings which she had so lately experienced, it seemed to her as if she might believe that this christening was, as it were, a pledge of pardon, and an earnest of better things.

Naylor, who had recovered much more slowly than Mr. Devereux, was at church for the first time, and after the service Mr. Mohun sought him out in the churchyard, and heartily shook hands with him. Lily would gladly have followed his example, but she only stood by Eleanor and Mrs. Weston, who were speaking to Mrs. Eden and Mrs. Naylor, admiring the little boy, and praising him for his good behaviour in church.

Love of babies was a strong bond between Mrs. Weston and Mrs. Hawkesworth, who seemed to become well acquainted from the first moment that little Henry was mentioned; and Lily was well pleased to see that in Jane's phrase Eleanor 'took to her friends so well.'

And yet this day brought with it some annoyances, which once would have fretted her so much as to interfere even with such joy as she now felt. The song, with which she had taken so much pains, ought to have been sent home a week before, but owing to the delay caused by Emily's carelessness, it had been burnt in the fire in the schoolroom, and Lily could not feel herself forgiven till she had talked the disaster over in private with her friend, and this was out of her power throughout the day, for something always prevented her from getting Alethea alone. In the morning Jane stuck close to her, and in the afternoon William walked to the school gate with them. But Alethea's manner was kinder towards her than ever, and she was quite satisfied about her.

It gave her more pain to perceive that Emily in every possible manner avoided being alone with her. It was by her desire that Phyllis came to sleep in their room; she would keep Jane talking there, give Esther some employment which kept her in their presence, linger in the drawing-room while Lilias was dressing, and at bedtime be too sleepy to say anything but good-night.

That Sunday was a sorrowful one to Eleanor; for in the course of the conversation with Ada, which Mr. Mohun had desired her to hold, she became conscious of the little girl's double-dealing ways. It was only by a very close cross-examination that she was able to extract from her a true account of the disaster, and though Ada never went so far as actually to tell a falsehood, it was evident that she was willing to conceal as much as possible, and to throw the blame on other people. And when the real facts were confessed she did not seem able to comprehend why she was regarded with displeasure; her instinct of truth and obedience was lost for the time, and Eleanor saw it with the utmost pain. Adeline had been her especial darling, and cold as her manner had often been towards the others, it ever was warm towards the motherless little one, whom she had tended and cherished with most anxious care from her earliest infancy. She had left her gentle, candid, and affectionate; a loving, engaging, little creature, and how did she find her now? Her fair bright face disfigured, her caresses affected, her mind turned to deceit and prevarication! Well might Eleanor feel it more than ever painful to leave her own little Henry to the care of others; and well it was for her that she had learned to find comfort in the consciousness that her duty was clear.

The next morning Emily learned what was Henry's destination.

'Oh! Eleanor,' said she, 'why do you not leave him here? We should be so rejoiced to have him.'

'Thank you, I am afraid it is out of the question,' answered Eleanor, quietly.

'Why, dear Eleanor? You know how glad we should be. I should have thought,' proceeded Emily, a little hurt, 'that you would have wished him to live in your own home.'

Eleanor did not speak, and Emily, who had the little boy in her arms, went on talking to him: 'Come, baby, let us persuade mamma to let you stay with Aunt Emily. Ask papa, Henry, won't you? Seriously, Eleanor, has Frank considered how much better it would be to have him in the country?'

'He has, Emily; he once wished much to leave him here.'

'I am sure grandpapa would like it,' said Emily. 'Do you observe, Eleanor, how fond he is of baby, always calling him Harry too, as if he liked the sound of the name?'

'It has all been talked over, Emily, and it cannot be.'

'With papa?' asked Emily in surprise.

'No, with Lily.'

'With Lily!' exclaimed Emily. 'Did not Aunt Lily wish to keep you, Harry? I thought she was very fond of you.'

'You had better inquire no further,' said Eleanor, 'except of your own conscience.'

'Did Lily think us unfit to take care of him?' asked Emily, in surprise.

As she spoke Lily herself came in, the key of the storeroom in her hand, and looks of consternation on her face. She came to announce a terrible deficiency in the preserved quinces, which she herself had carefully put aside on a shelf in the storeroom, and which Emily said she had not touched in her absence.

'Let me see,' said Eleanor, rising, and setting off to the storeroom; Emily and Lily followed, with a sad suspicion of the truth. On the way they looked into the nursery, to give little Henry to his nurse, and to ask Jane, who was sitting with Ada, what she remembered about it. Jane knew nothing, and they went on to the storeroom, where Eleanor, quite in her element, began rummaging, arranging, and sighing over the confusion, while Lily lent a helping hand, and Emily stood by, wishing that her sister would not trouble herself. Presently Jane came running up with a saucer in her hand, containing a quarter of a quince and some syrup, which she said she had found in the nursery cupboard, in searching for a puzzle which Ada wanted.

'And,' said Jane, 'I should guess that Miss Ada herself knew something about it, for when I could not find the puzzle in the right-hand cupboard, she was so very unwilling that I should look into that one; she said there was nothing there but the boys' old playthings and Esther's clothes. And I do not know whether you saw how she fidgeted when you were talking about the quinces, before you went up.'

'It is much too plain,' sighed Lily. 'Oh! Rachel, why did we not listen to you?'

'Do you suppose,' said Eleanor, 'that Ada has been in the habit of taking the key and helping herself?'

'No,' said Emily, 'but that Esther has helped her.'

'Ah!' said Eleanor, 'I never thought it wise to take her, but how could she get the key? You do not mean that you trusted it out of your own keeping.'

'It began while we were ill,' faltered Emily, 'and afterwards it was difficult to bring matters into their former order.'

'But oh, Eleanor, what is to be done?' sighed Lily.

'Speak to papa, of course,' said Eleanor. 'He is gone to the castle, and in the meantime we had better take an exact account of everything here.'

'And Esther? And Ada?' inquired the sisters.

'I think it will be better to speak to him before making so grave an accusation,' said Eleanor.

They now commenced that wearisome occupation—a complete setting-to-rights; Eleanor counted, weighed, and measured, and extended her cares from the stores to every other household matter. Emily made her escape, and went to sit with Ada; but Lily and Jane toiled for several hours with Eleanor, till Lily was so heated and wearied that she was obliged to give up a walk to Broomhill, and spend another day without a talk with Alethea. However, she was so patient, ready, and good-humoured, that Eleanor was well pleased with her. She could hardly think of the slight vexation, when her mind was full of sorrow and shame on Esther's account. It was she who, contrary to the advice of her elders, had insisted on bringing her into the house; she had allowed temptation to be set in her way, and had not taken sufficient pains to strengthen her principles; and how could she do otherwise than feel guilty of all Esther's faults, and of those into which she had led Adeline?

On Mr. Mohun's return Ada was interrogated. She pitied herself—said she did not think papa would be angry—prevaricated—and tried to coax away his inquiries, but all in vain; and at length, by slow degrees, the confession was drawn from her that she had been used to asking Esther for morsels of sweet things when she was sent to the storeroom; that afterwards she had seen her packing up some tea and sugar to take to her mother, and that Esther on that occasion, and several others, purchased her silence by giving her a share of pilfered sweetmeats. Telling her that he only spared her a very severe punishment for the present, on account of her illness, Mr. Mohun left her, and on his way downstairs met Phyllis.

'Phyl,' said he, 'did Esther ever give you sweet things out of the storeroom?'

'Once, papa, when she had been putting out some currant jam, she offered me what had been left in the spoon.'

'Did you take it?'

'No, papa, for Eleanor used to say it was a bad trick to lick out spoons.'

'Did you ever know that she took tea and sugar from the storeroom, for her mother?'

'Took home tea and sugar to her mother! She could not have done it, papa. It would be stealing!'

Esther, who was next called for, cried a great deal, and begged for pardon, pleading again and again that—

'It was mother,' an answer which made her young mistresses again sigh over the remembrance of Rachel's disregarded advice. Her fate was left for consideration and consultation with Mr. Devereux, for Mr. Mohun, seeing himself to blame for having allowed her to be placed in a situation of so much trial, and thinking that there was much that was good about her, did not like to send her to her home, where she was likely to learn nothing but what was bad.

CHAPTER XXIV
LOVE'S LABOUR LOST

'And well, with ready hand and heart,
  Each task of toilsome duty taking,
Did one dear inmate take her part,
  The last asleep, the earliest waking.'

In the course of the afternoon Lord Rotherwood and Florence called, to see Eleanor, inquire after Ada, and make the final arrangements for going to a morning concert at Raynham the next day. Lady Rotherwood was afraid of the fatigue, and Florence therefore wished to accompany her cousins, who, as Eleanor meant to stay at home, were to be under Mrs. Weston's protection. Lady Florence and her brother, therefore, agreed to ride home by Broomhill, and mention the plan to Mrs. Weston, and took their leave, appointing Adam's shop as the place of rendezvous.

Next morning Emily, Lilias, and Jane happened to be together in the drawing-room, when Mr. Mohun and Claude came in, the former saying to Lily, 'Here is the mason's account for the gravestone which you wished to have put up to Agnes Eden; it comes to two pounds. You undertook half the expense, and as Claude is going to Raynham, he will pay for it if you will give him your sovereign.'

'I will,' said Lily, 'but first I must ask Emily to pay me for the London commissions.'

Emily repented not having had a private conference with Lily.

'So you have not settled your accounts,' said Mr. Mohun. 'I hope Lily has not ruined you, Emily.'

'I thought her a mirror of prudence,' said Claude.

'Well, Emily, is the sovereign forthcoming? I am going directly, for Frank has something to do at Raynham, and William is going to try his gray in the phaeton.'

'I am afraid you will think me very silly,' said Emily, after some deliberation, 'but I hope Lily will not be very angry when I confess that seven shillings is the sum total of my property.'

'Oh, Emily,' cried Lily, in dismay, 'what has become of your five pounds?'

'I gave them as a subscription for a clergyman's widow in distress,' said Emily; 'it was the impulse of a moment, I could not help it, and, dear Lily, I hope it will not inconvenience you.'

'If papa will be kind enough to wait for this pound till Michaelmas,' said Lily.

'I would wait willingly,' said Mr. Mohun, 'but I will not see you cheated. How much does she owe you?'

'The commissions came to six pounds three,' said Lily, looking down.

'But, Lily,' said Jane, 'you forget the old debt.'

'Never mind,' whispered Lily; but Mr. Mohun asked what Jane had said, and Claude repeated her speech, upon which he inquired, 'What old debt?'

'Papa,' said Emily, in her most candid tone, 'I do not know what I should have done but for Lily's kindness. Really, I cannot get on with my present allowance; being the eldest, so many expenses come upon me.'

'Then am I to understand,' replied Mr. Mohun, 'that your foolish vanity has led you to encroach on your sister's kindness, and to borrow of her what you had no reasonable hope of repaying? Again, Lily, what does she owe you?'

Emily felt the difference between the sharp, curious eyes with which Jane regarded her, and the sorrowful downcast looks of Lily, who replied, 'The old debt is four pounds, but that does not signify.'

'Well,' resumed her father, 'I cannot blame you for your good-nature, though an older person might have acted otherwise. You must have managed wonderfully well, to look always so well dressed with only half your proper income. Here is the amount of the debt. Is it right? And, Lily, one thing more; I wish to thank you for what you have done towards keeping this house in order. You have worked hard, and endured much, and from all I can gather, you have prevented much mischief. Much has unfairly been thrown upon you, and you have well and steadily done your duty. For you, Emily, I have more to say to you, but I shall not enter on it at present, for it is late. You had better get ready, or you will keep the others waiting.'

'I do not think I can go,' sighed Emily.

'You are wanted,' said Mr. Mohun. 'I do not think your aunt would like Florence to go without you.'

Lily had trembled as much under her father's praise as Emily under his blame. She did not feel as if his commendation was merited, and longed to tell him of her faults and follies, but this was no fit time, and she hastened to prepare for her expedition, her spirits scarcely in time for a party of pleasure. Jane talked about the 30th, and asked questions about London, all the way to Raynham, and both Emily and Lily were glad to join in her chatter, in hopes of relieving their own embarrassment.

On arriving at the place of meeting they found Lady Florence watching for them.

'I am glad you are come,' said she, 'Rotherwood will always set out either too soon or too late, and this time it was too soon, so here we have been full a quarter of an hour, but he does not care. There he is, quite engrossed with his book.'

Lord Rotherwood was standing by the counter, reading so intently that he did not see his cousins' arrival. When they entered he just looked up, shook hands, asked after Ada, and went on reading. Lily began looking for some books for the school, which she had long wished for, and was now able to purchase; Emily sat down in a melancholy, abstracted mood, and Florence and Jane stood together talking.

'You know you are all to come early,' said the former, 'I do not know how we should manage without you. Rotherwood insists on having everything the same day—poor people first, and gentry and farmers altogether. Mamma does not like it, and I expect we shall be dreadfully tired; but he says he will not have the honest poor men put out for the fashionables; and you know we are all to dance with everybody. But Jenny, who is this crossing the street? Look, you have an eye for oddities.'

'Miss Fitchett, the subscription-hunter,' said Jane.

'She is actually coming to hunt us. I believe I have my purse. Oh! Emily is to be the first victim.'

Miss Fitchett advanced to Emily, and saying that she believed she had the honour to address Miss Mohun, began to tell her that her friend having been prematurely informed of her small efforts, had with a noble spirit of independence begged that the subscription might not be continued, and that what had already been given might be returned, and she rejoiced in this opportunity of making the explanation. But Miss Fitchett could not bear to relinquish the five-pound note, and added, that perhaps Miss Mohun might not object to apply her subscription to some other object, the Dorcas Society for instance.

'Thank you, I have no interest in the Dorcas Society,' said Emily; a reply which brought upon her a full account of all its aims and objects; and as still her polite looks spoke nothing of assent, Miss Fitchett went on with a string of other societies, speaking the louder and the more eagerly in the hope of attracting the attention of the young marquis and his sister. Emily was easily overwhelmed with words, and not thinking it lady-like to claim her money, yet feeling that none of these societies were fit objects for it, she stood confused and irresolute, unwilling either to consent or refuse. Jane, perceiving her difficulty, turned to Lord Rotherwood, and rousing him from his book, explained Emily's distress in a few words, and sent him to her rescue. He stepped forward just as Miss Fitchett, taking silence for consent, was proceeding to thank Emily; 'I think you misunderstand Miss Mohun,' said he. 'Since her subscription is not needed by the person for whom it was intended, she would be glad to have it restored. She does not wish to encourage any unauthorised societies.'

Boy as he was, in appearance still more than in age, there was a dignity in his manner which, together with the principle on which he spoke, overawed Miss Fitchett even more than his rank. She only said, 'Oh! my lord, I beg your pardon. Certainly, only—'

The note was placed in Emily's hands, and with a bow from Lord Rotherwood, she retreated, murmuring to herself the remonstrance which she had not courage to bestow upon the Marquis.

'Thank you, thank you, Rotherwood,' said Emily; 'you have done me a great service.'

'Well done, Rotherwood,' said Florence; 'you have given the old lady something to reflect upon.'

'Made a public announcement of principle,' said Lily.

'I was determined to give her a reason,' said the Marquis, laughing, 'but I assure you I felt like the stork with its head in the wolf's mouth, I thought she would give me a screed of doctrine. How came you to let your property get unto her clutches, Emily?'

'It was a subscription for Mrs. Aylmer,' said Emily.

'Our curate's wife!' cried he with a start; 'how was it? Florence, did you know anything? I thought she was in London. Why were we in the dark? Tell me all.'

'All I know is that she is living somewhere in Raynham, and last week there was a paper here to say that she was in want of the means of fitting out her son for India.'

'Yes, yes, Johnny, I know my father did get a promise for him—well!'

'That is all I know, except that she does not choose to be a beggar.'

'Poor Mrs. Aylmer! shameful neglect! she shall not be ill-used any longer, I will find her out this instant. Don't wait for me.'

And after a few words to Mr. Adams, off he went, walking as fast as he could, and leaving the young ladies not without fear of another invasion. Soon, however, the brothers came in, and presently after Mrs. Weston appeared. It was agreed that Lord Rotherwood should be left to his own devices, and they set out for the concert-room. Poor Florence lost much pleasure in disappointment at his non-appearance, but when the concert was over they found him sitting in the carriage, reading. As soon as they appeared he sprang out, and came to meet them, pouring rapidly out a history of his adventures.

'Then you have found them, and what can be done for them?'

'Everything ought to be done, but Mrs. Aylmer has a spirit of independence. That foolish woman's advertisement was unknown to her till Emily's five pounds came in, so fine a nest-egg that she could not help cackling, whereupon Mrs. Aylmer insisted on having every farthing returned.'

'Can she provide the boy's outfit?'

'She says so, or rather that her daughter can, but I shall see about that. It is worth while to be of age. Imagine! That bank which failed was the end of my father's legacy. They must have lived on a fraction of nothing! Edward went to sea. Miss Aylmer went out as a governess. Now she is at home.'

'Miss Aylmer!' exclaimed Miss Weston, 'I know she was a clergyman's daughter. Do you know the name of the family she lived with?'

'Was it Grant?' said William. 'I remember hearing of her going to some Grants.'

'It was,' said Alethea; 'she must be the same. Is she at home?'

'Yes,' said Lord Rotherwood, 'and you may soon see her, for I mean to have them all to stay at the castle as soon as our present visitors are gone. My mother and Florence shall call upon them on Friday.'

'Now,' said Claude, 'I have not found out what brought them back to Raynham.'

'Have you lived at Beechcroft all your life, and never discovered that there is a grammar-school at Raynham, with special privileges for the sons of clergymen of the diocese?'

A few more words, and the cousins parted; Emily by no means sorry that she had been obliged to go to Raynham. She tendered the five-pound note to her father, but he desired her to wait till Friday, and then to bring him a full account of her expenditure of the year. Her irregular ways made this almost impossible, especially as in the present state of affairs she wished to avoid a private conference with either Lily or Jane. She was glad that an invitation to dine and sleep at the castle on Wednesday would save her from the peril of having to talk to Lily in the evening. Reginald came home on Tuesday, to the great joy of all the party, and especially to that of Phyllis. This little maiden was more puzzled by the events that had taken place than conscious of the feeling which she had once thought must be so delightful. She could scarcely help perceiving that every one was much more kind to her than usual, especially Claude and Lily, and Lord Rotherwood said things which she could not at all understand. Her observation to Reginald was, 'Was it not lucky I had a cough on Twelfth Day, or Claude would not have told me what to do about gunpowder?'

Reginald troubled Phyllis much by declaring that nothing should induce him to kiss his nephew, and she was terribly shocked by the indifference with which Eleanor treated his neglect, even when it branched out into abuse of babies in general, and in particular of Henry's bald head and turned-up nose.

In the evening of Wednesday Phyllis was sitting with Ada in the nursery, when Reginald came up with the news that the party downstairs were going to practise country dances. Eleanor was to play, Claude was to dance with Lily, and Frank with Jane, and he himself wanted Phyllis for a partner.

'Oh!' sighed Ada, 'I wish I was there to dance with you, Redgie! What are the others doing?'

'Maurice is reading, and William went out as soon as dinner was over; make haste, Phyl.'

'Don't go,' said Ada, 'I shall be alone all to-morrow, and I want you.'

'Nonsense,' said Reginald, 'do you think she is to sit poking here all day, playing with those foolish London things of yours?'

'But I am ill, Redgie. I wish you would not be cross. Everybody is cross to me now, I think.'

'I will stay, Ada,' said Phyllis. 'You know, Redgie, I dance like a cow.'

'You dance better than nothing,' said Reginald, 'I must have you.'

'But you are not ill, Redgie,' said Phyllis.

He went down in displeasure, and was forced to consider Sir Maurice's picture as his partner, until presently the door opened, and Phyllis appeared. 'So you have thought better of it,' cried he.

'No,' said Phyllis, 'I cannot come to dance, but Ada wants you to leave off playing. She says the music makes her unhappy, for it makes her think about to-morrow.'

'Rather selfish, Miss Ada,' said Claude.

'Stay here, Phyllis, now you are come,' said Mr. Mohun, 'I will go and speak to Ada.'

Phyllis was now captured, and made to take her place opposite to Reginald; but more than once she sighed under the apprehension that Ada was receiving a lecture. This was the case; and very little did poor Ada comprehend the change that had taken place in the conduct of almost every one towards her; she did not perceive that she was particularly naughty, and yet she had suddenly become an object of blame, instead of a spoiled pet. Formerly her little slynesses had been unnoticed, and her overbearing ways towards Phyllis scarcely remarked, but now they were continually mentioned as grievous faults. Esther, her especial friend and comforter, was scarcely allowed to come into the same room with her; Hannah treated her with a kind of grave, silent respect, far from the familiarity which she liked; little Henry's nurse never would talk to her, and if it had not been for Phyllis, she would have been very miserable. On Phyllis, however, she repaid herself for all the mortifications that she received, while the sweet-tempered little girl took all her fretfulness and exactions as results of her illness, and went on pitying her, and striving to please her.

When Phyllis came up to wish her good-night, she was received with an exclamation at her lateness in a peevish tone: 'Yes, I am late,' said Phyllis, merrily, 'but we had not done dancing till tea-time, and then Eleanor was so kind as to say I might sit up to have some tea with them.'

'Ah! and you quite forgot how tiresome it is up here, with nobody to speak to,' said Ada. 'How cross they were not to stop the music when I said it made me miserable!'

'Claude said it was selfish to want to stop five people's pleasure for one,' said Phyllis.

'But I am so ill,' said Ada. 'If Claude was as uncomfortable as I am, he would know how to be sorry for me. And only think—Phyl, what are you doing? Do not you know I do not like the moonlight to come on me. It is like a great face laughing at me.'

'Well, I like the moon so much!' said Phyllis, creeping behind the curtain to look out, 'there is something so white and bright in it; when it comes on the bed-clothes, it makes me go to sleep, thinking about white robes, oh! and all sorts of nice things.'

'I can't bear the moon,' said Ada; 'do not you know, Maurice says that the moon makes the people go mad, and that is the reason it is called lunacy, after *la lune*?'

'I asked Miss Weston about that,' said Phyllis, 'because of the Psalm, and she said it was because it was dangerous to go to sleep in the open air in hot countries. Ada, I wish you could see now. There is the great round moon in the middle of the sky, and the sky such a beautiful colour, and a few such great bright stars, and the trees so dark, and the white lilies standing up on the black pond, and the lawn all white with dew! what a fine day it will be to-morrow!'

'A fine day for you!' said Ada, 'but only think of poor me all alone by myself.'

'You will have baby,' said Phyllis.

'Baby—if he could talk it would be all very well. It is just like the cross people in books. Here I shall lie and cry all the time, while you are dancing about as merry as can be.'

'No, no, Ada, you will not do that,' said Phyllis, with tears in her eyes. 'There is baby with all his pretty ways, and you may teach him to say Aunt Ada, and I will bring you in numbers of flowers, and there is your new doll, and all the pretty things that came from London, and the new book of Fairy Tales, and all sorts—oh! no, do not cry, Ada.'

'But I shall, for I shall think of you dancing, and not caring for me.'

'I do care, Ada—why do you say that I do not? I cannot bear it, Ada, dear Ada.'

'You don't, or you would not go and leave me alone.'

'Then, Ada, I will not go,' said Phyllis; 'I could not bear to leave you crying here all alone.'

'Thank you, dear good Phyl, but I think you will not have much loss. You know you do not like dancing, and you cannot do it well, and they will be sure to laugh at you.'

'And I daresay Redgie and Marianne will tell us all about it,' said Phyllis, sighing. 'I should rather like to have seen it, but they will tell us.'

'Then do you promise to stay?—there's a dear,' said Ada.

'Yes,' said Phyllis. 'Cousin Robert is coming in, and that will be very nice, and I hope he will not look as he did the day the gunpowder went off—oh, dear!' She went back to the window to get rid of her tears unperceived. 'Ah,' cried she, 'there is some one in the garden!'

'A man!' screamed Ada—'a thief, a robber—call somebody!'

'No, no,' said Phyllis, laughing, 'it is only William; he has been out all the evening, and now papa has come out to speak to him, and they are walking up and down together. I wonder whether he has been sitting with Cousin Robert or at Broomhill! Well, good-night, Ada. Here comes Hannah.'

CHAPTER XXV
THE THIRTIETH OF JULY

'The heir, with roses in his shoes,
That night might village partner choose.'

The 30th of July was bright and clear, and Phyllis was up early, gathering flowers, which, with the help of Jane's nimble fingers, she made into elegant little bouquets for each of her sisters, and for Claude.

'How is this?' said Mr. Hawkesworth, pretending to look disconsolate, 'am I to sing "Fair Phyllida flouts me," or why is my button-hole left destitute?'

'Perhaps that is for you on the side-table,' said Lily.

'Oh! no,' said Phyllis, 'those are some Provence roses for Miss Weston and Marianne, because Miss Weston likes those, and they have none at Broomhill. Redgie is going to take care of them. I will get you a nosegay, Frank. I did not know you liked it.'

She started up. 'How prudent, Phyllis,' said Eleanor, 'not to have put on your muslin frock yet.'

'Oh! I am not going,' said Phyllis.

'Not going!' was the general outcry.

'No, poor Ada cries so about being left at home with only baby, that I cannot bear it, and so I promised to stay.'

Away went Phyllis, and Reginald exclaimed, 'Well, she shall not be served so. I will go and tell Ada so this instant.'

Off he rushed, and putting in his head at the nursery door, shouted, 'Ada, I am come to tell you that Phyl is not to be made your black-a-moor slave! She shall go, that is settled.'

Down he went with equal speed, without waiting for an answer, and arrived while Eleanor was saying that she thought Ada was provided with amusement with the baby, her playthings, and books, and that Mr. Devereux had promised to make her a visit.

'Anybody ought to stay at home rather than Phyllis,' said Lily; 'I think I had better stay.'

'No, no, Lily,' said Jane, 'you are more wanted than I am; you are really worth talking to and dancing with; I had much better be at home.'

'I forgot!' exclaimed William. 'Mrs. Weston desired me to say that she is not going, and she will take care of Ada. Mr. Weston will set her down at half-past ten, and take up one of us.'

'I will be that one,' said Reginald, 'I have not seen Miss Weston since I came home. I meant to walk to Broomhill after dinner yesterday, only the Baron stopped me about that country-dance. Last Christmas I made her promise to dance with me to-day.'

Lily had hoped to be that one, but she did not oppose Reginald, and turned to listen to Eleanor, who was saying, 'Let us clearly understand how every one is to go, it will save a great deal of confusion. You and Jane, and Maurice, go in the phaeton, do not you? And who drives you?'

'William, I believe,' said Lily. 'Claude goes earlier, so he rides the gray. Then there is the chariot for you and Frank, and papa and Phyllis.'

So it was proposed, but matters turned out otherwise. The phaeton, which, with a promoted cart-horse, was rather a slow conveyance, was to set out first, but the whole of the freight was not ready in time. The ladies were in the hall as soon as it came to the door, but neither of the gentlemen were forthcoming. Reginald, who was wandering in the hall, was sent to summon them; but down he came in great wrath. Maurice had declared that he was not ready, and they must wait for him till he had tied his neckcloth, which Reginald opined would take three quarters of an hour, as he was doing it scientifically, and William had said that he was not going in the gig at all, that he had told Wat Greenwood to drive, and that Reginald must go instead of Maurice.

In confirmation of the startling fact Wat, who had had a special invitation from the Marquis, was sitting in the phaeton in his best black velvet coat. Jane only hoped that Emily would not look out of the window, or she would certainly go into fits on seeing them arrive with the old phaeton, the thick-legged cart-horse, and Wat Greenwood for a driver; and Reginald, after much growling at Maurice, much bawling at William's door, and, as Jane said, romping and roaring in all parts of the house, was forced to be resigned to his fate, and all the way to Hetherington held a very amusing conversation with his good-natured friend the keeper.

They were overtaken, nodded to, and passed by the rest of their party. Maurice had been reduced to ride the pony, William came with the Westons, and the chariot load was just as had been before arranged.

Claude came out to meet them at the door, saying, 'I need not have gone so early. What do you think has become of the hero of the day? Guess, I will just give you this hint,

"Though on pleasure he was bent, he had no selfish mind."'

'Oh! the Aylmers, I suppose,' said Lilias.

'Right, Lily, he heard something at dinner yesterday about a school for clergymen's sons, which struck him as likely to suit young Devereux Aylmer, and off he set at seven o'clock this morning to Raynham, to breakfast with Mrs. Aylmer, and talk to her about it. Never let me hear again that he is engrossed with his own affairs!'

'And why is he in such a hurry?' asked Lily.

''Tis his nature,' said Claude, 'besides Travers, who mentioned this school, goes away to-morrow. My aunt is in a fine fright lest he should not come back in time. Did not you hear her telling papa so in the drawing-room?'

'There he is, riding up to the door,' said Phyllis, who had joined them in the hall. Lord Rotherwood stopped for a few moments at the door to give some directions to the servants, and then came quickly in. 'Ah, there you are!—What time is it? It is all right, Claude—Devereux is just the right age. I asked him a few questions this morning, and he will stand a capital examination. Ha, Phyl, I am glad to see you.'

'I wish you many happy returns of the day, Cousin Rotherwood.'

'Thank you, Phyl, we had better see how we get through one such day before we wish it to return. Are the rest come?'

He went on into the drawing-room, and hastily informing his mother that he had sent the carriage to fetch Miss Aylmer and her brothers to the feast, called Claude to come out on the lawn to look at the preparations. The bowling-green was to serve as drawing-room, and at one end was pitched an immense tent where the dinner was to be.

'I say, Claude,' said he in his quickest and most confused way, 'I depend upon you for one thing. Do not let the Baron be too near me.'

'The Baron of Beef?' said Claude.

'No, the Baron of Beechcroft. If you wish my speech to be *radara tadara*, put him where I can imagine that he hears me.'

'Very well,' said Claude, laughing; 'have you any other commands?'

'No—yes, I have though. You know what we settled about the toasts. Hunt up old Farmer Elderfield as soon as he comes, and do not frighten him. If you could sit next to him and make him get up at the right time, it would be best. Tell him I will not let any one propose my health but my great-grandfather's tenant. You will manage it best. And tell Frank Hawkesworth, and Mr. Weston, or some of them, to manage so that the gentry may not sit together in a herd, two or three together would be best. Mind, Claude, I depend on you for being attentive to all the damsels. I cannot be everywhere at once, and I see your great Captain will be of no use to me.'

Here news was brought that the labourers had begun to arrive, and the party went to the walnut avenue, where the feast was spread. It was pleasant to see so many poor families enjoying their excellent dinner; but perhaps the pleasantest sight was the lord of the feast speaking to each poor man with all his bright good-natured cordiality. Mr. Mohun was surprised to see how well he knew them all, considering how short a time he had been among them, and Lilias found Florence rise in her estimation, when she perceived that the inside of the Hetherington cottages were not unknown to her.

'Do you know, Florence,' said she, as they walked back to the house together, 'I did you great injustice? I never expected you to know or care about poor people.'

'No more I did till this winter,' said Florence; 'I could not do anything, you know, before. Indeed, I do not do much now, only Rotherwood has made me go into the school now and then; and when first we came, he made it his especial request that whenever a poor woman came to ask for anything I would go and speak to her. And so I could not help being interested about those I knew.'

'How odd it is that we never talked about it,' said Lily.

'I never talk of it,' said Florence, 'because mamma never likes to hear of my going into cottages with Rotherwood. Besides, somehow I thought you did it as a matter of duty, and not of pleasure. Oh! Rotherwood, is that you?'

'The Aylmers are come,' said Lord Rotherwood, drawing her arm into his, 'and I want you to come and speak to them, Florence and Lily; I can't find any one; all the great elders have vanished. You know them of old, do not you, Lily?'

'Of old? Yes; but of so old that I do not suppose they will know me. You must introduce me.'

He hastened them to the drawing-room, where they found Miss Aylmer, a sensible, lady-like looking person, and two brothers, of about fifteen and thirteen.

'Well, Miss Aylmer, I have brought you two old friends; so old, that they think you have forgotten them—my cousin Lilias, and my sister Florence.'

'We have not forgotten you, Miss Aylmer,' said Florence, warmly shaking hands with her. 'You seem so entirely to belong to Hetherington that I scarcely knew the place without you.'

There was something that particularly pleased Lily in the manner in which Miss Aylmer answered. Florence talked a little while, and then proposed to adjourn to the supplementary drawing-room—the lawn—where the company were already assembling.

Florence was soon called off to receive some other guest, and Lilias spent a considerable time in sitting under a tree talking to Miss Aylmer, whom she found exceedingly pleasant and agreeable, remembering all that had happened during their former intercourse, and interested in everything that was going on. Lily was much amused when her companion asked her who that gentleman was—'that tall, thin young man, with dark hair, whom she had seen once or twice speaking to Lord Rotherwood?'

The tall gentleman advanced, spoke to Miss Aylmer, told Lily that the world was verging towards the tent, and giving one arm to her and the other to Miss Aylmer, took that direction. In the meantime Phyllis had been walking about with her eldest sister, and wondering what had become of all the others. In process of time she found herself seated on a high bench in the tent, with a most beautiful pink-and-white sugar temple on the table before her. She was between Eleanor and Frank. All along one side of the table was a row of faces which she had never seen before, and she gazed at them in search of some well-known countenance. At last Mr. Weston caught her eye, and nodded to her. Next to him she saw Marianne, then Reginald; on the other side Alethea and William. A little tranquillised by seeing that every one was not lost, she had courage to eat some cold chicken, to talk to Frank about the sugar temple, and to make an inventory in her mind of the smartest bonnets for Ada's benefit. She was rather unhappy at not having found out when grace was said before dinner, and she made Eleanor promise to tell her in time to stand up after dinner. She could not, however, hear much, though warned in time, and by this time more at ease and rather enjoying herself than otherwise. Now Eleanor told her to listen, for Cousin Rotherwood was going to speak. She listened, but knew not what was said, until Mr. Hawkesworth told her it was Church and Queen. What Church and Queen had to do with Cousin Rotherwood's birthday she could not imagine, and she laid it up in her mind to ask Claude. The next time she was told to listen she managed to hear more. By the help of Eleanor's directions, she found out the speaker, an aged farmer, in a drab greatcoat, his head bald, excepting a little silky white hair, which fell over the collar of his coat. It was Mr. Elderfield, the oldest tenant on the estate, and he was saying in a slow deliberate tone that he was told he was to propose his lordship's health. It was a great honour for the like of him, and his lordship must excuse him if he did not make a fine speech. All he could say was, that he had lived eighty-three years on the estate, and held his farm nearly sixty years; he had seen three marquises of Rotherwood besides his present lordship, and he had always found them very good landlords. He hoped and believed his lordship was like his fathers, and he was sure he could do no better than tread in their steps. He proposed the health of Lord Rotherwood, and many happy returns of the day to him.

The simplicity and earnestness of the old man's tones were appreciated by all, and the tremendous cheer, which almost terrified Phyllis, was a fit assent to the hearty good wishes of the old farmer.

'Now comes the trial!' whispered Claude to Lilias, after he had vehemently contributed his proportion to the noise. Lilias saw that his colour had risen, as much as if he had to make a speech himself, and he earnestly examined the coronet on his fork, while every other eye was fixed on the Marquis. Eloquence was not to be expected; but, at least, Lord Rotherwood spoke clearly and distinctly.

'My friends,' said he, 'you must not expect much of a speech from me; I can only thank you for your kindness, say how glad I am to see you here, and tell you of my earnest desire that I may not prove myself unworthy to be compared with my forefathers.' Here was a pause. Claude's hand shook, and Lily saw how anxious he was, but in another moment the Marquis went on smoothly. 'Now, I must ask you to drink the health of a gentleman who has done his utmost to compensate for the loss which we sustained nine years ago, and to whom I owe any good intentions which I may bring to the management of this property. I beg leave to propose the health of my uncle, Mr. Mohun, of Beechcroft.'

Claude was much surprised, for his cousin had never given him a hint of his intention. It was a moment of great delight to all the young Mohuns when the cheer rose as loud and hearty as for the young lord himself, and Phyllis smiled, and wondered, when she saw her papa rise to make answer. He said that he could not attempt to answer Lord Rotherwood, as he had not heard what he said, but that he was much gratified by his having thought of him on this occasion, and by the goodwill which all had expressed. This was the last speech that was interesting; Lady Rotherwood's health and a few more toasts followed, and the party then left the tent for the lawn, where the cool air was most refreshing, and the last beams of the evening sun were lighting the tops of the trees.

The dancing was now to begin, and this was the time for Claude to be useful. He had spent so much time at home, and had accompanied his father so often in his rides, that he knew every one, and he was inclined to make every exertion in the cause of his cousin, and on this occasion seemed to have laid aside his indolence and disinclination to speak to strangers.

Lady Florence was also indefatigable, darting about, with a wonderful perception who everybody was, and with whom each would like to dance. She seized upon little Devereux Aylmer for her own partner before any one else had time to ask her, and carried him about the lawn, hunting up and pairing other shy people.

'Why, Reginald, what are you about? You can manage a country-dance. Make haste; where is your partner?'

'I meant to dance with Miss Weston,' said Reginald, piteously.

'Miss Weston? Here she is.'

'That is only Marianne,' said Reginald.

'Oh! Miss Weston is dancing with William. Marianne, will you accept my apologies for this discourteous cousin of mine? I am perfectly horror-struck. There, Redgie, take her with a good grace; you will never have a better partner.'

Marianne was only too glad to have Reginald presented to her, ungracious as he was, but the poor little couple met with numerous disasters. They neither of them knew the way through a country-dance, and were almost run over every time they went down the middle; Reginald's heels were very inconvenient to his neighbours; so much so, that once Claude thought it expedient to admonish him, that dancing was not merely an elegant name for football without a ball. Every now and then some of their friends gave them a hasty intimation that they were all wrong, but that they knew already but too well. At last, just when Marianne had turned scarlet with vexation, and Reginald was growing so desperate that he had thoughts of running a way, the dance came to an end, and Reginald, with very scanty politeness to his partner, rushed away to her sister, saying, in rather a reproachful tone, 'Miss Weston, you promised to dance with me.'

'I have not forgotten my promise,' said Alethea, smiling.

At the same moment Claude hurried up, saying, 'William, I want a partner for Miss Wilkins, of the Wold Farm. Miss Wilkins, let me introduce Captain Mohun.'

'You see I have made the Captain available,' said Claude, presently after meeting Lord Rotherwood, as he speeded across the lawn.

'Have you? I did not think him fair game,' said the Marquis. 'Where is your heroine, Claude? I have not seen her dancing.'

'What heroine? What do you mean?'

'Honest Phyl, of course. Did you think I meant Miss Weston?'

'With Eleanor, somewhere. Is the next dance a quadrille?'

Lord Rotherwood ran up the bank to the terraced walks, where the undancing part of the company sat or walked about. Soon he spied Phyllis standing by Eleanor, looking rather wearied. 'Phyllis, can you dance a quadrille?'

Phyllis opened her eyes, and Eleanor desired her to answer.

'Come, Phyllis, let me see what M. Le Roi has done for you.'

He led her away, wondering greatly, and thinking how very good-natured Cousin Rotherwood was.

Emily was much surprised to find Phyllis her *vis à vis*. Emily was very generally known and liked, and had no lack of grand partners, but she would have liked to dance with the Marquis. When the quadrille was over, she was glad to put herself in his way, by coming up to take charge of Phyllis.

'Well done, Phyl,' said he; 'no mistakes. You must have another dance. Whom shall we find for you?'

'Oh! Rotherwood,' said Emily, 'you cannot think how you gratified us all with your speech.'

'Ah! I always set my heart on saying something of the kind; but I wished I could have dared to add the bride's health.'

'The bride!'

'Do not pretend to have no eyes,' said Lord Rotherwood, with a significant glance, which directed Emily's eyes to the terrace, where Mr. Mohun and Alethea were walking together in eager conversation.

Emily was ready to sink into the earth. Jane's surmises, and the mysterious words of her father, left her no further doubt. At this moment some one asked her to dance, and scarcely knowing what she did or said, she walked to her place. Lord Rotherwood now found a partner for Phyllis, and a farmer's daughter for himself.

This dance over, Phyllis's partner did not well know how to dispose of her, and she grew rather frightened on finding that none of her sisters were in sight. At last she perceived Reginald standing on the bank, and made her escape to him.

'Redgie, did you see who I have been dancing with? Cousin Rotherwood and Claude's grand Oxford friend—Mr. Travers.'

'It is all nonsense,' said Reginald. 'Come out of this mob of people.'

'But where is Eleanor?'

'Somewhere in the midst. They are all absurd together.'

'What is the matter, Redgie?' asked Phyllis, unable to account for this extraordinary fit of misanthropy.

'Papa and William both driving me about like a dog,' said Reginald; 'first I danced with Miss Weston—then she saw that woman—that Miss Aylmer—shook hands—talked—and then nothing would serve her but to find papa. As soon as the Baron sees me he cries out, "Why are not you dancing, Redgie? We do not want you!" Up and down they walk, ever so long, and presently papa turns off, and begins talking to Miss Aylmer. Then, of course, I went back to Miss Weston, but then up comes William, as savage as one of his Canadian bears; he orders me off too, and so here I am! I am sure I am not going to ask any one else to dance. Come and walk with me in peace, Phyl. Do you see them?—Miss Weston and Marianne under that tulip-tree, and the Captain helping them to ice.'

'Redgie, did you give Miss Weston her nosegay? Some one put such beautiful flowers in it, such as I never saw before.'

'How could I? They sent me off with Lily and Jane. I told William I had the flowers in charge, and he said he would take care of them. By the bye, Phyl,' and Reginald gave a wondrous spring, 'I have it! I have it! I have it! If he is not in love with Miss Weston you may call me an ass for the rest of my life.'

'I should not like to call you an ass, Redgie,' said Phyllis.

'Very likely; but do not make me call you one. Hurrah! Now ask Marianne if it is not so. Marianne must know. How jolly! I say, Phyl, stay there, and I will fetch Marianne.'

Away ran Reginald, and presently returned with Marianne, who was very glad to be invited to join Phyllis. She little knew what an examination awaited her.

'Marianne,' began Phyllis, 'I'll tell you what—'

'No, I will do it right,' said Reginald; 'you know nothing about it, Phyl. Marianne, is not something going on there?'

'Going on?' said Marianne, 'Alethea is speaking to Mrs. Hawkesworth.'

'Nonsense, I know better, Marianne. I have a suspicion that I could tell what the Captain was about yesterday when he walked off after dinner.'

'How very wise you think you look, Reginald!' said Marianne, laughing heartily.

'But tell us; do tell us, Marianne,' said Phyllis.

'Tell you whet?'

'Whether William is going to marry Miss Weston,' said the straightforward Phyllis. 'Redgie says so—only tell us. Oh! it would be so nice!'

'How you blurt it out, Phyl,' said Reginald. 'You do not know how those things are managed. Mind, I found it out all myself. Just say, Marianne. Am not I right?'

'I do not know whether I ought to tell,' said Marianne.

'Oh! then it is all right,' said Reginald, 'and I found it out. Now, Marianne, there is a good girl, tell us all about it.'

'You know I could not say "No" when you asked me,' said Marianne; 'I could not help it really; but pray do not tell anybody, or Captain Mohun will not like it.'

'Does any one know?' said Reginald.

'Only ourselves and Mr. Mohun; and I think Lord Rotherwood guesses, from something I heard him say to Jane.'

'To Jane?' said Reginald. 'That is provoking; she will think she found it out all herself, and be so conceited!'

'You need not be afraid,' said Marianne, laughing; 'Jane is on a wrong scent.'

'Jane? Oh! I should like to see her out in her reckonings! I should like to have a laugh against her. What does she think, Marianne?'

'Oh! I cannot tell you; it is too bad.'

'Oh! do; do, pray. You may whisper it if it is too bad for Phyllis to hear.'

'No, no,' said Marianne; 'it is nothing but nonsense. If you hear it, Phyllis shall too; but mind, you must promise not to say anything to anybody, or I do not know what will become of me.'

'Well, we will not,' said Reginald; 'boys can always keep secrets, and I'll engage for Phyl. Now for it.'

'She is in a terrible fright lest it should be Mr. Mohun. She got it into her head last autumn, and all I could say would not persuade her out of it. Why, she always calls me Aunt Marianne when we are alone. Now, Reginald, here comes Maurice. Do not say anything, I beg and entreat. It is my secret, you know. I daresay you will all be told to-morrow,—indeed, mamma said so,—but pray say nothing about me or Jane. It was only settled yesterday evening.'

At this moment Maurice came up, with a message that Miss Weston and Eleanor were going away, and wanted the little girls. They followed him to the tent, which had been cleared of the tables, and lighted up, in order that the dancing might continue there. Most of their own party were collected at the entrance, watching for them. Lilias came up just as they did, and exclaimed in a tone of disappointment, on finding them preparing to depart. She had enjoyed herself exceedingly, found plenty of partners, and was not in the least tired.

'Why should she not stay?' said William. 'Claude has engaged to stay to the end of everything, and he may as well drive her as ride the gray.'

'And you, Jenny,' said Mr. Mohun, 'do you like to stay or go? Alethea will make room for you in the pony-carriage, or you may go with Eleanor.

'With Eleanor, if you please,' said Jane.

'Already, Jane?' said Lily. 'Are you tired?'

Jane drew her aside. 'Tired of hearing that I was right about what you would not believe. Did you not hear what he called her? And Rotherwood has found it out.'

'It is all gossip and mistake,' said Lily.

Here Jane was called away by Eleanor, and departed with her; Lilias went to look for her aunt or Florence, but on the way was asked to dance by Mr. Carrington.

'I suppose I may congratulate you,' said he in one of the pauses in the quadrille.

Lily thought it best to misunderstand, and answered, 'Everything has gone off very well.'

'Very. Lord Rotherwood will be a popular man; but my congratulations refer to something nearer home. I think you owe us some thanks for having brought them into the neighbourhood.'

'Report is very kind in making arrangements,' said Lily, with something of Emily's haughty courtesy.

'I hope this is something more than report,' said her partner.

'Indeed, I believe not. I think I may safely say that it is at present quite unfounded,' said Lily.

Mr. Carrington, much surprised, said no more.

Lily did not believe the report sufficiently to be annoyed by it during the excitement and pleasure of the evening, and at present her principal vexation was caused by the rapid diminution of the company. She and her brother were the very last to depart, even Florence had gone to bed, and Lady Rotherwood, looking exceedingly tired, kissed Lily at the foot of the stairs, pitied her for going home in an open carriage, and wished her good-night in a very weary tone.

'I should think you were the fiftieth lady I have handed across the hall,' said Lord Rotherwood, as he gave Lily his arm.

'But where were the fireworks, Rotherwood?'

'Countermanded long ago. We have had enough of them. Well, I am sorry it is over.'

'I am very glad it is so well over,' said Claude.

'Thanks to your exertions, Claude,' said the Marquis. 'You acted like a hero.'

'Like a dancing dervish you mean,' said Claude. 'It will suffice for my whole life.'

'I hope you are not quite exhausted.'

'No, thank you. I have turned over a new leaf.'

'Talking of new leaves,' said the Marquis, 'I always had a presentiment that Emily's government would come to a crisis to-day.'

'Do you think it has?' said Claude.

'Trust my word, you will hear great news to-morrow. And that reminds me—can you come here to-morrow morning? Travers is going—I drive him to meet the coach at the town, and you were talking of wanting to see the new windows in the cathedral: it will be a good opportunity. And dine here afterwards to talk over the adventures.'

'Thank you—that last I cannot do. The Baron was saying it would be the first time of having us all together.'

'Very well, besides the great news. I wish I was going back with you; it is a tame conclusion, only to go to bed. If I was but to be on the scene of action to-morrow. Tell the Baron that—no, use your influence to get me invited to dinner on Saturday—I really want to speak to him.'

'Very well,' said Claude, 'I'll do my best. Good-night.'

'Good-night,' said the Marquis. 'You have both done wonders. Still, I wish it was to come over again.'

'Few people would say so,' said Lily, as they drove off.

'Few would say so if they thought so,' said Claude. 'I have been quite admiring the way Rotherwood has gone on—enjoying the fun as if he was nobody—just as Reginald might, making other people happy, and making no secret of his satisfaction in it all.'

'Very free from affectation and nonsense,' said Lily, 'as William said of him last Christmas. You were in a fine fright about his speech, Claude.'

'More than I ought to have been. I should have known that he is too simple-minded and straightforward to say anything but just what he ought. What a nice person that Miss Aylmer is.'

'Is not she, Claude? I was very glad you had her for a neighbour. Happy the children who have her for a governess. How sensible and gentle she seems. The Westons—But oh! Claude, tell me one thing, did you hear—'

'Well, what?'

'I am ashamed to say. That preposterous report about papa. Why, Rotherwood himself seems to believe it, and Mr. Carrington began to congratulate—'

'The public has bestowed so many ladies on the Baron, that I wonder it is not tired,' said Claude. 'It is time it should patronise William instead.'

'Rotherwood is not the public,' said Lily, 'and he is the last person to say anything impertinent of papa. And I myself heard papa call her Alethea, which he never used to do. Claude, what do you think?'

After a long pause Claude slowly replied, 'Think? Why, I think Miss Weston must be a person of great courage. She begins the world as a grandmother, to say nothing of her eldest daughter and son being considerably her seniors.'

'I do not believe it,' said Lily. 'Do you, Claude?'

'I cannot make up my mind—it is too amazing. My hair is still standing on end. When it comes down I may be able to tell you something.'

Such were the only answers that Lily could extract from him. He did not sufficiently disbelieve the report to treat it with scorn, yet he did not sufficiently credit it to resign himself to such a state of things.

On coming home Lily found Emily and Jane in her room, eagerly discussing the circumstances which, to their prejudiced eyes, seemed strong confirmation. While their tongues were in full career the door opened and Eleanor appeared. She told them it was twelve o'clock, turned Jane out of the room, and made Emily and Lily promise not to utter another syllable that night.

CHAPTER XXVI
THE CRISIS

'"Is this your care of the nest?" cried he,
"It comes of your gadding abroad," said she.'

To the consternation of the disconsolate damsels, the first news they heard the next morning was that Mr. Mohun was gone to breakfast at Broomhill, and the intelligence was received by Frank Hawkesworth with a smile which they thought perfectly malicious. Frank, William, and Reginald talked a little at breakfast about the *fête*, but no one joined them, and Claude looked so grave that Eleanor was convinced that he had a headache, and vainly tried to persuade him to stay at home, instead of setting off to Devereux Castle immediately after breakfast.

The past day had not been spent in vain by Ada. Mrs. Weston had led her by degrees to open her heart to her, had made her perceive the real cause of her father's displeasure, see her faults, and promise to confess them, a promise which she performed with many tears, as soon as she saw Eleanor in the morning.

On telling this to Emily Eleanor was surprised to find that she was not listened to with much satisfaction. Emily seemed to think it a piece of interference on the part of Mrs. Weston, and would not allow that it was likely to be the beginning of improvement in Ada.

'The words were put into her mouth,' said she; 'and they were an easy way of escaping from her present state of disgrace.'

'On the contrary,' said Eleanor, 'she seemed to think that she justly deserved to be in disgrace.'

'Did you think so?' said Emily, in a careless tone.

'You are in a strange mood to-day, Emily,' said Eleanor.

'Am I? I did not know it. I wonder where Lily is.'

Lily was in her own room, teaching Phyllis. Phyllis was rather wild and flighty that morning, scarcely able to command her attention, and every now and then bursting into an irrepressible fit of laughter. Reginald and Phyllis found it most difficult to avoid betraying Marianne, and as soon as luncheon was over, they agreed to set out on a long expedition into the woods, where they might enjoy their wonderful secret together. Just at this time Mr. Mohun returned. He came into the drawing-room, and Lilias, perceiving that the threatened conversation with Emily was about to take place, made her escape to her own room, whither she was presently followed by Jane, who could not help running after her to report the great news that Emily was to be deposed.

'I am sure of it,' said she. 'They sent me out of the room, but not before I had seen certain symptoms.'

'It is very hard that poor Emily should bear all the blame,' said Lily.

'You have managed to escape it very well,' said Jane, laughing. 'You have all the thanks and praise. I suppose it is because the intimacy with Miss Weston was your work.'

'I will not believe that nonsense,' said Lily.

'Seeing is believing, they say,' said Jane. 'Remember, it is not only me. Think of Rotherwood. And Maurice guesses it too, and Redgie told him great things were going on.'

While Jane was speaking they heard the drawing-room door open, and in another moment Emily came in.

It was true that, as Jane said, she had been deposed. Mr. Mohun had begun by saying, 'Emily, can you bring me such an account of your expenditure as I desired?'

'I scarcely think I can, papa,' said Emily. 'I am sorry to say that my accounts are rather in confusion.'

'That is to say, that you have been as irregular in the management of your own affairs as you have in mine. Well, I have paid your debt to Lilias, and from this time forward I require of you to reduce your expenses to the sum which I consider suitable, and which both Eleanor and Lilias have found perfectly sufficient. And now, Emily, what have you to say for the management of my affairs? Can you offer any excuse for your utter failure?'

'Indeed, papa, I am very sorry I vexed you,' said Emily. 'Our illness last autumn—different things—I know all has not been quite as it should be; but I hope that in future I shall profit by past experience.'

'I hope so,' said Mr. Mohun, 'but I am afraid to trust the management of the family to you any longer. Your trial is over, and you have failed, merely because you would not exert yourself from wilful indolence and negligence. You have not attended to any one thing committed to your charge—you have placed temptation in Esther's way—and allowed Ada to take up habits which will not be easily corrected. I should not think myself justified in leaving you in charge any longer, lest worse mischief should ensue. I wish you to give up the keys to Eleanor for the present.'

Mr. Mohun would perhaps have added something if Emily had shown signs of repentance, or even of sorrow. The moment was at least as painful to him as to her, and he had prepared himself to expect either hysterical tears, with vows of amendment, or else an argument on her side that she was right and everybody else wrong. But there was nothing of the kind; Emily neither spoke nor looked; she only carried the tokens of her authority to Eleanor, and left the room. She thought she knew well enough the cause of her deposition, considered it quite as a matter of course, and departed on purpose to avoid hearing the announcement which she expected to follow.

She was annoyed by finding her sisters in her room, and especially irritated by Jane's tone, as she eagerly asked, 'Well, what did he say?'

'Never mind,' replied Emily, pettishly.

'Was it about Miss Weston?' persisted Jane.

'Not actually, but I saw it was coming,' said Emily.

'Ah!' said Jane, 'I was just telling Lily that she owes all her present favour to her having been Alethea's bosom friend.'

'I confess I thought Miss Weston was assuming authority long ago,' said Emily.

'Emily, how can you say so?' cried Lily. 'How can you be so unjust and ungrateful? I do not believe this report; but if it should be true, are not these foolish expressions of dislike so many attempts to make yourself undutiful?'

'I have rather more sincerity, more dignity, more attachment to my own mother, than to try to gain favour by affecting what I do not feel,' said Emily.

'Rather cutting, Emily,' said Jane.

'Do not give that speech an application which Emily did not intend,' said Lily, sadly.

'What makes you think I did not intend it?' said Emily, coldly.

'Emily!' exclaimed Lily, starting up, and colouring violently, 'are you thinking what you are saying?'

'I do not know what you mean,' replied Emily quietly, in her soft, unchanging voice; 'I only mean that if you can feel satisfied with the new arrangement you are more easily pleased than I am.'

'Only tell me, Emily, do you accuse me of attempting to gain favour in an unworthy manner?'

'I only congratulate you on standing so well with every one.'

Lily hid her face in her hands. At this moment Eleanor opened the door, saying, 'Can you come down? Mrs. Burnet is here.' Eleanor went without observing Lily, and Emily was obliged to follow. Jane lingered in order to comfort Lily.

'You know she did not quite mean it,' said she; 'she is only very much provoked.'

'I know, I know,' said Lily; 'she is very sorry herself by this time. Of course she did not mean it, but it is the first unkind thing she ever said to me. It is very silly, and very unjust to take it seriously, but I cannot help it.'

'It is a very abominable shame,' said Jane, 'and so I shall tell Emily.'

'No, do not, Jenny, I beg. I know she thinks so herself, and grieves too much over it. No wonder she is vexed. All my faults have come upon her. You had better go down, Jane; Mrs. Burnet is always vexed if she does not see a good many of us, and I am sure I cannot go. Besides, Emily dislikes having that girl to entertain.'

'Lily, you are so very gentle and forgiving, that I wonder how any one can say what grieves you,' said Jane, for once struck with admiration.

She went, and Lily remained, weeping over the injustice which she had forgiven, and feeling as if, all the time, it was fair that the rule of 'love' should, as it were, recoil upon her. Her tears flowed fast, as she went over the long line of faults and follies which lay heavy on her conscience. And Emily against her! That sister who, from her infancy, had soothed her in every trouble, of whose sympathy she had always felt sure, whose gentleness had been her admiration in her days of sharp answers and violent temper, who had seemed her own beyond all the others; this wound from her gave Lily a bitter feeling of desertion and loneliness. It was like a completion of her punishment—the broken reed on which she leant had pierced her deeply.

She was still sitting on the side of her bed, weeping, when a slight tap at the door made her start—a gentle tap, the sound of which she had learned to love in her illness. The next moment Alethea stood before her, with outstretched arms. This was a time to feel the value of such a friend, and every suspicion passing from her mind, she flew to Alethea, kissed her again and again, and laid her head on her shoulder. Her caress was returned with equal warmth.

'But how is this?' said Alethea, now perceiving that her face was pale, and marked by tears. 'How is this, my dear Lily?'

'Oh, Alethea! I cannot tell you, but it is all misery. The full effect of my baneful principle has appeared!'

'Has anything happened?' exclaimed Alethea.

'No,' said Lily. 'There is nothing new, except the—Oh! I cannot tell you.'

'I wish I could do anything for you, my poor Lily,' said Alethea.

'You can look kind,' said Lily, 'and that is a great comfort. Oh! Alethea, it was very kind of you to come and speak to me. I shall do now—I can bear it all better. You have a comforting face and voice like nobody else. When did you come? Have you been in the drawing-room?'

'No,' said Alethea. 'I walked here with Marianne, and finding there were visitors in the drawing-room we went to Ada, and she told me where to find you. I had something to tell you—but perhaps you know already.'

The colour on her cheek recalled all Lily's fears, and to hear the news from herself was an unexpected trial. She felt as if what she had said justified Emily's reproach, and turning away her head, replied, 'Yes, I know.'

Alethea was a little hurt by her coldness, but she ascribed it to dejection and embarrassment, and blamed herself for hurrying on what she had to tell without sufficient regard for Lily's distress. There was an awkward pause, which Alethea broke, by saying, 'Your brother thought you would like to hear it from me.'

'My brother!' cried Lily, with a most sudden change of tone. 'William? Oh, Alethea! dearest Alethea; I beg your pardon. They almost made me believe it was papa. Oh! I am so very glad!'

Alethea could not help laughing, and Lily joined her heartily. It was one of the brightest hours of her life, as she sat with her hand in her friend's, pouring out her eager expressions of delight and affection. All her troubles were forgotten—how should they not, when Alethea was to be her sister! It seemed as if but a few minutes had passed, when the sound of the great clock warned Alethea that it was time to return to Broomhill, and she asked Lilias to walk back with her. After summoning Marianne, they set out through the garden, where, on being joined by William, Lily thought it expedient to betake herself to Marianne, who was but too glad to be able freely to communicate many interesting particulars. At Broomhill she had a very enjoyable talk with Mrs. Weston, but her chief delight was in her walk home with her brother. She was high in his favour, as Alethea's chief friend. Though usually reserved, he was now open, and Lily wondered to find herself honoured with confidence. His attachment had begun in very early days, when first he knew the Westons in Brighton. Harry's death had suddenly called him away, and a few guarded expressions of his wishes in the course of the next winter had been cut short by his father. He then went to Canada, and had had no opportunity of renewing his acquaintance till the last winter, when, on coming home, to his great joy and surprise he found the Westons on the most intimate terms with his family.

He then spoke to his father, who wished him to take a little more time for consideration, and he had accordingly waited till the summer. Lily longed to know his plans for the future, and presently he went on to say that his father wished him to leave the army, live at home, and let Alethea be the head of the household.

'Oh, William! it is perfect. There is an end of all our troubles. It is as if a great black curtain was drawn up.'

'They say such plans never succeed,' said William; 'but we mean to prove the contrary.'

'How good it will be for the children!' said Lily.

'Oh! why had we not such a guide at first?'

'She has all that Eleanor wants,' said William.

'My follies were not Eleanor's fault,' said Lily; 'but I do think I should not have been quite so silly if I had known Alethea from the first.'

It was not in the power of William himself to say more in her praise than Lily. In the eagerness of their conversation they walked slowly, and as they were crossing the last field the dinner-bell rang. As they quickened their steps they saw Mr. Mohun looking at his wheat. Lily told him how late it was.

'There,' said he, 'I am always looking after other people's affairs. Between Rotherwood and William I have not a moment for my own crops. However, my turn is coming. William will have it all on his hands, and the old deaf useless Baron will sit in his great chair and take his ease.'

'Not a bit, papa,' said Lily, 'the Baron will grow young, and take to dancing. He is talking nonsense already.'

'Eh! Miss Lily turned saucy? Mrs. William Mohun must take her in hand. Well, Lily, has he your consent and approbation?'

'I only wish this was eighteen months ago, papa.'

'We shall soon come into order, Lily. With Miss Aylmer for the little ones, and Mrs. Mohun for the great ones, I have little fear.'

'Miss Aylmer, papa!'

'Yes, if all turns out well. We propose to find a house for her mother in the village, and let her come every day to teach the little ones.'

'Oh! I am very glad. We liked her so much.'

'I hope,' said Mr. Mohun, 'that this plan will please Claude better than my proposal of a governess last month. He looked as if he expected Minerva with helmet, and Ægis and all. Now make haste and dress. Do not let us shock Eleanor by keeping dinner waiting longer than we can help.'

Lilias found that her sisters had long been dressed and gone down. She dressed alone, every now and then smiling at her own happy looks reflected in the glass. Just as she had finished, Claude knocked at the door, and putting in his head, said, 'Well, Lily, has the wonderful news come forth? I see it has, by your face.'

'And do you know what it is, Claude?' said Lily.

'I know what Rotherwood meant, and I cannot think where all our senses were.'

'And, Claude, only say that you like her.'

'I think it is a very good thing indeed.'

'Only say that you cordially like her.'

'I do. I admire her sense and her gentleness very much, and I think you owe a great deal to her.'

'Then you allow that you were unjust last summer?'

'I do; but it was owing to you. You were somewhat foolish, and I thought it was her fault. Besides, I was quite tired of hearing that extraordinary name of hers for ever repeated.'

Here they were summoned to dinner, and hurried down. The dinner passed very strangely; some were in very high spirits, others in a very melancholy mood; Eleanor and Maurice alone preserved the golden mean; and the behaviour of the merry ones was perfectly unintelligible to the rest. Reginald, still bound by his promise to Marianne, was wild to make his discovery known, and behaved in such a strange and comical manner as to call forth various reproofs from Eleanor, which provoked double mirth from the others. The cause of their amusement was ostensibly the talking over of yesterday's *fête*, but the laughing was more than adequate, even to the wonderful collection of odd speeches and adventures which were detailed. Emily and Jane could not guess what had come to Lily, and thought her merriment very ill-placed. Yet, in justice to Lily, it must be said that her joy no longer made her wild and thoughtless. There was something guarded and subdued about her, which made Claude reflect how different she was from the untamed girl of last summer, who could not be happy without a sort of intoxication.

The ladies returned to the drawing-room, where Ada now appeared for the first time, and while they were congratulating her Mr. Mohun summoned Eleanor away. Jane followed at a safe distance to see where they went. They shut themselves into the study, and Jane, now meeting Maurice, went into the garden with him. 'It must be coming now,' said she; 'oh! there are William and Claude talking under the plane-tree.'

'Claude has his cunning smile on,' said Maurice.

'No wonder,' said Jane, 'it is very absurd. I daresay William will hardly ever come home now. One comfort is, they will see I was right from the first.'

Jane and Maurice remained in the garden till teatime, and thus missed hearing the whole affair discussed in the drawing-room between Emily, Lilias, and Frank. This was the first news that Emily heard of it, and a very great relief it was, for she could imagine liking, and even loving, Alethea as a sister-in-law. Her chief annoyance was at present from the perception of the difference between her own position and that of Lilias. Last year how was Lily regarded in the family, and what was her opinion worth? Almost nothing; she was only a clever, romantic, silly girl, while Emily had credit at least for discretion. Now Lily was consulted and sought out by father, brothers, Eleanor—no longer treated as a child. And what was Emily? Blamed or pitied on every side, and left to hear this important news from the chance mention of her brother-in-law, himself not fully informed. She had become nobody, and had even lost the satisfaction, such as it was, of fancying that her father only made her bad management an excuse for his marriage. She heard many particulars from Lily in the course of the evening, as they were going to bed; and the sisters talked with all their wonted affection, although Emily had not thought it worth while to revive an old grievance, by asking Lily's pardon for her unkind speech, and rested satisfied with the knowledge that her sister knew her heart too well to care for what she said in a moment of irritation. On the other hand, Lily did not think that she had a right to mention the plan of Alethea's government, and the next day she was glad of her reserve, for her father called her to share his early walk for the purpose of talking over the scheme, telling her that he thought she understood the state of things better than Eleanor could, and that he considered that she had sufficient influence with Emily to prevent her from making Alethea uncomfortable. The conclusion of the conversation was, that they thought they might depend upon Emily's amiability, her courtesy, and her dislike of trouble, to balance her love of importance and dignity. And that Alethea would do nothing to hurt her feelings, and would assume no authority that she could help, they felt convinced.

After breakfast Mr. Mohun called Emily into his study, informed her of his resolution, to which she listened with her usual submissive manner, and told her that he trusted to her good sense and right feeling to obviate any collisions of authority which might be unpleasant to Alethea and hurtful to the younger ones. She promised all that was desired, and though at the moment she felt hurt and grieved, she almost immediately recovered her usual spirits, never high, but always serene, and only seeking for easy amusement and comfort in whatever happened. There was no public disgrace in her deposition; it would not seem unnatural to the neighbours that her brother's wife should be at the head of the house. She would gain credit for her amiability, and she would no longer be responsible or obliged to exert herself; and as to Alethea herself, she could not help respecting and almost loving her. It was very well it was no worse.

In the meantime Lily, struck by a sudden thought, had hastened to her mother's little deserted morning-room, to see if it could not be made a delightful abode for Alethea; and she was considering of its capabilities when she started at the sound of an approaching step. It was the rapid and measured tread of the Captain, and in a few moments he entered. 'Thank you,' said he, smiling, 'you are on the same errand as myself.'

'Exactly so,' said Lily; 'it will do capitally; how pretty Long Acre looks, and what a beautiful view of the church!'

'This room used once to be prėtty,' said William, looking round, disappointed; 'it is very forlorn.'

'Ah! but it will look very different when the chairs do not stand with their backs to the wall. I do not think Alethea knows of this room, for nobody has sat in it for years, and we will make it a surprise. And here is your own picture, at ten years old, over the fireplace! I have such a vision, you will not know the room when I have set it to rights.'

They went on talking eagerly of the improvements that might be made, and from thence came to other subjects—Alethea herself, and the future plans. At last William asked if Lily knew what made Jane look as deplorable as she had done for the last two days, and Lily was obliged to tell him, with the addition that Eleanor had begun to inform her of the real fact, but that she had stopped her by declaring that she had known it all from the first. Just as they had mentioned her, Jane, attracted by the unusual sound of voices in Lady Emily's room, came in, asking what they could be doing there. Lily would scarcely have dared to reply, but William said in a grave, matter-of-fact way, 'We are thinking of having this room newly fitted up.'

'For Alethea Weston?' said Jane; 'how can you, Lily? I should have thought, at least, it was no laughing matter.'

'I advise you to follow Lily's example and make the best of it,' said William.

'I do, but it is another thing to stand laughing here. I see one thing that I shall do—I shall take away your picture and hang it in my room.'

'We shall see,' said William, following Lilias, who had left the room to hide her laughter.

To mystify Jane was the great amusement of the day; Reginald, finding Maurice possessed with the same notion, did more to maintain it than the others would have thought right, and Maurice reporting his speeches to Jane, she had not the least doubt that her idea was correct. Lord Rotherwood came to dinner, and no sooner had he entered the drawing-room than Reginald, rejoicing in the absence of the parties concerned, informed him of the joke, much to his diversion, though rather to the discomfiture of the more prudent spectators, who might have wished it confined to themselves.

'It has gone far enough,' said Claude; 'she will say something she will repent if we do not take care.'

'I should like to reduce her to humble herself to ask an explanation from Marianne,' said Lily.

'And pray don't spoil the joke before I have enjoyed it,' said Lord Rotherwood. 'My years of discretion are not such centuries of wisdom as those of that gentleman who looks as grim as his namesake the Emperor on a coin.'

The entrance of Eleanor and Jane here put an end to the conversation, which was not renewed till the evening, when the younger, or as Claude called it, the middle-aged part of the company were sitting on the lawn, leaving the drawing-room to the elder and more prudent, and the terrace to the wilder and more active. Emily was talking of Mrs. Burnet's visit of the day before, and her opinion of the Hetherington festivities. 'And what an interminable visit it was,' said Jane; 'I thought they would never go!'

'People always inflict themselves in a most merciless manner when there is anything going on,' said Emily.

'I wonder if they guessed anything,' said Lily.

'To be sure they did, and stayed out of curiosity,' said Lord Rotherwood. 'In spite of Emily's dignified contradictions of the report, every one knew it the other evening. It was all in vain that she behaved as if I was speaking treason—people have eyes.'

'Ah! I am very sorry for that contradiction,' said Lily; 'I hope people will not fancy we do not like it.'

'No, it will only prove my greatness,' said Lord Rotherwood. 'Your Marques, was China in the map, so absorbing all beholders that the magnanimous Mohuns themselves—'

'What nonsense, Rotherwood,' said Jane, sharply; 'can't you suppose that one may shut one's eyes to what one does not wish to see.'

The singular inappropriateness of this answer occasioned a general roar of laughter, and she looked in perplexity. Every one whom she asked why they laughed replied by saying, 'Ask Marianne Weston;' and at length, after much puzzling and guessing, and being more laughed at than had ever before happened to her in her life, she was obliged to seek an explanation from Marianne, who might well have triumphed had she been so disposed. Jane's character for penetration was entirely destroyed, and the next morning she received, as a present from Claude, an old book, which had long belonged to the nursery, entitled, *A Puzzle for a Curious Girl.*

CHAPTER XXVII
CONCLUSION

'There let Hymen oft appear
In saffron robe, with taper clear,
And pomp, and feast, and revelry,
And mask, and antique pageantry;
Such sights as useful poets dream
On summer eves, by haunted stream.'

On the morning of a fine day, late in September, the Beechcroft bells were ringing merrily, and a wedding procession was entering the gate of the churchyard.

In the afternoon there was a great feast on the top of the hill, attended by all the Mohuns, who were forced, to Lily's great satisfaction, to give it there, as there was no space in the grounds at the New Court. All was wonderfully suitable to old times, inasmuch as the Baron was actually persuaded to sit for five minutes under the yew-tree where 'Mohun's chair' ought to have been, and the cricketers were of all ranks, from the Marquis of Rotherwood to little Dick Grey.

The wedding had been hurried on, and the wedding tour was shortened, in order that Mrs. William Mohun might be installed as mistress of the New Court before Eleanor's departure, which took place early in October; and shortly after Mrs. Ridley, who had come on a visit to Beechcroft, to take leave of her brother, returned to the north, taking with her the little Harry. He was nearly a year old, and it gave great pain to his young aunts to part with him, now that he had endeared himself to them by many engaging ways, but Lily felt herself too unequal to the task of training him up to make any objection, and there were many promises that he should not be a stranger to his grandfather's home.

Mrs. and Miss Aylmer had been about a month settled at a superior sort of cottage, near the New Court, with Mrs. Eden for their servant. Lord Rotherwood had fitted out the second son, who sailed for India with Mr. and Mrs. Hawkesworth, had sent Devereux to school, and was lying in wait to see what could be done for the two others, and Jane was congratulated far more than she wished, on having been the means of discovering such an excellent governess. Jane was now a regular inhabitant of the schoolroom, as much tied down to lessons and schoolroom hours as her two little sisters, with the prospect of so continuing for two years, if not for three. She made one attempt to be pert to Miss Aylmer; but something in the manner of her governess quite baffled her, and she was obliged to be more obedient than she had ever been. The mischief which Emily and Lilias had done to her, by throwing off their allegiance to Eleanor, and thus unconsciously leading her to set her at nought, was, at her age, not to be so easily repaired; yet with no opportunity for gossiping, and with involuntary respect for her governess, there were hopes that she would lose the habit of her two great faults. There certainly was an improvement in her general tone and manner, which made Mr. Devereux hope that he might soon resume with her the preparation for confirmation which had been cut short the year before.

Phyllis and Adeline had been possessed by Reginald with a great dread of governesses; and they were agreeably surprised in Miss Aylmer, whom they found neither cross nor strict, and always willing to forward their amusements, and let them go out with their papa and sisters whenever they were asked. Phyllis, without much annoyance to one so obedient, was trained into more civilisation, and Ada's more serious faults were duly watched and guarded against. The removal of Esther was a great advantage to Ada; an older and more steady person was taken in her place; while to the great relief of Mr. Mohun and Lilias, Rachel Harvey took Esther to her brother's farmhouse, where she promised to watch and teach her, and hoped in time to make her a good servant.

Of Emily there is little to say. She ate, drank, and slept, talked agreeably, read idle books, and looked nice in the drawing-room, wasting time, throwing away talents, weakening the powers of her mind, and laying up a store of sad reflections for herself against the time when she must awake from her selfish apathy.

As to Lilias Mohun, the heroine of this tale, the history of the formation of her character has been told, and all that remains to be said of her is, that the memory of her faults and her sorrows did not fleet away like a morning cloud, though followed by many happy and prosperous days, and though the effects of many were repaired. Agnes's death, Esther's theft, Ada's accident, the schism in the parish, and her own numerous mistakes, were constantly recalled, and never without a thought of the danger of being wise above her elders, and taking mere feeling for Christian charity.